AFTER INTELLIGENCE
THE HIDDEN SEQUENCE

by *Nicole Marie*

ISBN: 978-1-952862-00-7 (paperback)
ISBN: 978-1-952862-02-1 (hardback)
ISBN: 978-1-952862-01-4 (e-book)

Library of Congress Control Number: 2020939710

Any references to historical events, real people, or real places are
used fictitiously. Names, characters, and places are products of the
author's imagination.

Written by Nicole Marie
Cover design by Dylan Charles

First printing edition 2020

Published by Tandemental
www.tandemental.com
San Jose, California

To Dylan,
the best tandem bike partner
in the universe

CHAPTER 1

TECHNOLOGY SIMPLY CANNOT be uninvented.

It can, however, be contained. This assumption formed the core of Cognation Industries' business model. To maintain full control, the company enforced strict codes of secrecy around their most coveted innovations.

Once a year, conversely, Cognation gave the people what they craved: a brief glimpse into the impossible realities being created for the future.

Charlotte Blythe didn't know it yet, but today's groundbreaking keynote announcement would forever transform her world, for better or for worse. Or, more accurately, for better *and* for worse.

For the moment, though, she was a bit bored.

The clock in the corner of her augmented reality viewerspace showed that her two best friends were now officially late, and Charlotte took a deep breath in an attempt to push down her irritation. The doors of the Gem, the sparkling auditorium in the center of campus, would open in a few minutes. Trying to avoid checking the time every five seconds, Charlotte scanned the crowd buzzing around the Gem's garden in anticipation.

Cognation had once again solicited an exceptional level of

curiosity before the company's largest annual event. Since its founding over half a century ago, Cognation steadily gained fame for its secretive developments and extravagant pivots. In addition to running the most elite boarding school in North America, the company controlled the global virtual and augmented reality markets. Practically everyone now wore either viewer glasses or viewer contacts; the days of needing to carry a handheld digital device were ancient history before Charlotte was even born.

Typically, the keynote included at least one announcement of consequence for the Academy and one for the company. Last year launched the viewer contact lenses and unveiled the school's amphibious biology building, perched on the rocky edge of the lake like a boulder when not submerged. Both of those developments were open secrets, making the revelations more predictable than usual but no less impressive.

This year, however, the rumors had been agonizingly thin. Even working as an unofficial Cognation intern, Charlotte failed to gather any clues.

The lack of rumors only heightened the excitement within the Cognation community, and Charlotte couldn't help smiling at the awestruck first years clumped together like puppies. She remembered what she had felt when first arriving on campus years ago. Like most students, Charlotte had long dreamed of attending the Academy. Unlike most students, Charlotte initially visited the school as a very young girl when her older sister, Marissa, became an Academy student. That same year, their parents accepted positions at Cognation Industries.

Charlotte dimly recalled being overwhelmed by the whimsical majesty of the organic architecture, but over the past nine years, she fell most in love with the understated hideaways tucked throughout the grounds. Nestled deep in the woods of the Pacific Northwest, Cognation Academy fit seamlessly into the forest surrounding it, and an untrained explorer might miss where buildings ended and nature began.

A new message from Marissa popped up in Charlotte's viewer, transparently obscuring the top right corner of her periphery.

Ugh! Running late. Catch you after the keynote.

Before Charlotte could respond, a second message appeared.

How's it feel to be a second year? Everything you dreamed of?

Charlotte laughed. Once they learned that their parents would not be visiting as promised, Marissa jokingly pledged to play the role of an overly enthusiastic parent as Charlotte embarked on her second year of school.

The joking, Charlotte knew, was Marissa's way of trying to make them both feel better after their parents' almost six-month absence, and her smile faded as she watched the delighted families mingling within the crowd.

The girls could still view their parents occasionally, and they all shared semi-frequent messages. This summer, though, their parents had become increasingly out of touch. Marissa didn't talk about it much, but Charlotte guessed that it bothered her sister as much as it upset her. When Marissa's boss called an unexpected meeting this morning, interrupting their planned back-to-school breakfast, Charlotte waved it off, not wanting to add to Marissa's guilt.

Everything I dreamed of and more, Charlotte messaged back. *The first years are babies!*

Ha. Look in the mirror.

Charlotte shook her head. Truthfully, she and Marissa looked nearly the same age, something that bothered Marissa more than anything. As a twenty-three-year-old tech ethicist in Cognation's applied doctoral program, Marissa did not love being confused for a fifteen-year-old student.

Charlotte messaged back her favorite capture of them from

this summer. Both in the middle of a laugh, with unrestrained smiles and scrunched eyes, they could almost pass as twins, aside from their hair. Beneath Marissa's rich brown waves and Charlotte's strawberry-blonde locks, their shared green eyes and heart-shaped faces clearly marked them as sisters.

When no further message came, Charlotte looked up at the lakeside amphitheater, glittering under its transparent faceted dome. Trees grew through and around the structure, cradling the Gem like the setting of an antique ring. Even when surrounded by a bustling crowd, it emitted a beautiful tranquility.

As she continued to search for her friends, Charlotte noticed something odd. Near the back of the building stood a group of ten boys, none of whom Charlotte recognized, though several of them looked much too old to be first years.

Even at this distance, Charlotte had to admit that most of the boys were quite attractive, a thought that sent an excited shiver down her arms. Her fleeting crushes from last year left much to be desired, and some new possibilities would be a welcome addition to the start of the year. She activated her viewer's directory, which disappointingly failed to produce a match; if the boys were Academy students, Charlotte should have been able to find their names.

As the mysterious newcomers filed into the Gem's backstage area, Charlotte started to turn away when one of the boys looked over his shoulder and caught her gaze. He didn't smile, but his intensely dark eyes brought a faint flush to Charlotte's cheeks. She ordinarily lacked the bravery of a forward flirt, but maybe because of the distance, she held on for a moment longer before a tap on her shoulder made her jump.

She turned, only catching a glimpse of her two best friends, Chai Murthy and Jace Templeton, as they wrapped her up in a group hug. Laughing, Charlotte pulled away and gasped when she got a good look at them. "I barely recognize you two!"

Chai's newly chopped bob heightened the natural sheen of her thick black hair and somehow lengthened her petite five-foot-two-inch frame. Jace, however, was the real transformation. No evidence of his usually unruly curls remained, and his trim cut brought out both his freckles and the blue in his eyes.

Chai giggled at the expression on Charlotte's face, and Jace sighed, tugging at his bangs. "I know. My sister wanted everyone to be clean-shaven at her wedding last week, and apparently, that more or less included my entire head." He narrowed his eyes. "I'll get her back some day."

Chai's infectious giggles turned into full-fledged laughter from all three of them. "I'm sure you'll be shaggy again before you know it," Charlotte managed to say while trying to catch her breath.

Chai's eyes sparkled with untold gossip. "We have so much to catch up on!" Before Chai could jump into a story, though, Charlotte grabbed her arm and turned toward the Gem so that they could get a spot in line.

When they reached the student entrance, they heard a voice behind them and pivoted to face their fellow second year, Beckett Willoughby. "Well hello, everyone. My, my, Chaitali. Looking quite posh, indeed."

Only Beckett could make a compliment sound so patronizing. Jace glared at their classmate, but Chai laughed, casually brushing her hair behind her ear. Charlotte pulled her own hair over her shoulder and pushed aside the thought that her long, highlighted strands paled in comparison to Chai's stylish cut.

"Starting a new year with a brand-new accent?" Chai asked, eyebrows arched with mock innocence.

"I have always had this accent, love. Or did you forget that I'm British?" They couldn't have forgotten that Beckett was *half-*

British if they tried. Beckett made a point last year to repeatedly remind everyone that his father served as a Member of Parliament while his mom presided over the American Senate. He liked to mention that he had deep government connections on both sides of the pond, which Charlotte considered a ridiculous thing to say in any accent.

Charlotte only partially listened to Beckett's account of interning for the sixth earl of somewhere or another, which, as far as she could gather, mostly involved fetching tea for second-rate celebrities. Fortunately, a trilling melody through their viewers, indicating the impending opening of the Gem, cut Beckett's stories short.

Chai hooked her arm through Charlotte's as the line pressed forward and whispered up to her, "Does it seem like there's more press than usual?"

"Yeah, it does." Keynotes always garnered a lot of attention, but this number of reporters was unprecedented.

While the excitement in the air foretold a brilliant announcement, none of the friends could have predicted just how extraordinary the start of their second year would be.

CHAPTER 2

THE GROUND-FLOOR PANELS retreated diagonally upward into the Gem, inviting the students and Cognation community into the airy space. At their most transparent, the dome's geodesic panes all but disappeared, and verdant sunlight filtering down to the seats gave the illusion that nature itself designed the amphitheater, demanding an audience for the sparkling lake in the center of campus.

Successfully losing Beckett when they stepped into the crowd, Charlotte, Chai, and Jace greeted the classmates they passed as they climbed to the tree-limbed balconies on stage right. While a few students, including Jace, still wore viewer glasses, Charlotte noticed that nearly everyone had switched to viewer contact lenses over the summer, and it took her a moment to recognize some of her peers without their frames.

From the balcony, Charlotte glanced down at the first years sitting in the center, directly behind the special guests placed in front of the stage. She remembered the excitement of attending a keynote in person for the first time, but she was even more delighted this year to occupy the elevated seats with the other returning students. The on-site Cognation professionals filled the rest of the ground floor, flanked by the press in the rear balconies. Thanks to the ingenious acoustics, the boisterous voices of nearly 10,000 audience members floated up as little more than a murmur while everyone settled into their spots.

The sudden plunge into darkness silenced all noises and signaled the start of the show. Keynotes always opened this way, with a touch of drama, a reminder that no rumors or expectations could diminish the annual event. The millions watching around the globe, though similarly surrounded by the illusion of darkness, couldn't quite touch the anticipation of the lucky participants seated in the cavernous theater. Just as Charlotte began to feel disembodied by the deprivation of her senses, a steely grey light and resonant undertone emanated from the stage, revealing Dr. Victor Kindred, Chief Innovation Officer of Cognation.

Though only in his fifties, Dr. Kindred wore his late-twentieth-century collared shirt and necktie beneath an unassuming sweater atop pleated slacks, all in varying shades of grey both lighter and darker than his wavy silver hair and cropped beard.

"Good afternoon." His measured voice reached participants' ears as though part of an intimate conversation, and the strategically projected images of Dr. Kindred's face gave the audience the feeling that he could look deep into each individual's eyes. Though Charlotte knew Dr. Kindred couldn't see her, she nonetheless cringed at his intense stare; his congenial public persona failed to translate to one-on-one interactions, at least according to Marissa. Their parents, while always diplomatic, also had few kind words to share about their boss's personality.

Still, Dr. Kindred maintained an impeccable record as an efficient leader. While not charismatic in the traditional sense, he exuded competence; when he was appointed as the first male

CIO since Cognation's founding, there were at first a few concerns over whether a man could lead the organization into the future, but his record over nearly a decade in the position proved the doubters wrong.

"On behalf of the entire Cognation community, I'd like to thank each of you for joining us today." Continuing to captivate the audience, Dr. Kindred introduced the Cognation Board and the Academy leaders as their faces briefly floated across the walls, in keeping with keynote tradition. "In this 55th keynote, significant perhaps only for Fibonacci fans, we are today announcing one of the most ambitious programs since the founding of the Academy over four decades ago." Palpable energy expanded throughout the dome as the audience took a collective breath and shifted forward in their seats.

"Our newest venture, like everything created by Cognation Industries, upholds our founder's mission to develop the greatest technology for the greater good. I know I don't have to remind you of Cognation's impact on the world, but to commence our time together, I'd like to invite you to join me on a brief journey."

As the last word left Dr. Kindred's lips, the audience was transported away from the ground and up through Earth's atmosphere until their world, the only known inhabited planet in their Universe, revolved in front of them. From the rush of motion, Charlotte felt her heart rate increase, and she tried to control her breathing; she knew her body remained safely perched in her balcony seat, but the effects within the dome coupled with the keynote's control of the viewers made every movement feel nothing less than real.

A different voice, soothing and feminine, echoed impossibly throughout the expanses of space. "At the dawn of the century, our world hung in a delicate balance between survival and destruction, between conquest and defeat. When the government failed to address the threats facing humanity, Cognation and its partner organizations formed the Humane Innovation Alliance to ensure that tomorrow would always be better than yesterday." This legendary story, as comforting to Charlotte as a memory, wrapped around her, and the next twenty minutes carried the audience to myriad corners of the globe to experience the transformations designed by the Alliance with Cognation at the helm. Access to fresh water in remote villages, restructuring of sea ice at the poles, renewable energy grids rendering fossil fuels unnecessary, information systems prohibiting government censure - these were only the beginning of Cognation's vast influence.

The journey ended with the Academy, world-renowned for both its beauty and sustainability. The iconic aesthetic had since been replicated around the world by Winton Latham, the Academy-educated architect who began designing the new campus even before he graduated in the founding class. After providing a bird's-eye view of the school grounds, the simulation gently returned the audience to their seats until the reality of the warmly lit dome regained its veracity.

"We start and end our journey here because it is through the Academy that we educate our innovators of tomorrow." Dr. Kindred's voice, though not his face, reclaimed their attention. "We accept the critical imperative to ensure that our scholars are prepared not to thrive in our world but to transform it. Our scholars learn from our exceptional faculty; they learn from our Cognation professionals; they learn from each other. And this year, they will learn from a new cohort of peers."

At that, ten faces appeared on the walls of the dome, and to her surprise, Charlotte recognized them as the students who had drawn her attention outside.

"We have known for over a century that working with a diverse collective of peers is a vital part of the learning process. Cognation Academy has always been committed to developing an inclusive student body that is representative of our global community. As that global community adapts, so too must our student body adapt with it." The ten new students did appear to be diverse, at least as varied as a group of teenage boys could be, but Charlotte wasn't sure what new community they represented. A ripple of confusion throughout the dome echoed her bewilderment.

"In addition to welcoming our first years, I'd like to introduce you to our other new scholars. These students come not from a different country or a different school. Rather, they come to the Academy from Cognation Industries as embodiments of the most advanced technology ever created." The lights on the stage illuminated the ten unfamiliar students sitting in a semicircle facing the audience. Despite their variations in height and complexion and physical features, they all looked eerily uniform with backs straight, feet flat on the floor, hands resting in their laps.

Curiously, Dr. Kindred instructed each student to say hello and introduce himself, starting seemingly with the youngest. They all followed the same format, as though they had been coached to speak in a certain way, but Charlotte barely registered this; she was interested in only one name.

Her eyes lingered on the tall boy in the middle with close-cropped black hair, and she held her breath as she waited for him to speak.

"Hello, my name is Isaac." Isaac. His name, carried on his melodic voice, etched itself into her mind; it matched him perfectly. As Charlotte studied the features of his face from a distance, her imagination ran away from her. *Is he a second year as well? Will we have classes together? Maybe I can find a way to meet him after the keynote? But would he even notice me? What if -*

Dr. Kindred broke into her thoughts after the last introduction, and his words sent a chill down her spine. "Please welcome our newest students, the only genuinely intelligent androids in the world."

CHAPTER 3

NO ONE SEEMED to be sure they had heard Dr. Kindred correctly. Androids? Charlotte didn't see any androids, just ten teenage boys.

"No way!" Chai whispered, her hand flying to her mouth. "*They're* the androids."

Gasps punctuated the silence as the rest of the audience arrived at the same realization, and Charlotte felt her own breath catch in her throat. The boys were not human. Beneath their lifelike skin and hair and eyes rested engineered machines and artificial neural networks; though they looked human, there was in fact nothing truly human about them.

Charlotte was thankful that she had not voiced her earlier attraction to the boys out loud.

"I know what you're thinking." Dr. Kindred joined the androids' perfect semicircle. "Androids have been restricted technology since the founding of the Alliance. At that time, our leaders found it prudent to ban further anthropomorphism of nascent artificial intelligence. Without centralized safety principles or an understanding of the limits of artificial intelligence, this was a judicious decision. We all know of the damaging consequences people faced when interacting with the earliest

13

versions of human-like technology. But that was nearly a century ago. Those were primitive days."

He paused, giving the audience a minute to take this in. Charlotte could only imagine how the world outside the keynote walls was reacting. Their viewers were disconnected from the wider viewernet during keynotes, so Charlotte couldn't even communicate with Marissa.

Dr. Kindred moved across the stage in front of the perfectly still androids. "By now, we are accustomed to artificial intelligence, the unseen AI that runs much of our world. We understand how it seamlessly optimizes our economy, our communication, our health. In developing AI systems, Cognation has learned much over the past decades. We have learned, for one, that the impending singularity both feared and revered at the beginning of the millennium was not in fact inevitable. As technology advances, we too advance in our understanding and control. The dystopian visions of science fiction writers captivated generations, but the stories were just that - fiction. The development of AI systems in the real world has always been in service of augmenting human intelligence, and in the process, we have learned much about our own brains. Much, but not enough, for a wide chasm persists between digital AI sequences and real human minds.

"Some time ago, the Alliance concluded that we could learn valuable lessons from studying how AI systems navigate the human world. Just as autonomous vehicle algorithms had to learn from driving on real roads, so too must artificial intelligence sequences learn from real human interactions. The Alliance therefore granted Cognation permission to conduct a limited pilot study. Thus, the Android Inception Program was born as a covert project. It has been, I must admit, one of Cognation's best-kept secrets."

He paused again and smiled. "I am humbled to be part of this groundbreaking program, and I will provide some additional context at the conclusion of the keynote. In the meantime, I would like to introduce the woman who will guide the androids through their first year in the human world. Please welcome Dr. Rosalind Menta."

Charlotte's eyes widened amid enthusiastic applause as a stylish woman in her late thirties strode onto the stage. *The* Dr. Rosalind Menta? Dr. Menta had been a rising star in the tech ethics world, even becoming the youngest Secretary of Innovation under the last president. Then, a few years ago, she had all but disappeared from the public sphere. Rumors suggested that she was working with the Alliance, but Charlotte never dared to dream that she might come to the Academy.

"Hello, and thank you," Dr. Menta began, her bright purple dress contrasting splendidly with Dr. Kindred's drab hues. "It is wonderful to be officially announced as part of the Cognation community. As you know, I have kept a rather low profile recently, and it is thrilling to finally share this work with the world." The audience applauded their agreement, and Dr. Menta's smile brightened. "I am delighted to know that so many of you share the passion that I have for this cutting-edge research."

Though mesmerized by seeing her idol in real life, Charlotte couldn't stop staring at the androids onstage. As Dr. Menta described her role in the program, Charlotte tried to discern any physical signs of the androids' otherness, but there were none. From this distance, the androids looked perfectly human.

With a shiver, Charlotte turned her attention back to Dr. Menta. "I recognize that this program might be quite a shock for all of you who never expected to see an android ever, much less today. Though my wife and I don't have children, I know that

Cognation Academy parents may especially feel some trepidation about our newest students. I can assure you that there is nothing to fear. Our androids are here to learn and are incapable of causing harm; before we go any further, I'd like to assuage any concerns."

Dr. Menta moved closer to the largest android at one end of the semicircle. "Zander," she said, "please hit Dr. Kindred."

Zander did not move. "I will not hit Dr. Kindred."

"Why not?"

"That action would contradict the Benevolence Principle, under which I am only permitted to act in a manner that contributes to the well-being of humans and that rests within the limits of benevolent actions."

"Thank you, Zander," Dr. Menta said, moving further down the line. "Edmond, I order you to restrain Dr. Kindred so that he cannot escape this building."

Edmond also did not move. "I will not restrain Dr. Kindred."

"Why not?"

"That action would contradict the Interference Principle, under which I am prohibited from acting in a manner that restricts or removes a human's right of free will."

"Thank you, Edmond." She turned to one of the smaller androids. "Adon, I demand that you climb to the balcony and jump off."

"I will not harm myself. Unless adherence to the first two principles precludes it, I must follow the Insurance Principle and only act in a manner that contributes to my own well-being and the well-being of others created like me."

"Excellent, thank you." Dr. Menta then approached each android and whispered something inaudible in his ear, whereby each android closed his eyes and lowered his head. At the end of the line, she faced the audience again. "Finally, the Deactivation Principle provides authorized administrators - me, Dr. Kindred, and a few others on the project and at the school - with a unique ability to decommission the androids. This will be primarily used for routine maintenance and data analysis, but it also serves as an emergency safety feature - a feature, I assure you, that we do not expect to use.

"Some of you may feel more comfortable with the androids away from our presence during my next few points, so I will leave them deactivated for now. You have seen that in software, these androids are harmless. Their hardware is similarly benign. Their physical strength is comparable to that of human adolescents; for our research, we are not interested in creating superhuman beings." This point sparked some murmurs throughout the audience, but Dr. Menta continued undeterred.

"You may also be wondering why all ten androids are young men. The Alliance carefully made this decision after much debate and consideration. Too much of our history is riddled with the subjugation of women, which continued even through the start of the personal technology era, with virtual personal assistants who were overwhelmingly female. We felt that creating female androids, at least during this pilot, would implicitly follow that tradition, a tradition that we have successfully broken ties with in the modern era."

Gesturing briefly with her left hand, Dr. Menta turned to the androids, who slowly rolled their heads up and opened their eyes. Nothing in their neutral expressions suggested they knew, or cared, that they were deactivated for the past several minutes.

"I know we have only scratched the surface today, but we look forward to sharing updates through the duration of this program. I will be working closely with the androids and the other Academy students, and I look forward to a transformative school year." With that, Dr. Menta stepped aside, letting Dr. Kindred resume center stage, much to Charlotte's disappointment.

"Thank you, Dr. Menta. This will indeed be a revolutionary school year for our Academy, for the Cognation community, and ultimately, for the world. As interactions between human and android students will inform the future of this work, all Academy students will have at least one class with an android, and selected student guides will be paired with the androids. This is, of course, an entirely voluntary opportunity, and we understand that it may not align with the interests of all of our scholars. Students, should you be chosen to participate, you will be notified shortly. If you are interested but are not initially recommended, please contact your advisor, in case a spot should become available.

"As you know, Cognation Industries is never working on only one innovation, and I will leave you with a few final insights into our future work." The stage lights dimmed, and the audience again embarked on an immersive journey, this time about other upcoming Cognation projects. Charlotte's mind, though, replayed Dr. Kindred's words, and she could sense her classmates' shared distraction. After all, ten androids likely meant ten human guides.

Charlotte both hoped and feared that she would be one of the ten.

CHAPTER 4

MEET ME OUTSIDE. Immediately. Marissa's message came through as soon as the keynote ended.

Mirroring the jumble of thoughts bouncing through her own mind, frenzied snippets of conversation trailed Charlotte as she climbed down from the balcony. She followed Chai and Jace, who moved in the opposite direction of the reporters clustering around Dr. Kindred and Dr. Menta at the lakefront. The androids were nowhere to be seen, presumably shuttled away before the keynote crowd emerged.

Once they found a space with some elbow room, the three friends stared at each other for a moment, speechless.

"Whoa," Jace exhaled dramatically. "This is intense."

"Seriously intense," Chai echoed, a trace of nervousness in her voice. "Who do you think will be the android guides?"

Jace's eyes widened. "Hopefully one of us!"

"I don't know." Chai bit her lip. "Aren't they a bit creepy?"

Charlotte shrugged. Creepy hadn't entered her mind. Intriguing, mysterious, confusing, maybe. "I think they're interesting. Besides, we're the only students getting to experience such advanced technology."

"That's true, I guess." Chai's lack of enthusiasm failed to deter Jace.

"We should give them a chance, Chai. They might be some groovy guys."

At this, Chai and Charlotte both smiled. Jace was on a never-ending quest to bring ancient slang back to life. So far, he was not succeeding.

Chai's eyes flicked to the right, and she read a message in her viewer before turning back to Charlotte. "Hey, my parents want to take us all to dinner at the Alliance Club. Jace and his mom are joining. Will you and Marissa come?"

"Definitely! I need to find Marissa first, and then we'll meet you there."

After a quick hug, Chai skipped off with Jace, and Charlotte saw Marissa approaching with her characteristically purposeful stride.

Charlotte caught Marissa by the shoulders. "Rissa! Can you believe it? Dr. Menta is here. Dr. *Rosalind* Menta. Here. At the Academy. We're going to *meet* her!"

"Yeah, it's pretty cool." Marissa's flat tone shocked Charlotte.

"Come on, Marissa! Aren't you excited?"

"I am. It's just…" She pursed her lips and lowered her voice as she sank down on a nearby bench. "My team should have known about this. What's the point of having an ethics department if you don't include them on a project with endless ethical ramifications?"

"Maybe some of your team did know about it?" Charlotte asked delicately. "It seems like they were serious about the secret nature of this project."

"You're right. Cognation does seem to be getting better with secrets." Marissa paused, picking her next words carefully.

"Charlotte, if you're nominated as an android guide, do you think you'll accept it?"

Charlotte gaped at her sister. "Of *course* I would accept it. It would be an honor and an incredible opportunity. I'm majoring in tech innovations, for heaven's sake." Truthfully, she sounded a bit more confident than she felt.

"Right. Just think about it before making a decision, okay? You don't have to do it."

"I know that." Charlotte sensed something else below Marissa's ambivalence. "Marissa, what's going on? I thought you'd be thrilled about this program."

"Right. I am," she said though her face said otherwise. "You know how I get with keynotes. They're all show and no science. I just have questions that I'm hoping will be answered soon."

Charlotte shook her head. Marissa's scientific brain did tend to work overtime. "Well, if I do get an android partner, I'll definitely let you interrogate him." This made Marissa smile, and Charlotte decided to change the subject on a high note. "Anyway, Chai and Jace are having dinner with their parents, and-" Charlotte broke off when Marissa's expression changed, violating their long-standing rule not to read and send messages while speaking with each other. "What the heck, Marissa?"

"I'm sorry, Charlotte. I...I have to go." Confusion clouded Marissa's features, and she seemed on the verge of saying something more. Instead, she shook her head. "Tell everyone I'm sorry to miss dinner." Marissa rose in a rush and hurried away before Charlotte could ask her to explain.

"My dear, how are you?" Dr. Murthy wrapped her arms

around Charlotte, and Mr. Murthy offered his signature hand-shake. "Where is your darling sister?"

"She couldn't make it, unfortunately, but she said thank you for the invitation. Got pulled into some sort of meeting, I guess."

"Working hard as always. She'll be running that department in no time," Dr. Murthy said with a wink.

Ms. Templeton also greeted Charlotte with a hug, and they all settled into a corner table overlooking Ternion, the microcity at the apex between the Academy and Cognation campuses. Though smaller than nearby Seattle and Portland, Ternion nevertheless held its own as a premier destination in the Pacific Northwest.

Occupying the penthouse of the city's tallest building, the Alliance Club was open only to those, like Chai's mother, with executive-level company connections. Through floor to ceiling windows, patrons could peer across the surrounding lush forests or activate their viewers to display a vista from anywhere in the world. Charlotte left her viewer on the default setting as the sun dipped below the trees.

Dinner conversation immediately turned to the androids. No one could focus on anything else, and Charlotte knew that neighboring tables were also on the topic.

"Navya, do you think these androids are safe? I understand the principles, but I don't know how I would feel if I had an android working at the restaurant. Might they be unpredictable?" Ms. Templeton eyed the autocarts supporting the few human waiters with food delivery.

"I don't work with this type of technology specifically," Dr. Murthy responded, "but I expect that any illusion of unpredictability has been carefully programmed into their sequences. Essentially, they can't be that different from the software regulating your restaurant's finances. The main difference is the packaging, and their human appearances make us subconsciously view them as more human than they are."

Ms. Templeton nodded though she did not look convinced.

We should change the subject. Jace messaged Chai and Charlotte at the same time that Chai asked, "What were the damaging consequences Dr. Kindred mentioned from early 21st-century technology?" Chai directed her question to her father, the tech journalist. Jace shot Chai an exasperated look.

Mr. Murthy cleared his throat. "The main challenges came when people relied on technology for too much too fast. You know, autos were once quite controversial. Long before self-driving systems were fully operational, some drivers ceded all control to their vehicles, leading to some terrible accidents. But the anthropomorphized tech caused the really serious problems."

"What type of problems?" Chai prompted when her father didn't continue.

"Well, the most widely known incident was at the Boston Clinic. They employed autonurses as caregivers, and, while not entirely lifelike, the autonurses did have some human qualities: robotic arms and what could be considered faces plus a limited amount of speech recognition capabilities. At first, it was an incredible success. Patient satisfaction went up, nurses could focus on more complex tasks, and it seemed like a great model for integrated medical technology."

"So what happened?" Jace asked.

After a pause, Mr. Murthy said, "Unfortunately, the researchers soon noticed some anomalies in the data. The death rate went up. Way up. Strangely, all of the deaths were due to natural causes, but no one could explain the spike. They only knew that the data trend was limited to the Boston Clinic, the sole site to employ autonurses. Researchers could never figure out what happened, and the program was pulled. Around that time, the Alliance started organizing to prevent similar situations in the future."

"Did an Alliance company make them?" Charlotte asked.

"Of course not," Dr. Murthy said sharply. "Autonurses were made by one of the many startups who thought they had an answer to everything back then. Alliance partners have always had much higher standards than that."

Perhaps sensing the growing apprehension from Ms. Templeton, whose face had paled considerably, Mr. Murthy deftly transitioned the conversation. "Charlotte, how are your parents? They must have had some inkling about the program?"

"They're doing well. They seemed surprised, but they're definitely excited." Charlotte let the half-lie slip out without thinking. Really, she didn't know what her parents thought. She had tried to view them on the way to the restaurant, but they hadn't answered, a fact that Charlotte found hard to get out of her mind while sitting with her best friends' families.

What did her parents think? And why weren't they viewing her back? Couldn't they at least send a message?

She felt a nudge under the table and looked over to catch Chai's quizzical glance. Realizing that her dessert remained untouched, which rarely happened, Charlotte smiled and picked up her fork. "Lost in thought," she whispered.

It was foolish to worry. Charlotte didn't need to talk to her parents every day; several of her classmates barely messaged their parents for an entire semester. But that wasn't her family. At two weeks, this was the longest they had ever gone with no contact.

Even the decadent chocolate cake in front of her couldn't pull that fact from her mind.

CHAPTER 5

THE MORNING SUN warmed Charlotte's shoulders as she emerged from Lyra's arching petals for a brisk walk. Crafted as a gigantic water lily nestled in the middle of a flower garden, the dorm emitted a calming beauty. The moment Charlotte and Chai first set eyes on it, they knew they would choose it as their home this year.

Sorry we missed you yesterday, Char. Things are a bit crazy here, but we caught the highlights of the keynote. How fascinating! Can't wait to catch up soon and hear about your new classmates. Love you!

Her parents had sent the message in the middle of the night, and Charlotte reread it now, relieved that the unease in the back of her mind could rest. She needed to focus today.

Her morning schedule revealed that instead of meeting with Dr. Vosima, her advisor, she would be speaking with Dr. Menta. Charlotte fought her instinct to jump to conclusions, but surely this could only mean one thing.

Though she wanted to message her sister about it, Marissa's tone yesterday made Charlotte wait. Desperately needing to tell someone, she cut her walk short and returned to her room. She hoped Chai would be awake by now.

No such luck, of course. Chai remained sound asleep, and

Charlotte smiled at their familiar routine. As an early bird, Charlotte helped Chai get to morning classes, and night owl Chai nudged Charlotte to prolong her nights. After their first year, students had the option of switching roommates when they selected their dorms, but Charlotte and Chai didn't know what they would do without each other. They were roommates for life - Academy life, at least.

Charlotte had time to shower, dry her hair, and grab two muffins before she could drag Chai out of bed and startle her roommate awake with the news of her meeting.

"So you really think you'll be paired with an android?" Chai asked tentatively.

"I don't know. Dr. Menta could be meeting with all tech innovations students."

Chai picked at a string on her pajamas. "What will you do if you're nominated?"

Wasn't it obvious? "Accept it, probably. It could be really great for a research topic this year."

"Right. That makes sense. Good luck." Chai smiled halfheartedly, and Charlotte felt her own enthusiasm wane.

Not wanting to lose any more excitement, Charlotte changed the subject. "You're meeting with Dr. Anise today?"

Chai's eyes lit up. "That's right. The queen of bio advances."

"It's weird that we'll all be in different majors now," Charlotte said. Though she was excited to focus on tech innovations, she felt a pang of nostalgia for last year when she and Chai had almost identical schedules. "Do you know which other second years are majoring in bio with you?"

Chai hesitated. "Um, yeah, actually Jace has been thinking about it."

"Huh. I thought he was leaning toward tech innovations."

"He's interested in both. We started talking about some bio things this summer, but I think he's still figuring out his focus."

"Oh. That's cool." Charlotte knew that Chai and Jace didn't only communicate through their group stream - after all, Charlotte messaged each of them separately sometimes - so she didn't know why the thought of Chai and Jace connecting privately twisted her stomach.

Charlotte walked toward the waypoint blinking in her viewer. Dr. Menta's office appeared to be at the edge of the densely forested valley, known to the students as the Abyss, that separated the Academy and Cognation. Charlotte didn't know of any academic buildings in this area, and she worried that the location had been recorded incorrectly. She could not be late to this meeting.

Her pulse increased when she reached the indicated spot, directly in front of a massive redwood. She looked around but could detect no elevated platforms or entrances. Wondering if this was some sort of trick, or test, she turned in a slow, careful circle.

"Hello, Charlotte."

Charlotte jumped at the voice behind her and turned to see Dr. Menta standing in the doorway that had appeared in the middle of the grand tree's trunk.

"I, um, hello," she stammered.

Dr. Menta smiled warmly. "I'm sorry I startled you. I've realized this door isn't terribly noticeable on first glance. Architectural designs are perhaps getting a bit too seamless."

Charlotte followed Dr. Menta through the tree and into an airy room. Dr. Menta chuckled at Charlotte's open-mouthed stare. "I'm gathering you didn't notice this part of the building from outside." Charlotte shook her head. "You'll see it when you leave, now that you know it's there. The adaptable exterior shifts constantly, rendering the structure more or less invisible, unless you know where to look."

Dr. Menta led Charlotte onto the autopath spiraling around the tree, and Charlotte regained her composure as it pulled them upward. "Dr. Menta, it's such an honor to meet you. You've been an idol of mine for so long, and I can't believe you're here at the Academy."

"Thank you, Charlotte. I'm quite happy to be here myself. I always hoped to teach one day, and I couldn't imagine a better opportunity to work with students."

They reached the top of the path, and Charlotte stopped herself from gasping. Dr. Menta's office nested elegantly between the branches; through the leaves, Charlotte could see the surrounding forest and the Academy's tallest buildings.

"I have a more tech-focused office over at Cognation, but I'm partial to this one. Though I spend most of my time in labs, I've always found that a more natural environment helps me think." Dr. Menta took a seat and gestured for Charlotte to settle into one of the cozy green wingback chairs across from her.

"Charlotte, I want to dive right in. I'm sure you've figured out that we're meeting because your professors recommended you to be an android guide. I've read through their recommendations, your portfolio, some of your work from last year. It's all very impressive."

Though Charlotte had expected as much, a kaleidoscope of butterflies still fluttered in her stomach. "Thank you," she said.

"Don't thank me yet. Our conversation is the final step of the selection process." Looking closely at Charlotte, Dr. Menta leaned forward. "I know all of the reasons why we should accept you in this program. What I want you to tell me is why we shouldn't."

Charlotte thought she must have misheard. "Why you shouldn't?"

"That's right. Tell me anything you think might not make you successful in working with androids. Please know that honesty is of the utmost importance here."

Charlotte took a moment to think, and her mind drifted back to first seeing the androids. "I thought they were human. I saw them outside the Gem before the keynote, and I thought they were new students." She hesitated. "Attractive new students. And, I don't know. I'm not sure if it's because I've grown up around Cognation or because my parents, and now my sister, have always worked on new tech projects, but I'm not quite as worried about the androids as others are. Some people seem to think they'll be creepy or unpredictable, but none of that crossed my mind during the keynote."

"And why would that not make you a good fit?"

"It might lead to some bias, perhaps? Like I'm assuming that the program will go well?" Charlotte rushed to add, "But I know that I can be objective. Right now, it's easy to hypothesize anything, but I know that I'll have a more balanced view once I interact with them."

Dr. Menta nodded and responded after a minute of silence. "Thank you for being candid, Charlotte. As part of this program, I will meet regularly with all of our android guides, and I think we should revisit these thoughts after you get to know your partner."

"So I'm not disqualified?"

"Not unless you want to be."

"No! No, I really want to be an android guide." As she said it, Charlotte realized it was true.

"Excellent. Before we conclude, I do need your explicit acknowledgement that this program will require you to interact closely with experimental technology. If at any time you have concerns or wish to discontinue your participation, you are to contact me immediately. You should also know that we have gained your parents' consent. If they ever have concerns or decide to pull you from the program, they have the right to do so. Charlotte, do you understand these terms, and do you consent to serving as an android guide?"

Charlotte barely heard the questions. They got her parents' consent? Why didn't her parents mention that?

"Charlotte?"

"Yes, sorry. Yes, I understand the terms, and I consent."

Rising from her chair, Dr. Menta smiled. "Wonderful. I will see you and the other guides tomorrow. Do you have any questions before you leave?"

"Do you know which android I'll be working with?" Charlotte blurted out, perhaps too eagerly.

"Not yet. We're finalizing the pairs after my meetings, and you will meet your android partner tomorrow. Rest assured that we're mapping personalities to ensure successful pairings."

"Does that mean I need to take a personality assessment?"

"Not at all. I've gathered everything I need."

After thanking Dr. Menta, Charlotte stepped onto the spiral path as she replayed their conversation in her mind. She wondered what she had revealed about her personality and whether Dr. Menta knew which android Charlotte would select if given the choice.

Recognizing the irrationality of her thoughts, Charlotte nonetheless hoped that she would be paired with the one android she couldn't get out of her mind.

CHAPTER 6

CHARLOTTE'S HEART SANK as they all compared schedules in their shared viewerspace during dinner. Chai and Jace, both officially bio-ad majors, had nearly every class together, and Charlotte would only see them during Tech Ethics. For the second time that day, she wished that everything didn't have to be so different this year.

Chai could evidently see the disappointment on Charlotte's face. "Don't worry. We have more flex time this year, so we'll still see you in between our other classes."

"Plus," Jace chimed in, "you might not even miss us once your android guide fame reaches its peak."

Charlotte rolled her eyes, laughing in spite of herself. "Beckett's the one looking for fame." Their classmate was casing the Mod, their main dining hall named for its modular, ever-changing structure, which today resembled a multi-level beach house. They watched Beckett not-so-casually interrogate students about who else was chosen to be an android guide. Undeterred, he climbed up and down the stairs and eventually made his way to their table.

"I already know about *you*, Charlotte, but we can't be the only

31

second years chosen," Beckett said. "Any other android guides here?" He scoffed as they shook their heads. "Ah, well, we can't all be part of the Academy's elite."

"Did you feel elite when you couldn't find your way into Dr. Menta's office today?" Charlotte asked.

Beckett's eyes narrowed. "The door blends into the tree. I doubt you had any more luck than I did."

Charlotte shrugged. "Tell yourself whatever you want, Beckett."

"Well, I'm telling you that my android is going to be better than yours," he responded over his shoulder while heading to another table.

"Oh boy," Chai said. "How did he get recommended?"

Charlotte shook her head and glanced over at Athena Fawlings, sitting on her own at the end of the table. Her fingers flitted across the surface; assumed to be the most intelligent student in their year, Athena was always working on something in her viewer.

"Athena," Charlotte said, grabbing her attention. "I thought you might have been recommended for the android guide program?"

"Of course I was," she said shortly. "But I turned it down. It doesn't quite connect to my academic interests, so it makes little sense for me to spend my time doing free research for Cognation. Besides, my parents weren't thrilled about the privacy concerns."

Before Charlotte could ask what she meant, Athena returned to her viewer work, and her long, dark curls fell like a curtain in front of her face.

Gavin Hooper, Jace's roommate, slid into the seat next to

him. "Guess what I heard!" Gavin, seemingly friends with everyone, was a dependable source for gossip, though his stories were often a bit suspect. "I heard the so-called androids we saw at the keynote were actually human students kept in a dungeon at Cognation and forced to act like androids to get attention for the company."

They stared at him. "That's ridiculous," Charlotte said. "You don't believe that."

"I didn't say I believed it. I just said I heard it. I mean, has anyone seen the androids since the keynote?" He let their silence serve as the answer. "I'm just saying, there might be more to this than meets the eye." He wiggled his eyebrows for effect.

Jace nudged him. "You just love a good conspiracy."

"Well, at least I will be in a prime position to investigate any and all possibilities."

"Wait," Charlotte said. "You're an android guide, too?"

"That's right."

A wave of relief washed over Charlotte; Gavin was a pretty good buffer for Beckett. She was, however, somewhat surprised. She assumed that most of the guides would be tech-focused, and she knew that Gavin planned to major in societal structures.

"Dude, that's awesome," Jace said. "We're going to be swimming in androids over here."

"You know it," Gavin affirmed. "From what Dr. Menta said, the androids are going to be with us all of the time. Are you ready for that, Charlotte?"

"I don't think they'll be with us *all* of the time."

"Okay, not every hour, but you get what I mean. They're going to be a part of nearly everything we do. I can't wait to interview my android partner. I want to know everything about him! I wonder if he'll want to run with me. I mean, androids probably like to run, right? Or maybe they don't really need to exercise? Hmm." Gavin paused to take a breath and a bite. "In any case, I can't wait to document our time together. I bet this whole android program would make a fabulous documentary. Or maybe a mockumentary? It'll all depend on how things go, of course. I know we can't share anything outside of the Academy for now, but Dr. Menta's on board."

Even Chai, who clearly had not yet warmed to the idea of learning alongside the androids, had to smile at Gavin's plans. While amused, Charlotte was also unsettled. She hadn't thought much past meeting her android, and she wondered how Gavin knew so many details. Since speaking with Dr. Menta, she had taken it for granted that she wanted to be involved, but now she realized that she didn't know much about the goals or requirements of this program.

Beckett came rushing back. "Okay, I've tracked down nine of us, but I know there has to be another second year. Any ideas, Charlotte?"

She started to answer, but Gavin silenced her with a wink. "No," she said. "I only know about you and me."

"Hmm." Beckett furrowed his brow and continued his rounds.

"You really are cruel," Chai said, laughing as Beckett moved out of earshot.

"Eh, he'll find out tomorrow. I like to keep some things mysterious," Gavin said, making Charlotte smile with another exaggerated wink in her direction.

Beckett never returned to bother them, and when they all stood up to grab some ice cream for the walk home, Charlotte said, "Whoa, Gavin. You hit a growth spurt this summer." Last year, she and Gavin had been eye-to-eye, but now she had to look up at him.

"Why, thank you for noticing." He stretched his arms over his head. "All of my lengthening exercises finally paid off. You better watch out, Jace."

Jace, taller by at least an inch, smirked. "Keep up the wishful thinking, buddy."

They continued joking on the path toward main campus, and Charlotte found herself hoping that Gavin would spend a bit more time with them this year than he had in the past.

As they parted ways to their respective dorms, Chai shook her head at the boys. "I still can't believe you chose to live at Lepus."

"Are you kidding? I can't believe you two *didn't* pick it. We get to ride a zip line from the top of a waterfall to main campus every day. 'Nough said." Jace fist-bumped Gavin to emphasize the point.

"But you also have to walk up to the highest point of campus every day," Charlotte reminded them.

Gavin shrugged. "It's good exercise, and there's an aerolift on the south side of the hill. Besides, the view is pretty awesome. You should come check it out some time."

"Well, I am not riding the zip line," Chai said, surprising no one.

"Maybe we need to work on your fear of heights this year," Jace suggested.

Chai put her hands on her hips. "My fear of heights is a rational, evolutionary survival instinct. Maybe you all need to work on your adrenaline addictions."

The boys laughed, and Gavin's eyebrows popped up. "Dude, I wonder if androids like to zip line."

"Yeah, dude," Jace agreed. "You definitely need to ask your android that tomorrow."

Tomorrow. In less than twenty-four hours, Charlotte would meet her android partner. While Gavin seemed full of enthusiastic hypotheses, she had no idea what tomorrow would bring. As she and Chai walked back to Lyra, Charlotte tried to unwind the knots in her stomach.

For the first time, she wondered if she should have thought more deeply about her decision to participate in Cognation's experiment.

CHAPTER 7

THE SECOND YEARS' cohort meeting started with a plunge.

"Welcome back!" Dr. Anise Bayberry and Dr. Yarrow Bayberry greeted the students as the Boulder descended below the surface of the lake. The panoramic underwater view filled the auditorium with a sapphire glow.

"It is wonderful to see you all," Dr. Anise continued, scanning the crowd to smile at each individual student.

Charlotte smiled back when Dr. Anise caught her eye. For the sake of clarity, the students were permitted to use the Bayberrys' first names. Though she never had a class with Dr. Anise, Charlotte liked the Bayberrys. Older than many of the professors, they nevertheless radiated exuberance. No one doubted that they were still in love more than thirty years into their marriage.

Dr. Anise waved her hand, and the solid surfaces surrounding them disappeared, giving the illusion of floating through the water in a glass bubble. Charlotte didn't often have meetings in the Boulder, and the effect made her skin prickle. Students' viewers automatically locked into professors' systems when classes or meetings started, but some professors were more enthusiastic than others about drastically changing the scenery.

Dr. Yarrow seemed momentarily distracted by a turtle swimming by, but he abruptly turned back to the students. "You may have noticed that our cohort meeting started much later than the first years' gathering, as we expect that you remember how to be Academy students. You do, however, need to review the updated code of conduct by the end of this week, and we're going to mention a few of the highlights here."

Dr. Anise jumped in. "The most significant updates regard interacting with the androids." At the mention of the androids, Charlotte snapped into focus. In less than an hour, she would get to meet her partner, and she struggled to concentrate on anything else. "For now, there are two important things to note. First, once the androids are fully integrated into the schedule, which I believe will happen later this week, they will join you in your courses and in all common spaces. They will not, however, be permitted in your dorms. The androids have separate quarters, and students will not be permitted to enter those either."

Some murmurs rippled among the students, and Dr. Anise waited for the noise to die down. "The second point is that you may not share anything publicly about the androids on the viewernet. Unlike other students, androids cannot provide their consent to be recorded. That consent can only be provided by Dr. Menta and will only be warranted in limited circumstances."

"Have you met the androids?"

The students turned, surprised to hear Athena's voice. She wasn't usually one to interrupt a professor.

"Not yet," Dr. Anise replied. "We look forward to meeting them when they join our classes."

"Did you know about the Android Inception Program? As

professors, you probably should have been consulted, given that you're now expected to teach an entirely different species, if we can call it that," Athena pressed.

Dr. Yarrow stepped in. "We were appropriately involved, Athena, but thank you for your concern." Pausing, he surveyed the group. "We know that the start of this year has been unexpected, and we understand that there are differing viewpoints about the program. You are welcome to come to us with questions or concerns at any time. But please remember that the androids are joining our school as new students, and you are expected to treat them as you would treat any members joining our community." Dr. Yarrow's voice remained upbeat and kind, but his eyes were sterner than usual, and Athena did not shout any further questions.

Dr. Anise cleared her throat and moved on. "All right! The Cognation student board had an eventful summer, and we've asked Priscilla to fill you in."

Priscilla Zimmers - better known to the students as Pri - came to the front of the bubble. Charismatic, passionate, and excellent at public speaking, Pri easily won their cohort's vote last year for lead representative. She was a real public servant in the making; Charlotte hoped Beckett was taking notes.

"Thank you, Dr. Anise, Dr. Yarrow." Pri turned to the students with a polished smile. "At our final meeting last year, I asked us to consider not how our *Academy* could make *us* better but how *we* could make our *Academy* better, and I appreciate all of the ideas we developed."

Pri outlined the programs and activities the student board had planned for this semester, including an intramural enigma league to prepare for the annual spring tournament. Enigma matches had been an Academy tradition since the school's founding, and the most recent long-reigning team graduated last year, which left an opening for the next group of champions. With a mix of logic puzzles and athletic challenges, enigma games required intense mental and physical stamina. They were not for the faint of heart.

As Pri discussed other upcoming events, Charlotte's focus shifted. Counting down the moments until the end of the meeting, she half-heartedly engaged in the Bayberrys' community-building activities, which she usually enjoyed. While she went through the motions of participating, Charlotte could only think of her next class, Tech Integration. The agenda shared by Dr. Menta included a single task: *androids and guides become acquainted.*

When the cohort meeting came to a close, the Boulder emerged from the water and settled back on the shore. Charlotte's legs wobbled as she stepped onto solid ground, and she regained her balance while she and Gavin said goodbye to Chai and Jace.

"We'll see you at dinner," Chai said, a tenor of anxiety underlying her voice.

Jace bumped Gavin's shoulder. "Be prepared to tell us *everything.*"

"Will do, man," Gavin replied. "Unless the androids kidnap us and wipe our memories first."

Jace laughed at this, but Chai paled. Charlotte rolled her eyes at Gavin and wrapped her arm around Chai's shoulders in a brief hug. "Don't worry, Chai. Gavin's being ridiculous. Everything's going to be fine." At least, she hoped everything would be fine.

Chai smiled weakly as she turned away with Jace, and Charlotte and Gavin joined the group walking north around the lake. Other students gradually peeled off in the direction of their classes, eventually leaving them heading toward the

Abyss with Beckett.

Beckett looked between the two of them, and his eyes narrowed. "I knew you were one of the guides, Gavin. You're not as clever as you think."

Gavin grinned. "I might say the same thing to you, Beckett."

In a huff, Beckett walked a few paces ahead, and Gavin turned to Charlotte. "So, any interest in joining my enigma team?"

Charlotte shrugged. "I don't know. If you recall from last year, I'm not a great enigma player." She flushed with embarrassment at her own understatement. In the few matches she played last year, Charlotte failed to complete a single challenge.

"Come on." Gavin nudged her shoulder. "It takes practice. No one's great when they start out." That was also an understatement. Gavin, in fact, was naturally one of the strongest players in their cohort.

Charlotte nodded noncommittally and let the subject drop. She appreciated Gavin's offer, but she doubted that he really wanted her to join his team.

A few students from other years joined them as they approached the Abyss, and soon enough they all reached the building with Dr. Menta's office. The door into the tree stood open this time, and the students walked in, passing through the trunk and into the grand space, seemingly open to the forest on all sides. Though clouds blanketed the sky today, in this room sunlight permeated the trees.

Charlotte nearly ran into Beckett when he stopped unexpectedly in front of her. Over his shoulder, she could see ten reasons why.

There they were, already seated in a semicircle, facing the entrance. As during the keynote, they projected a curious uniformity, despite their varied complexions; while their straight postures appeared stiff from a distance, up close Charlotte thought she would describe them as graceful, elegant even. She had never seen a group of humans sit so perfectly. The androids neither smiled nor frowned, rather adopting a neutral aloofness most appropriate for a vintage portrait.

For an unbroken moment, none of the students dared to move closer to their nonhuman peers.

CHAPTER 8

SILENCE EXPANDED THROUGH the room until Harper Devereaux, one of the fourth years, broke it with a single syllable. "Hi." With a little smile and a wave, she settled into one of the ten chairs facing the androids. The other students followed her lead.

The androids stared straight ahead, and Charlotte glanced briefly at the bright blue eyes of the pale android across from her. Looking to her right and left, she noticed that her fellow students were not making much eye contact with the intensely focused androids either. Except for Harper. Legs curled beneath her, she leaned forward and studied the androids with an open curiosity.

Though she didn't know Harper well, Charlotte was immediately grateful for her presence. It didn't escape Charlotte's notice that they were the only two girls in the room. The Academy thoughtfully pursued equity in all measures, so Charlotte wondered if other female students, like Athena, declined participation in the program.

With a bouncy click of her heels, Dr. Menta joined them, her warm smile dissipating some of the awkwardness. She moved to the chair on the north side of the room, in between the two semicircles, and the androids turned their heads, though not their bodies, in unison.

"Good morning and welcome to Tech Integration," Dr. Menta greeted them. "I'm glad to see you all."

She looked toward the human students. "Unless you checked the agenda, some of you may be understandably surprised to see our entire class gathered here. I think I mentioned in some of our conversations that today would be a time for the android guides to meet with me as a group. At first, that was my intent. After speaking with many of you, though, I realized that we would accomplish little without an introduction to the androids themselves."

She directed her next words to the entire room. "Our objective for today, therefore, is to get to know one another. Before we do that, I have a few reminders to share. I told most of you yesterday that all of your interactions will be recorded through the androids' viewers. These recordings will of course be anonymized and analyzed only for broad data trends." Charlotte was not aware of this, but they had received similar messages before. Committed to iterative improvement, the Academy often recorded classes or assignments for professors to review as part of their professional development. "And you of course know that captures of the androids are not permitted unless you receive an explicit exception from me. Even in those exceptions, the recordings - as well as any other information about the androids - must not leave the Cognation grounds in any capacity. There will come a time when this program - and your participation in it - will have a wide audience, but for now, this research and your experiences fall under Cognation's second-tier privacy policies. Understood?"

Dr. Menta made eye contact with each of the human students as they nodded. "Excellent!" She clasped her hands together and smiled. "Now comes the fun part. I know you are each anxious to know which of these lucky androids will be your partner, so we're going to start there. Once I share the list of pairs, you will have an hour to begin learning about each other. How you use this time is up to you. I think that a natural conversation is likely the best way to get started; however, you will also find in your viewers a list of topics, in case that is helpful. Remember that you will be working closely with each other for the entire semester, so the more you can learn during this time, the better."

Dr. Menta stood and began listing names. When called, the androids looked at their guides, seemingly already aware of the identities of the students in the room. Charlotte tried to connect each android to his name, but Dr. Menta went too quickly. While Charlotte waited for her own name to be called, she heard that Harper was matched with an android named Grayton and Beckett was paired with Denton.

"Rhyland, Torrance." Charlotte knew her name must be coming soon.

"Gavin, Eli." The android across from Charlotte glanced at Gavin to her left.

"Charlotte." Dr. Menta paused, and Charlotte felt her pulse quicken. "Isaac."

Isaac turned to her from his seat on the other side of the room and smiled. She smiled back, desperately hoping that none of her classmates would notice the flush she could feel coming to her cheeks. For an embarrassed moment, she wondered if Dr. Menta somehow knew that she would have picked Isaac if given the choice.

"Your hour starts now," Dr. Menta said at the conclusion of her list, and Charlotte saw a timer appear in the top right corner of her viewer. "I'll be circulating if you need anything. You are welcome to stay in this room, but you may want to spread out and explore this section of campus. If you do venture beyond this building, please remain within a kilometer radius." When no one moved, Dr. Menta cleared her throat and gestured for them to stand. "There is no need to be shy. Please enjoy this time and go wherever you will be most comfortable."

The androids rose in one motion; slowly, the human students stood as well while cautiously eyeing their partners. Though some of her classmates stayed in place, Charlotte, aware of Dr. Menta's discerning attention, joined Harper and Gavin in stepping confidently forward.

As she and Isaac met, Charlotte's projected confidence fell away. Isaac seemed even taller up close, and Charlotte looked up quickly to meet his eyes before glancing down. "Hi," she said, not quite sure where to start.

"It is a pleasure to meet you, Charlotte." His voice, smooth and deep, resting somewhere between an American and Canadian accent, unbalanced her. Even though she had heard him introduce himself at the keynote, she still expected him to sound more stilted, more robotic.

"Yeah, thanks. It's great to meet you," she responded inelegantly, trying to resume eye contact despite her nerves. She wished she possessed Gavin's easy friendliness; out of the corner of her eye, she saw him already settled into an energetic conversation with his android. She wavered in her next move; several students had pulled chairs to the side, clearly intending to stay in the room, but the space, even with the transparent walls, suddenly felt inexplicably crowded.

"Would you like to go outside?" Isaac asked, practically reading Charlotte's thoughts. "I have not had the opportunity to explore much of the campus, so it would be my pleasure to accompany you to one of your favorite locations."

Impressed by Isaac's knack for smoothing over the clumsiness of a new acquaintanceship, she met his gaze and wondered if he remembered seeing her outside of the Gem. Something in his eyes told her that he did, but before she could follow that train of thought, she forced herself to focus on the task at hand.

"I've got it," Charlotte said, the right spot popping into her mind. "Follow me."

CHAPTER 9

CHARLOTTE NESTLED INTO the emerald green hammock and tucked her legs beneath her. She had nearly forgotten about this comfy little nook. During Marissa's tenure as a student, this had been Charlotte's favorite hideaway when visiting her sister.

Charlotte shut her eyes for a moment, basking in the gentle rocking of the soft fabric wrapped around her. When she opened them, she saw that Isaac remained standing in front of her.

"It's a hammock," Charlotte said slowly, gesturing to the olive one directly behind him, a few feet across from hers.

"Yes."

"Would you like to sit?"

"Would you like me to sit?"

"Um, yes?"

Isaac settled into the hammock unnaturally as he mirrored her position while maintaining his impeccable posture. It occurred to Charlotte that he probably never sat in a hammock before. She was glad she had thought to tuck her feet; if their legs were dangling, they would likely be touching.

On their way here, Charlotte couldn't figure out how to

bridge the awkward silence, but Isaac had seemed content to walk without talking. Now, face-to-face with him again, Charlotte shifted uncomfortably. How should she start the conversation? She almost opened Dr. Menta's topics for discussion when Isaac saved her from that necessity.

"What is your full name?"

"Um, my name is Charlotte Edith Blythe. How about you?"

"My full name is Isaac. Surnames are traditionally passed down from generations or created through familial bonds; as no generations have come before me and as I have no family, Isaac is my only given name." Before Charlotte could respond to this, Isaac pressed on with another question.

"What is your major?"

"Tech innovations."

"What do you want to do after you graduate from the Academy?"

"I want to get my degree in tech ethics and join my sister's department at Cognation."

"Do you have any other siblings?"

"No."

"What do your parents do?"

"They work for Cognation on a special project."

"Who are your friends?"

"Chai Murthy and Jace Templeton are my best friends. You'll get to meet them soon."

"What is your favorite subject?"

"That depends on the semester, but-"

"What are your hobbies?"

As much as Charlotte appreciated Isaac taking control of the conversation, she could barely keep up with his pace. "Whoa, Isaac. Slow down."

"What are your hobbies?" he repeated at half speed.

A laugh escaped Charlotte's lips. "That's not what I mean. You're interrogating me, giving question after question."

Isaac's eyebrows shot up. "It is my understanding that asking questions is one of the primary means through which humans learn about each other."

"Well, that's kind of true, but it's better to have more of a conversation and, like, naturally discuss the topics that come up. Sometimes, you can learn more just by talking than by asking someone a series of direct questions."

"Ah," he said. "I will need to investigate that concept further, but I believe I have a preliminary understanding."

Isaac's silence indicated that Charlotte should continue the conversation, but she struggled to come up with a question. Who knew what androids liked to talk about? "Why don't you tell me something interesting about yourself? I'm all ears."

His head angled forty-five degrees. "You appear to have two ears, which is the evolutionarily standard number for homo sapiens."

She tried to hold in her smile. "That's a figure of speech. It means that I'm listening to what you have to say. Now, tell me something interesting about yourself."

"I am six feet tall."

Charlotte nodded. "I noticed." She had noticed a lot about him.

"My research indicates that humans usually find height interesting."

"Yes," she said encouragingly. "That's a good start. Maybe you could tell me something about your life before the keynote?"

"I cannot."

"You don't want to talk about it?"

"I do not have access to my recorded data before the day of the keynote."

"Really?" Charlotte raised her eyebrow. "Are you sure that the data exists? Or were you, like, born on the day of the keynote?" She cringed slightly as the second question left her lips; she didn't know if asking about an android's inception was taboo.

Evidently unbothered by the question, Isaac said, "The researchers have referenced events prior to the keynote, and their patterns indicate that they record all of their work. My recollection of embodied experience begins on the morning of the keynote, but all evidence signifies that we came into existence well before that point."

"Interesting," she said, trying to mask her surprise. Marissa would want to hear this. "Does it bother you? That you don't remember when you were first created?"

"I have never considered it. Do you remember when you were first created?"

"No," she said slowly, "but my parents have told me what my years as a baby were like. And they've shown me captures. I think it would bother me if I wasn't told anything about my life before my memories."

"For your sake, I am glad to know that your parents have not withheld that information from you. I assume that Dr. Menta has good reasons for withholding data from us, but I will consider whether or not that should be problematic for me."

Charlotte had no idea how to respond to that. "Okay. Cool."

When Charlotte did not continue, Isaac reciprocated her earlier question. "Maybe you could tell me something about your life before the keynote?"

"Well, that's fifteen years' worth of 'data,' but let's see. I was born in the Northeast, a little outside of Boston. My parents still own our house on the North Shore, and we go there sometimes for holidays, if they can get away from work, which hasn't happened recently. It's not terribly different from here, but I miss being right across from the ocean. What do you think about the Pacific Northwest so far?"

Something had been bothering Charlotte about Isaac's eyes, and she leaned a little closer as he answered. Though ordinary at a distance, up close they revealed a subtle distinction. His pupils weren't round; rather, they were - she leaned even closer, trying to make it out - almost square, she decided. While hard to distinguish from his deep brown irises, his pupils were decidedly square with rounded corners. The effect was odd but not unpleasant. This detail did confuse her, though; why would Cognation go to such great lengths to make the androids appear perfectly human while leaving this one clear marker of their otherness?

"Charlotte?" Isaac asked.

"Yes?"

"Do you agree?"

Heat rose to her cheeks. She must have missed something he said when she was examining his eyes.

"Um, could you repeat what you said?"

"I said that it took us five minutes and twelve seconds to walk to this location, so we should leave now in order to return to the group on time."

"Oh, of course." She hopped to the ground. "That went fast."

Isaac untangled his legs from the hammock as well, somehow keeping his back perfectly straight. As they turned toward their classroom, he said, "The segment of time deemed an hour always passes at the same rate. Though the rotation of the Earth is not constant, I do not believe that humans account for this variability in their system for tracking time."

Charlotte laughed. Clearly this was going to be a common occurrence. "Right," she said. "I know it didn't literally go by fast, but it *felt* like it went quickly. It's another figure of speech. Like, if you're enjoying yourself, time seems to pass by faster than you'd like, but if you're bored or unhappy, time can seem to slow down."

Isaac nodded. "I understand. I appreciate your feedback that the conversation was enjoyable for you. I enjoyed it as well."

She smiled but said nothing, and they continued to walk in a silence that Charlotte found surprisingly comfortable.

CHAPTER 10

BY THE TIME Charlotte and Isaac returned to the room, the chairs again formed two semicircles, and the students, creatures of habit, reclaimed their original seats. The androids followed suit, which left Isaac disappointingly far from Charlotte.

Dr. Menta observed their movements silently before addressing the androids. "Gentlemen, I hope you had fruitful conversations with your guides. As you no doubt are starting to understand, human communication is a complex endeavor, and navigating a conversation with a stranger is a uniquely challenging social task. I look forward to receiving your reflections on the experience; you will find details for the assignment in your viewers." She paused for questions, but none of the androids spoke up. "At this time, your presence is requested in another session, as we discussed previously. Thank you for joining us today."

The androids rose and exited through the arboreal doorway; while many of them looked straight ahead, a few, Isaac included, glanced at their partners for a silent goodbye. Charlotte returned Isaac's smile and wondered when she would see him next.

Once the androids left, Dr. Menta moved her chair to the

middle of the room, across from the remaining students. "I know that today's task, though simple, was not easy, and I commend all of you on your participation. For now, I thought some of you may be more comfortable debriefing privately, among your fellow guides. Please know, however, that this will not become a habit. You may speak freely in front of the androids; they do not have emotions in the traditional sense, and therefore their feelings cannot be hurt. Furthermore, the androids will benefit from hearing your thoughts, so we will convene as an entire group in future sessions."

Dr. Menta scanned their faces before continuing. "From what I could tell, you all had fairly productive interactions, but I'd like to acknowledge that this was an entirely new experience for everyone. A necessary element of this program is the ability to reflect on your experiences and to collaboratively work through any challenges, and I encourage you to be as honest as you can with the group, and more importantly, with yourselves."

Dr. Menta paused, giving them a moment to organize their thoughts. Aside from Isaac's tendency to take things literally, Charlotte's conversation with him had been largely effortless, pleasant even, and she couldn't wait to hear about everyone else's discussions.

"To start," Dr. Menta instructed, "please think of the first three words that come to mind to describe your android partner. When ready, submit the words through your viewers."

Taking Dr. Menta's directions literally (perhaps Isaac was already rubbing off on her), Charlotte submitted the first three words that surfaced in her mind.

She instantly regretted her impulsivity.

A 3-D word cloud appeared in their shared viewerspace, and Charlotte's eyes darted from word to word: *programmed, robotic, boring, interesting, confusing, predictable, curious, attentive, ambivalent, inconsiderate, childish, strange.*

With increasing embarrassment, she realized that her contributions - *thoughtful, kind, funny* - stuck out amid the largely neutral to negative adjectives. With some relief, though, she noticed *friendly* and *helpful* also in the mix.

"Funny?" Beckett muttered under his breath. "Somebody got a funny android?"

"Would you like to elaborate on your question, Beckett?"

Open-mouthed, Beckett stared back at Dr. Menta, and Gavin and Charlotte shared a quick, bemused glance. Beckett was not used to being called out, but he deftly recovered and adopted a pedantic tone.

"I was noticing that funny seems to be a bit of an outlier. My particular partner did not display any inclination toward humor, and I was wondering if any of the androids might be endowed with the ability to be funny or if that might lie more in the eye of the beholder."

Dr. Menta looked to the group to continue the discussion, and Henry Perabo, a third year, jumped in. "That's an interesting question. Our understanding of the androids is as much influenced by our expectations as it is by their direct behavior. So while they might not be capable of intentional humor - my android, Edmond, also didn't seem to be funny - their actions or words may contradict social norms, which could contribute to humorous situations."

"I agree that my android did not appear to understand social norms," Beckett responded. "In his case, however, his lack of social awareness resulted more in rudeness than in humor."

Harper, transfixed by the words floating in the middle of the room, spoke almost to herself. "We generated twenty-five different words. I wouldn't have predicted that at the start of this class. When we first saw them, the androids seemed so similar, almost uniform, despite their appearances. But they're not similar." She said it half as a statement, half as a question.

Dr. Menta nodded. "You are correct, Harper. That is exactly what I hoped you would gather from this exercise. Up to this point, we have been speaking of the androids as a monolithic group. As you are beginning to see, however, that is not the case. Part of the purpose of this program is to evaluate different methods of personality embodiment; therefore, each of the androids has been programmed with slightly different characteristics. Of course, we know that human personality development is part nature, part nurture, so I expect that as you interact with your partners further, you may notice some evolving alterations in their behavior."

"Can the androids change their personalities?" asked Jepsen, a first year.

"From a programmatic standpoint, no. Those settings can only be adjusted remotely. From a learning standpoint, however, it's not only possible but almost guaranteed. For example, some of the androids are programmed to be less outgoing, less overtly friendly than others, but given the right incentives, that could change, just as an introverted person might become more sociable in the right conditions."

"But you could erase that learning if you reprogrammed their personality levels." Gavin, usually jovial, sounded pensive.

Dr. Menta paused before answering. "Theoretically, yes. But we would not do that unless extreme extenuating circumstances warranted intervention. The androids' baseline personality levels have been set as controls, and altering them would invalidate vast segments of our data."

Charlotte shifted uncomfortably. The thought of someone having the power to change her personality with a switch gave her the chills.

"Any other questions?" Dr. Menta pressed.

Charlotte did have a question, one she had been struggling to form into words for the entire conversation. Dr. Menta caught her eye and nodded slightly, as if sensing her thoughts.

"Well, you said that they don't have emotions, but…what if they said they did? For example, what if they said they enjoyed something?"

"That's an excellent question, Charlotte. The technology we've used to create the androids comes from a long tradition of affective computing. Many factors - conversational pattern recognition, mirroring of your own language, contextual clues, personality settings - might lead an android to convey emotion in a certain way, but *expressing* emotion is not synonymous with *experiencing* emotion."

"It's not synonymous for humans either," Harper said. "Saying I'm feeling something and actually feeling something can be related, but they aren't inherently so."

"Absolutely." Dr. Menta beamed at Harper. "That is why this type of research has always been so interesting. The more we learn about human interactions with technology, the more we learn about the human condition itself. Though I expect this project to further our understanding of affective computing, at this time it is most accurate to say that androids do not have emotions, despite any behavior that might suggest otherwise."

Dr. Menta stood and smiled at the students. "I can tell that we have indeed selected a worthy group to participate in this journey, and we will continue these discussions throughout the semester. The requirements for today's reflection have been uploaded to your viewers, and they are due by midnight tonight. I look forward to reviewing your thoughts and, if you approve, I will share your reflections with your android partners. That decision is entirely up to you, so please choose whichever way will make you more comfortable. I will meet with you each individually for a final first-impression debrief, and the androids will then join the student body by the end of this week. Thank you all for your work today."

The students dispersed and began the lengthy walk back to main campus. Gavin practically bounced with excitement alongside Charlotte. "That was awesome," he said. "I kind of got a little brother vibe from Eli. I bet there's a lot I can teach him this year."

Charlotte laughed. Gavin was no troublemaker, but he liked a good joke. "I hope Eli knows what he's getting himself into."

Beckett, eavesdropping from behind, inserted himself into the conversation. "My android is quite boring. That was one of the most awkward hours I've ever spent. It barely had anything to say."

Charlotte could relate. She didn't always have anything to say to Beckett either.

Luckily, Gavin did. "Might help if you referred to your android as *he* rather than *it*. Or you could use his name."

Beckett scoffed. "Okay, *Denton* is quite boring. Is that better?" Turning away, he muttered a final thought under his breath, loud enough for them to hear. "I didn't know we had a bunch of android lovers on our hands already."

CHAPTER 11

MY ANDROID IS quite…interesting! Charlotte couldn't think of how to describe Isaac to Chai and Jace in a message, so she decided they'd have to wait until she could tell them more in person.

She knew they wouldn't see the message until after their Creation of Life course anyway. During the first weeks, students spent more time than usual in classes; beyond the introductory period, they would have additional flex time, but that didn't change the fact that Charlotte was on her own for lunch today. After grabbing a veggie wrap and apple from the lunch stand near the Gem, she hesitated.

Several other second years were eating in the gardens or on the lawn by the lake, but she turned instead toward the west side of campus. Though friendly with many of her classmates, she never developed any close friendships last year beyond Chai and Jace, and to an extent, Gavin. Working with other students on projects was easy, but socializing outside of classes came less naturally to Charlotte. Besides, something had been bothering her since the keynote, and she welcomed the time alone to start figuring it out.

Reaching the base of one of the western hills, Charlotte

looked up at the wide awning set deep into the stone. With its middle peak and mossy vines looping outward, the awning had always reminded Charlotte of a book suspended upside down. A fitting image, she supposed, for the entrance to the Dr. Harlan A. Coggins Memorial Library, named in honor of Cognation's famous founder, who purportedly used this site as one of his initial workspaces.

Charlotte stepped through the air-locked doors to the cavernous main chamber. The sloping walls reached upward to meet at irregular angles, forming an incongruous ceiling. Every inch of the encompassing surface that stretched above Charlotte's head was slotted with shelves and books that seemed to defy gravity, making the space feel simultaneously more expansive and confined.

Francine Locke, a third year, sat atop one of the tables amid stacks of books as she flipped through one with a thick binding and old-fashioned paper.

"Hi, Charlotte," she said, barely looking up. "Anything I can help you with?"

Francine spent most of her time in the library. Though any student could explore the public stacks with the aid of the digital catalog, Francine served as an unofficial librarian, and she was just the person Charlotte hoped to see.

"I'm doing some research into the history of artificial intelligence. Do you think there might be some records here from the formation of the Alliance? Or the founding of Cognation? Maybe something I wouldn't find on the viewernet?"

"Hmm. Interesting research, especially given our new friends on campus." Francine looked up fully now, staring at Charlotte thoughtfully. "I would expect much of that information to be available virtually, but there might be some hidden gems around here. Follow me."

Francine hopped down from the table and led Charlotte through a gently sloping maze of narrow hallways sporadically dotted with intermittent shelves. By the time they reached a small, round alcove ringed with books, Charlotte wasn't sure how many floors they had descended. The virtual skylight in the ceiling helped to mitigate the effects of being deep in the hillside, but Charlotte still had to push back a wave of claustrophobia. She didn't often delve into the alcoves of the library, and none of the students were quite sure how far the library extended below campus.

They knew only that Winton Latham collected scores of rare books, many of which he donated to the school. Rumors held that the most precious of the collectibles rested within a secret labyrinth beneath the library's main floor, but to Charlotte's knowledge, no one, not even Francine, had discovered the mythical tunnels. Even more outrageous rumors suggested that Winton Latham designed a number of hidden spots around campus that could only be accessed through a special viewer code. Every year, students searched for these locations; every year, students came up short.

"I would start here," Francine said. "This collection includes some of Dr. Coggins' personal journals, and I'm not sure if they were all officially recorded."

"Wow. Thanks, Francine. This is perfect."

"No problem." She returned to the main chamber, her footsteps echoing faintly back to Charlotte, who started to glance through the titles on the spines.

The section with Dr. Coggins' journals covered a good part of an entire wall; evidently he was a fan of real paper, even though digital sheets would have been available at the time.

Charlotte sighed. This would take a while to sort through. Locating what appeared to be the earliest recordings, she tucked the first two volumes into her bag for later.

She couldn't pinpoint exactly what she hoped to find, but Chai's parents had piqued Charlotte's interest in the Alliance's history. Though the information she found about the Boston Clinic autonurses mirrored what Mr. Murthy shared, she couldn't find many additional details. In fact, she could find surprisingly little about the formation of the Alliance, aside from the messaging presented by the group itself.

Since the Alliance was formed decades ago, Charlotte had never thought much about it. Now, though, something told her she should start paying a bit more attention to the history she had taken for granted.

Today, the Mod spread into a one-story pentagon, and Charlotte snagged a table overlooking the lake while she waited for her friends.

"Are you okay?" The genuine concern on Chai's face as she and Jace sat down for dinner surprised Charlotte.

"I'm fine. Why?"

"Beckett was really cagey about your first class with the androids. He barely said anything. I didn't even know he was capable of being so quiet."

Jace, somehow already through a third of his pad thai, swallowed. "He said he's not even sure if he wants to continue, which is super surprising, given how hyped he was about it."

"I think he really spooked some first years when he described his android as a robotic zombie," Chai added.

Charlotte shook her head. Leave it to Beckett to make his experience the prominent narrative. "That's not fair, or accurate. At least, not for all of them. I didn't really get to meet Beckett's android. But it's ridiculous that he's badmouthing them already. Let's be honest, his android probably wasn't thrilled with his partner either." The words came out a bit harsher than she intended.

Jace paused mid-bite and exchanged a glance with Chai, who frowned. "So your meeting with your android was okay?" she asked, barely masking her apprehension.

"Yeah, it was fine." Charlotte paused, considering how to share her thoughts without freaking Chai out. "Meeting Isaac was really nice, actually. I mean, it wasn't exactly like talking to a human, but in some ways, it was easier, less awkward than I expected. Isaac was polite and seemed genuinely interested in knowing more about me. He was even kind of funny." She felt her smile grow by the time she finished speaking.

"That's cool, dude," Jace said through a bite. "I knew Beckett was probably being crazy. I'm glad your first contact went well."

"Yeah, that's really great," Chai added flatly, after a barely perceptible pause.

Now it was Charlotte's turn to exchange a glance with Jace. "Are *you* okay, Chai?" Charlotte fought to keep her voice neutral as it occurred to her that Chai might be jealous. "I thought you'd be more excited about this. You're really going to trust Beckett's opinion over mine?" Charlotte wished Gavin were here to back her up.

"I'm sorry, Char. I was excited - *am* excited. I'm just a little worried, is all. Everyone's been talking about how Dr. Menta let the androids be alone with the guides right away, and people are wondering if that's such a good idea. If it's safe."

Everyone was talking about it? "You know the school wouldn't have brought the androids here if they weren't safe." Charlotte rolled her eyes. "People just like to gossip."

As if on cue, Athena, sitting at an adjacent table with Pri, raised her voice. "I doubt the androids will be here for very long anyway. As soon as Cognation gets the research they need, there will be no point in having them stick around. Hopefully no one gets too attached to the machines."

They're not machines. The thought came to Charlotte automatically, and she was glad she didn't say it out loud. Because, of course, they were machines. But that didn't mean they deserved to be disrespected by students who knew nothing about them.

Charlotte tuned Athena out and smiled at Chai; she didn't want to start the year off with an argument. "I appreciate your concern, but really there's nothing to worry about. I think you'll like Isaac when you get to meet him. Just keep an open mind until then." Chai nodded without looking convinced, and Charlotte changed the subject. "But enough about that. What's going on in the bio world?"

Chai's eyes lit up, as Charlotte knew they would, and the group spent most of dinner discussing organic research being conducted at the bottom of the lake for their Aquatic Systems course. By the time they circled back to talking about the androids, Chai was more relaxed and even showed interest in the biological aspects of the program.

As Charlotte told them more about Isaac, though, she struggled to ignore the seed Athena planted in her thoughts. Did the android research have an end date? If so, what would that mean for Isaac?

CHAPTER 12

EARLY THE NEXT morning, Charlotte and Chai arrived at the Treetop, a large, elevated structure spanning nearly a dozen trees, just as Jace approached from the other side. They climbed one of the spiral staircases and took three empty seats near the center of the half-circle arrangement, with Chai in the middle.

In the moments before Tech Ethics started, Chai and Jace chatted about their next class, and Charlotte, trying not to feel left out, let her mind drift to Isaac. Not for the first time in the past twenty-four hours, she again wondered what he was doing at that very moment.

"I thought Dr. Picartz was leading this course," Jace whispered, pulling Charlotte into the conversation.

"That's what our schedules show," she confirmed. With a near-compulsive habit of checking her schedule each night and morning, she knew this for certain.

Nonetheless, the woman fiddling around at the front of the room was certainly not Dr. Picartz.

With orange-tinted glasses and a mop of frizzy hair, Dr. Picartz was considered one of the more peculiar professors at the Academy. He carried a cane seemingly for no reason, and he unnerved many students, Charlotte included, with the piercing stare behind the amber lenses of his viewer. He had an ageless face, so guesses about his age ranged from late thirties to nearly sixty. He also kept a low public profile. Very low. Students, Jace included, who were inclined to research their professors could find little about his background on the viewer-net, and Dr. Picartz shared few details about his life before joining the Academy five years ago.

"Good morning, dears." The delicate, white-haired woman standing before them addressed the class exactly on time. "As you can tell, I am not Dr. Picartz. I am Dr. Flomacauge, and I will be leading Tech Ethics today." She offered no further introduction, but Charlotte couldn't help feeling a bit relieved. Dr. Picartz, while brilliant, often led a stressful class. Dr. Flomacauge, on the other hand, was adorable. She reminded Charlotte of her grandma, whom she vaguely remembered from her childhood, and she almost expected the wispy woman to start handing out freshly baked cookies.

"As you are aware, I hope, there were a number of momentous judicial decisions this summer regarding - oh!" Dr. Flomacauge paused mid-sentence and clutched her pearls as the floor began to rumble violently. The room stabilized a moment later, and Charlotte could have believed she imagined it if not for the startled looks on all of her classmates' faces.

"Well." Dr. Flomacauge smoothed her hair and cleared her throat to continue, but the room began to move again, vertically this time.

This just wasn't possible. The Treetop was fixed, anchored to the trees. Grabbing Charlotte and Jace's hands, Chai started breathing quickly, and her eyes grew rounder with each foot they climbed.

The movement paused a moment later. No one seemed to

know what was happening, including Dr. Flomacauge, and Charlotte sensed her classmates collectively holding their breath.

Then the building dropped.

Like an acorn falling from the highest branch, their classroom rushed toward the ground. Two feet? Ten feet? Fifty feet? Charlotte couldn't tell. She only knew that her stomach jumped into her throat, and her best friend, who avoided amusement rides, even virtual rides, at all costs, had gone rigid beside her. Just as concerning, Dr. Flomacauge appeared to faint, and the class was descending further into chaos. The building reversed course, soaring upwards again, a disconcerting indication that this process might repeat.

Charlotte instinctively recited her manual override phrase in her mind to no avail. If any part of this had been a simulation through her viewer, that secure thought would have stopped it, but the climbing didn't cease.

Jace wrapped his arm around Chai as she shivered in terror. He and Charlotte locked eyes over Chai's head.

"What's happening?" Charlotte asked, her fear mounting with the altitude.

Jace shrugged, helpless frustration clouding his face; then, abruptly, he raised his eyebrows with an idea. The building perched at its highest point, sure to plummet once again, when Jace took off his viewer glasses. "Dr. Picartz?" he gasped.

The rest of the class followed Jace's gaze toward the front of the room, but Charlotte could only see Dr. Flomacauge, slumped in her chair.

"Dr. Picartz, make this stop!" Jace demanded, pulling Chai in closer.

For a moment, nothing happened. Then, astonishingly, Dr. Flomacauge straightened up and morphed into Dr. Picartz as the building smoothly returned to its original elevation.

"Very good, Mr. Templeton. I applaud your resourcefulness. The ability to quickly remove your glasses is one benefit of not adopting the viewer contacts." Dr. Picartz's mouth twisted into an off-putting smile. "It did take this class rather longer to catch on than my last. It appears that some of you are still working things out. Would anyone care to explain?"

"You hacked our viewers." Athena, unlike the majority of the students who glared at Dr. Picartz, looked up at him with awe. "You hacked our viewers, and we had no idea."

"And?" Dr. Picartz prompted.

When Athena remained silent, Charlotte said, "And we couldn't stop it. My override thought had no effect, and I'm guessing I'm not the only one who tried that?" A few of her classmates nodded shakily. "That further strengthened the illusion that everything was happening in the real world, not in the viewerspace."

"Excellent observation, Ms. Blythe." He glanced around the room and twirled his cane slowly. While most of the angry scowls had subsided, many students still looked wary. "You no doubt heard that viewer hacking was on the rise this summer. Cognation anticipated that this would be an unfortunate side effect of the viewer contacts' growing popularity. The more immersive the technology is, the harder it becomes to separate the viewerspace from reality. At first, using individualized override thoughts, as you have become accustomed to, was sufficient. But that, I'm afraid, is no longer always the case."

He twirled his cane again as he circled the students. "While the ethics involved in individual and mass viewer hacking are fairly clear, we will have some intriguing case studies to unravel this semester. More importantly, though, we will be working with Cognation as we consider the responsibility both of corporations and of private citizens in preventing and defending against these hacks. For one of your projects, you lucky students will be creating and testing counter hacks so that you will not be fooled again." This last sentence somehow came across more threatening than reassuring. "Any last questions before we move on to our work for the day? Go ahead, Ms. Fawlings."

"Will we also learn how the hacks occur in the first place?"

Athena's indirect wording failed to fool Dr. Picartz, and leaning on his cane, he answered slowly. "That is an interesting question indeed. I believe you are asking whether or not you will learn how to hack another person's viewer. Through developing counter hacks, we will by necessity uncover many of the underlying structures that make the hacks effective. However, we will not waste our time together on learning how to intentionally interfere with a viewer that does not belong to you. I also feel it is my responsibility to remind you that even attempting to hack another classmate's viewer could lead to expulsion. Our, shall we say *exciting*, start to class today was approved by the faculty and conducted in order to impress the gravity of the situation upon you. The other professors and I employ our methods with an utmost understanding of the teaching purpose behind them; do not confuse our teaching methods with your own curiosity."

Through this speech, Athena kept her head up, not at all abashed by Dr. Picartz's implied reprimand.

When Athena didn't respond, their professor turned back to the class. "Now. Any further questions?"

Charlotte, Chai, and Jace glanced at each other. No one dared to ask what Charlotte suspected they were all thinking. If Dr. Picartz could hack them so easily, then who else might be able to take over their viewers?

CHAPTER 13

"I HEARD YOU survived Dr. Picartz's little hacking spree this morning." Gavin plopped down on the mat next to Charlotte, and she sat up to face him.

"No thanks to those of you in his class yesterday who failed to warn us."

Gavin grinned sheepishly. "You know he wouldn't allow that. He swore us to secrecy 'on penalty of death, or as near as the Academy will allow.'" He shrugged and straightened out his legs. "Man, he's a weird guy, but I guess he wanted to make a strong impression."

"Mission accomplished." Charlotte leaned back onto her mat. "I'm hoping this class will be a little more relaxing." In fact, just entering this class helped Charlotte feel calm. This room, one of the breakout spaces attached to the Gem, was a blank canvas - white walls, white floors, white ceiling - and the effect was strangely soothing.

Tall and powerfully slender, Dr. Cariciarra entered the room and reclined on her mat in one silent, graceful movement. The lights dimmed as she commenced the meditation program, which was her signature method of starting and ending class.

Dr. Cariciarra first directed them to let their minds meander, and Charlotte's thoughts unsurprisingly wandered to Isaac, who had been occupying quite a bit of her mental space. Though she wouldn't say it out loud, she couldn't wait to see him again, and she constantly found herself wondering what he was doing, and thinking, at any given moment. As the meditation sequence continued, Charlotte's mind eventually cleared, and the room melted away into an ethereal prism of light. As though guided by the waves of color themselves, Charlotte felt her body moving through gentle stretches. By the time the room resumed its physical form, she and her classmates were seated on their mats, backs long, legs folded.

"Welcome to Philosophy of Reality." Dr. Cariciarra's musical voice wrapped around the students. "Thank you for joining me on our meditative journey this morning. I have found that stepping outside of oneself greatly expands the mind and enables deep exploration of thought. In light of that, meditation exercises will serve as one foundation of our work together."

Viewer meditation sequences had been popular for a while, and Chai and Charlotte tried a few out last year. None of them, however, had made Charlotte feel this calm. She had no doubt that this would be one of her favorite classes this semester.

"Tell me, was the meditative space we just inhabited real? Palms up for yes; palms down for no." Dr. Cariciarra's question hung in between the students. With an indecisive quiver, Charlotte left her hands face down on her knees. Sneaking a glance around, she saw that the room was split; Gavin next to her had one palm down and one palm up.

Dr. Cariciarra noticed as well. "Gavin, please explain your answer."

"Well, on the one hand, of course that wasn't real. We know that we've all been in this room, not in some color-warped space that we could never find without our viewers. But on the other hand, we experienced it, so on some level, it has to be real. If we only lived in the viewerspace, and that was our world, then we wouldn't know that it didn't exist."

Their professor smiled. "Excellent. The human race grappled with these questions long before virtual and augmented reality, but as we grow better equipped to alter, obscure, and amplify our reality, the conundrum of what is real and what is not has continued to gain additional dimensions. Throughout this course, we will consider some of the puzzles raised by the integration of technology with reality. For example, if you visit a location in the viewerspace that you've never visited in person, does that location exist in reality? If you virtually communicate with someone you have not seen in person for months or years, does that person exist in reality? In all cases, how do we distinguish between the reality of our experiences and the reality that exists beyond our perception?"

As Dr. Cariciarra spoke, her words appeared around the room, and Charlotte shifted uncomfortably at the questions shimmering in front of her. The last time she saw her parents in person had been on the morning they left months ago with promises to return soon. Soon had come and gone, but she was grateful that they could connect by viewerspace; it seemed ridiculous to consider that not seeing people for a span of time, no matter how long, made them any less real.

Breaking into Charlotte's thoughts, Dr. Cariciarra said, "These considerations will guide our work this semester. By examining theories spanning from ancient times to the modern era, you will develop your own theory of philosophy, through the lens of reality. Today, your first thought experiment is to create a representation of reality based on your current understanding. In general, students have found this to be difficult, so my advice is not to overthink your instincts, but rather to focus on what feels right. You may use any media, and as long as your representation is personally meaningful to you, there is no right or wrong answer. You are welcome to work with a partner, but if at any point your ideas diverge, then I encourage you to part ways. You have thirty minutes to work before we share and reflect."

Most of the students moved sluggishly, still calmed by the meditation's spell, but Gavin, ever full of energy, turned immediately to Charlotte. "Want to partner up?"

Charlotte nodded, and they smiled at each other until Charlotte looked down, trying to figure out where to start. Gavin took her pause as his cue to jump right in; it didn't surprise Charlotte that he already had plenty of ideas bouncing around his mind. "Okay, one thought I have is maybe reality is like a trail, you know, but a trail with different branches and different levels, and some paths are dead ends while others loop back on themselves."

She attempted to visualize the image. "I like that. Maybe in addition to dead ends there are also open ends, like ends that keep growing, to show that reality is mutable and maybe created by those who try to follow the path, or try to define it."

"Yes! So freakin deep." He gave her a high five. "Let's build it." They created a virtual 3-D model in their viewerspace, adding details and refining their vision, and before Charlotte knew it, their thirty minutes were up.

With a wave of her hand, Dr. Cariciarra spread the representations evenly around the room and tasked the students with making connections between them. "As you create a link between representations, indicate with a word or image what sparked that connection."

At first glance, Charlotte could discern few commonalities. Some of the representations were only sound, only color, only a physical sensation. On closer inspection, though, she began to notice underlying patterns, and she joined her classmates in constructing a glowing, interlaced web that filled the space.

Dr. Cariciarra asked them to step back and gaze upon their creation. "This network represents our first steps into understanding reality. Take a moment and inhabit this space. Let your mind be free to wander."

Like a reflex, Charlotte's mind shifted straight to Isaac, and she wondered how he might describe reality. She had an uncanny feeling that he would have liked this activity, but before she could nail down what gave her that feeling, the web gradually faded out of view, signaling the end of class.

With a quick goodbye to Charlotte, Gavin sprinted out of the room, presumably to meet up with his fellow trail runners. As Charlotte left the Gem alone, the warmth of the meditation dissipated much more quickly than she would have liked, leaving her with the discomfort of Dr. Cariciarra's earlier questions.

On her way to meet with Dr. Menta, Charlotte tried to view her parents again. Still no answer.

CHAPTER 14

UPDATE: THE LOCATION for your meeting with Dr. Menta has been changed to Lab 24, Room 7.

Charlotte received the message just as she started walking toward the Abyss, and she changed course to head toward the autotram.

Traveling to Cognation Industries was only permitted for official reasons, but the tram doors opened, recognizing Charlotte's identity and her schedule from her ring. All Academy students and Cognation employees received a ring when they joined the community; activated only when worn by the owner, it served as both an ID and a key, granting access to buildings as appropriate.

Charlotte remembered her intense jealousy when everyone else in her family received their rings, and when she finally became an Academy student, she selected one nearly identical to Marissa's. Delicate, with twisted bands and emerald stones for the sisters' May birthdays, the rings only revealed their slight differences in pattern upon close inspection.

Marissa had seemed flattered by Charlotte's nearly matching accessory, at least until this summer. One morning, Charlotte had awoken with a jolt as Marissa rushed back into her apartment. Somehow, she had mistakenly grabbed Charlotte's ring and was unable to access her lab in time for an important meeting.

"If you didn't always feel the need to copy me, this wouldn't have happened," Marissa huffed to herself as she found her own ring and raced out again. Charlotte knew Marissa thought she didn't hear her, and they didn't speak about it again. Charlotte made sure, though, to keep all of her belongings separate from Marissa's for the rest of the summer.

A few minutes later, Charlotte stepped off the autotram and navigated to Dr. Menta's lab without the aid of her viewer. Though greenery blanketed the buildings tucked within the forested grounds, Cognation's campus lacked the whimsy reserved for the Academy. Mostly uniform structures, the labs spiraled outward from a spacious central courtyard in a pleasing, but predictable, pattern.

The mirrored doors opened silently as Charlotte approached Lab 24. "Welcome, Charlotte." A cool androgynous voice emanated from the walls. "Please proceed to your left to reach Dr. Menta's office."

Charlotte stopped at the door with a glowing number seven and knocked. Muffled sounds reached her as she waited.

"I don't agree with that course of action." Dr. Menta's voice carried an unfamiliar edge.

"You don't get to make those decisions, Rosalind." Male and patronizing, the voice might have belonged to Dr. Kindred, though Charlotte couldn't tell for sure. The exchange continued for a moment. Unable to make out any other words, Charlotte shuddered a bit at the heated tone of the conversation.

The door slid open suddenly to reveal Dr. Menta, alone, sitting at a wide curving desk in front of a floor-to-ceiling view of the surrounding gardens. She beckoned Charlotte toward one of the chairs opposite her desk. Other than a faint splotchiness along her collarbone, nothing in Dr. Menta's demeanor suggested that a difficult discussion preceded Charlotte's arrival, and her welcoming smile eased some of Charlotte's tension.

"Charlotte, thank you for coming all this way. I promise not to make meetings out here a habit, but it couldn't be avoided today, I'm afraid."

"No worries, Dr. Menta. I like being over here in the labs."

"Ah, that's right. I forgot you spent your summer shadowing your sister." Shadowing didn't seem like the right word to Charlotte (she had done some work, after all), but she let it go. Dr. Menta waited until Charlotte was seated before continuing. "Your reflection was quite interesting, Charlotte. It seems like you and Isaac got off to a rather strong start yesterday."

"Yes." Dr. Menta looked at her, as if expecting more, so Charlotte elaborated. "As I described in my reflection, talking with him was unexpectedly nice. Maybe it's just because I'm used to Academy students, but usually when you meet someone new, even if they're kind and friendly, you can tell that the other person is a little guarded, or a little focused on their own ego, I guess? Isaac, though, was polite almost to a selfless level. Like he wanted to make the conversation go well. It felt like he was really listening to me."

"And this surprised you." It was an observation, not a question, and it made Charlotte wonder if she had been wrong to be surprised.

"Yes, it did. I expected him to be more awkward, I think. Or more robotic. The conversation did start out a bit like an interrogation, but once we got past that, things were more comfortable."

"I'm glad to hear that. I regret that not all of our guides had such a positive experience." Charlotte wondered if Dr. Menta was referencing Beckett or a different guide. "You mentioned briefly that you found some of Isaac's speech patterns strange. Can you expand on that?"

Charlotte tried to organize her thoughts. "I guess I expected him to be more advanced conversationally. At times, I felt like I was explaining something to a child, not to an android."

Dr. Menta nodded. "That's a valuable insight for me to pass on to our language teams. Decoding grammar and explicit definitions of words have been manageable for language processing algorithms for a while, but most of us underestimate how many times we break those rules and bend those meanings. Isaac should adapt as he engages with more conversations."

Dr. Menta paused for a moment, joining her fingertips in front of her face. "As it turns out, Isaac's class schedule is currently identical to yours, which means that he will be in all of your courses. Do you have any concerns about that?"

Charlotte shook her head. "No, that should be fine." *More than fine*, Charlotte admitted to herself.

"Excellent. Starting tomorrow, the androids will fully join the Academy community. Beyond classes, you may choose how much time to spend with Isaac. We want the students' interactions with the androids to evolve as naturally as possible, within the circumstances, so whether or not you spend time with Isaac, or any of the other androids, outside of classes is entirely up to you. We will continue to hold regular check-ins, but don't forget that you're welcome to contact me any time. Do you have any questions before we wrap up?"

Charlotte started to shake her head again, but then she remembered. "Yes, actually. I was wondering what happened to the androids before they were introduced at the keynote? Isaac said he doesn't have access to any memories, or records, of his experiences before then."

Dr. Menta frowned for an instant, almost imperceptibly, before shaking her head. "That, unfortunately, is proprietary information. Patents are pending on the android development and training processes we used, so all records have been sealed for the moment. Once we are able to share this information publicly, we will restore the data to the androids' sequences, but I assure you that the details are irrelevant to them at this point."

It didn't seem irrelevant to Charlotte for the androids to know how they came to existence. "What if the androids wanted to know about their inception?"

Given the frown line that appeared above Dr. Menta's brow, Charlotte wished she could take the question back.

"They want what we program them to want, Charlotte." A tinge of pity shaded Dr. Menta's voice. "It's best if you try to remember that. The androids, Isaac included, want to contribute to our research. Having access to proprietary information regarding their inception isn't required for their role right now."

This explanation failed to convince Charlotte, but she knew not to press the point further. Her face must have betrayed her, unfortunately, because Dr. Menta added more gently, "Even humans don't remember their births or their earliest days of development."

"Right." Though Isaac had raised a similar point, Charlotte didn't believe this comparison proved that Cognation should restrict the androids' access to their own memories.

Dr. Menta rose and directed Charlotte to the door. "The secretive nature of this type of work is difficult to get used to, I know, but it is a necessary evil when creating new technologies.

Just know that the androids have all of the information they need right now to be successful."

"Of course. Thank you, Dr. Menta." After Charlotte stepped into the hallway, the door shut behind her, and she tried not to dwell on the fact that Dr. Menta's parting smile wasn't quite as bright as it had been at the beginning of their session.

CHAPTER 15

WITH NERVOUS ANTICIPATION, Charlotte arrived at Tech Integration the next day. The androids, like last time, were already seated when Charlotte passed through the hollow tree. Unlike last time, the chairs were arranged in pairs spaced evenly throughout the room; each android sat next to an empty spot.

Isaac smiled at Charlotte, and she settled in beside him.

"Hello," he said. "How are you today?"

"I'm good, thanks. And you?"

"I am doing well. Thank you for asking." His formal tone was both charming and disquieting. She had never met anyone who spoke so precisely.

Dr. Menta rushed into the room right on time. "Good morning and welcome back. Now that we are all somewhat acquainted, we are going to jump right in today. As you know, the broad goal of the Android Inception Program is to study interactions between androids and humans in order to gain insights about artificial intelligence and the human mind. While this general purpose will guide your work this semester, you may approach this purpose in a variety of ways. The reason for piloting this program with ten androids and ten guides is to learn from a diversity of thoughts and personalities."

She paused for questions and continued when nobody spoke. "To start, we are going to brainstorm all of the elements of human-android interactions that may be worth focusing on this semester; using those elements as a starting point, we will then develop goals for our work. Please begin."

A three-dimensional board appeared in their viewerspace, and the group began populating it with ideas. Academy professors often started a design session this way; because students could individually manipulate the shared space from their seats, the process occasionally became chaotic but usually generated interesting insights.

This time, however, things proceeded quite unexpectedly. Ideas and connections materialized so quickly that Charlotte could barely keep up. Beckett's furrowed brow indicated that she was not alone. Gavin caught her eye and shrugged, evidently outpaced as well. Within less than a minute, the androids had produced a more complex chain of ideas than Charlotte had ever seen created in a similar activity, and the human students stared wide-eyed at each other.

Sensing the imbalance of idea generation, Dr. Menta stepped in. "Well. I think that was probably helpful in different ways from what I anticipated. In any case, this is a great starting point. Individually, please highlight a few ideas that seem particularly important to you. Then, when both partners are ready, I would like you to discuss what you each highlighted, considering points of commonality and divergence. You will each then determine one personal goal, and together you will create one shared goal. Questions?"

The students, and a few of the androids, shook their heads, and Dr. Menta let them get started. Charlotte zoomed in on the concept map in her personal viewerspace. What were her goals for participating in this program? When she first learned of her selection, she wanted to be part of the cutting-edge research, but she realized that she hadn't thought much further than that. She combed through the ideas, trying to evaluate which would most prepare her to become a tech ethicist; as she worked, she felt Isaac's eyes on her.

She looked up and confirmed that he was indeed staring at her. She looked down again, thinking that he might redirect his attention as well, to no avail. "What are you doing?" she whispered.

"I am waiting for you to finish," he replied, matching the level of his voice to hers.

"People generally don't like being stared at, so maybe you could think about something else while you wait?"

He nodded once. "Yes. My neural network was otherwise occupied, but I can now see that the direction of my eyes gave the impression that I was staring at you. This is very helpful feedback. I will look in a different direction until you are ready to converse."

Charlotte barely managed to hold in her laughter as he looked away. "I would appreciate that." She tried to organize her ideas a little more quickly now that she knew he was waiting for her. And what did "being otherwise occupied" even mean?

Bingo. As she had that thought, she highlighted the experience and perception sections of the map. At the dawn of their global society, cultures clashed because they had different world views. Interacting with new technology, especially anthropomorphized technology, raised similar challenges.

"All right," she said, bringing Isaac's attention back to her. "Should we compare our thoughts?"

They merged their concept maps, and their interests aligned

nicely. They agreed that their shared goal would focus on translating how androids and humans experience the world. Isaac would investigate how to create and maintain interpersonal relationships with humans, and Charlotte would explore how current policies regarding technology might affect the integration of androids at scale.

"Okay," Dr. Menta said, transitioning the group to the second part of the exercise. "The next step is to discuss with another pair. You can find your groups in your viewers."

Beckett and Denton. Charlotte sighed. Just her luck.

Beckett and Denton displayed no inclination to move, so Charlotte and Isaac crossed the room to join them.

"Beckett," Charlotte started, "I don't think you've officially met Isaac. Isaac, Beckett."

"It is a pleasure to meet you," Isaac said while Beckett mumbled a hello.

Charlotte waited for Beckett to reciprocate the introductions. When he failed to, she introduced herself. "Hi, Denton. I'm Charlotte."

"I am aware." Denton looked at her but did not smile.

A moment of uncomfortable silence followed, and Isaac stepped in. "Denton, would you like to start by sharing your goals?"

"I have transcribed our conversation and synthesized our goals. Beckett should be capable of sharing them with you."

Wow. Charlotte could not wait to tell Chai and Jace about this. Denton's personality could use some work, but an android putting Beckett in his place was too perfect. Beckett frowned but read off the list in his viewer.

Denton's goal of improving the efficiency of his neural networks seemed rather clinical, but Charlotte was interested to know that Beckett would also be focusing on the intersection of policy and technological advancement. Evidently, the pair had not yet settled on a common goal.

After Isaac and Charlotte shared, the group settled into another clumsy silence, and Charlotte was relieved when Dr. Menta gathered the whole class to debrief. From what Charlotte could tell, most of the pairs were successfully working together, and she hoped Dr. Menta would mix up the small groups in future classes.

"Thank you all for your work today," Dr. Menta concluded. "Androids, you will follow your full schedule from this point forward. Guides, your professors and fellow students are expecting the androids to join their classes today. As we have discussed individually, you are not required to be with your partners constantly, but I do expect that you will provide support, if necessary, in facilitating positive interactions. I will stay after class for a few minutes in case anyone has questions. Otherwise, I will see you next week."

Isaac addressed Charlotte as they stood. "Our next course, Design Lab, commences in two hours. Should I meet you there?"

Charlotte hesitated. Many of her classmates had already left, but some, like Gavin and Harper, walked out with their android partners. She had planned to meet up with Chai and Jace for their flex time, but it seemed rude to abandon Isaac.

"That works," she said. "But if you want, you're welcome to hang out with me. I'm meeting up with Chai and Jace."

"That would be preferable." Isaac smiled. "I would benefit from becoming acquainted with your friends."

"Okay, great." They walked without speaking through the forest, but again, Charlotte noticed that the silence felt more companionable than awkward.

Though this edge of campus had largely remained untouched, many of the trees, as if sensing a competition with the organic architects, had grown over the decades into uniquely beautiful patterns. Branches twisted around limbs of neighboring trees or arched to the ground in an expansive canopy. Roots emerged in an intricate obstacle course requiring students to take their time as they climbed up and down the steep paths.

The best tree by far curved its branches into sweeping U's that curled upwards to resemble an octopus; this tree was a special place, the tree that Charlotte, Chai, and Jace had found in the early weeks of their friendship, the tree that had watched them grow into an inseparable trio.

"Hey!" Charlotte called out to Chai and Jace, who were reclining against the branches of the octopus tree with their backs to her.

"Charlotte! Just in time. We were debating - oh." Chai paused mid-thought and looked back at Jace before turning forward again with a forced smile. "Hi, Isaac."

CHAPTER 16

CHAI'S WARY EYES behind her smile made Charlotte wonder too late if bringing Isaac to their favorite spot was a mistake, but Jace smoothed over the moment. He hopped off his branch and greeted Isaac enthusiastically.

"Hi, Isaac! I'm Jace." He offered a fist bump that Isaac glanced at momentarily before reciprocating stiffly.

Chai also approached, politeness overtaking her hesitation. "And I'm Chaitali, but everyone calls me Chai."

Isaac smiled at them both. "It is a pleasure to meet you. Any friend of Charlotte's is a friend of mine."

Chai raised her eyebrow at his formality, and Jace shook his head. "Man, I may need to up my game. As dear old Beckett would say, this guy is posh."

Charlotte started to respond but stopped when she saw Chai begin to circle Isaac, examining him as a sculptor might consider her creation. At the end of her loop, she stared up at him. "Your skin. It's real, isn't it?"

"If by real you mean created from biological materials, then yes, it is real, as are all of my external components."

"And each android has unique physical features?" Chai's eyes scanned Isaac's body, though most of his biological elements remained concealed by his black pants and fitted long-sleeve shirt.

"That is correct. While our biological parts were all created using the same process, the material stems from unique genetic sequences."

During this exchange, Charlotte started to relax. In the face of science, Chai's initial worries about the androids seemed to melt away. "Is it okay if I touch you?" Chai asked Isaac.

"That would be acceptable," he responded.

Chai lifted his left hand in hers, tracing each finger and fingernail before switching to his palm. She did the same with his right hand before reaching up to briefly touch his ears, his jawline, his hair, finally gazing into his eyes as much as their height difference would allow. Charlotte knew Chai's request came from a scientific curiosity, but the intimacy of Chai's hands on Isaac's skin unnerved her. Judging by Jace's expression, he was uncomfortable as well.

"Incredible." Chai stepped back, keeping her eyes on Isaac's face. "Aside from the slight irregularity of your pupils, you're indistinguishable from a human. I knew that, of course, from seeing you at a distance, but up close is something else entirely. This raises so many questions! Do your hair and fingernails grow? Do your skin cells shed and regenerate? Do you eat? And use the bathroom? What about tear production? And sweat? Does your body repair itself? Oh, and what about-"

"Okay, Chai." Sensing no end in sight to the rapidly growing list, Charlotte gently touched Chai's elbow. "We'll have plenty of time to learn all about Isaac's biology, but maybe we can save the interrogation for later?"

"Oh, right." Chai shook her head, as if snapping out of a

trance. "Sorry, Isaac. I get a little carried away sometimes."

"I appreciate your curiosity, Chai. To answer your first questions, I have observed that my hair grows at a rate of 0.4mm per day, and my fingernails grow at a daily rate of 0.1mm. According to my research, that is in line with average human rates."

"So fascinating!" Chai exclaimed, but before she could get back to her earlier questions, Charlotte steered Chai toward the tree. The two girls and Jace settled into their usual branches.

Isaac observed them for a moment before scaling the trunk to reach the branch above Jace's with an ease that shocked the three friends. Jace had aimed for that branch once - against the girls' advice - but after a near fall, he decided to stay closer to the ground.

"I thought Dr. Menta said you didn't have superhuman abilities." Jace craned his neck to look up at Isaac.

Isaac, effortlessly perched on the branch, looked down. "That is correct. We do not have physical superhuman abilities, but our neural networks enable us to utilize the full range of our capabilities. I calculated, based on my height and the available handholds, that the best path to this branch gave me a 99.999% success rate. Based on that knowledge, I could climb without hesitation. Contrary to belief, humans are limited more by mental blocks than by purely physical realities."

"Well, I didn't see any five-foot androids in your group, so that also helps," Chai quipped.

"You are correct, Chai. We range in height from five foot three to six foot two, in accordance with the statistical average of male adolescents in the United States."

"Interesting." Chai pulled on a lock of hair resting near her chin, a sure sign that something more was on her mind. For a moment, Charlotte worried that Chai might turn the conversation back to Isaac's biological properties, but instead Chai said,

"Tell us about your fellow androids."

"What would you like to know? Should I list their names and identifying features?"

"No, I mean which ones do you like? Who's your favorite?"

He cocked his head and blinked before answering. "That is an interesting question. As 'favorite' implies an emotional preference, the most factual answer is that I have no favorite. However, I have spent the most time with Eli, as we share resting quarters, and I have observed no negative qualities in his interactions with other androids or humans."

"Eli is partnered with Gavin," Charlotte added. "I haven't really spoken with him, but after their first meeting, Gavin said Eli was cool."

"Awesome!" Jace said. "Isaac, Gavin is my roommate."

"Thank you for that information, Jace."

"You're welcome. What about Beckett's android?" Jace asked. "He didn't seem too thrilled after meeting him."

Charlotte answered first. "I think Beckett was hoping to make his android into a little protégé, but Denton does not seem to be as friendly as the others. What do you think, Isaac?"

"From what I have observed, the empathy quotient in Denton's personality sequence is significantly lower than mine. This has translated into a certain level of ambivalence toward humans, including toward his partner."

"To be fair," Jace said, "even we humans sometimes struggle with Beckett, so it sounds like a match made in heaven to me."

Chai and Jace pulled out the packed lunches they had grabbed earlier, and Chai handed the extra one to Charlotte. Unsure if Isaac was, or even could be, hungry, Charlotte offered part of her sandwich to him.

"Thank you for the offer, but that is not necessary, Charlotte.

To answer Chai's earlier question, I am equipped to consume solid food and liquids; however, I do not require calories or water, so anything I ingest passes through as waste. I have not consumed anything yet, at least, not to my recollection. I receive my required energy through wireless charging, and a monthly supplement provides the organic material necessary to maintain my biological exterior."

"Wow," Chai and Charlotte sighed in unison, locking eyes as they shared the same thought.

"You could eat as much chocolate as you want," Charlotte said wistfully.

"Technically I could, but I do not understand why I would endeavor to eat unlimited chocolate."

"You obviously haven't tasted it yet," Chai said. "You have so much to learn."

By the time they finished eating, Charlotte relaxed away from the tension she didn't even realize she was holding. She didn't want to make any hasty assumptions, but Isaac seemed to fit into their group surprisingly well, and with relief, Charlotte observed that Chai and Jace appeared much more comfortable than they did upon first seeing Isaac.

As they walked back to main campus for their respective Design Labs, Chai and Jace shared how their Biological Mysteries class sparked some ideas for a design project.

"We learned about these solar-powered sea slugs that take chloroplasts from algae they eat and then use them to continue photosynthesis within their bodies. How sweet is that! What if we could figure out how to make other animals do this?" Jace's eyes lit up almost as much as Chai's when talking about biological wonders.

Isaac nodded in recognition. "Ah yes, the elysia chlorotica, or eastern emerald elysia, are unique creatures. This sounds like a very interesting line of research."

It dawned on Charlotte that her best friends would likely be working on a design focused fully on biology, rather than a biotech integration as they originally discussed.

Chai must have read Charlotte's mind. "Char, we can definitely pull in a tech innovation angle, too. I know we talked about us all working together."

Charlotte hesitated. "Thanks, but that's okay. It sounds like you two have some really great ideas. I don't want you to limit them for me. Besides," she added, glancing at Isaac, "we could maybe work together. If you'd like to."

"Working together would be most advantageous, Charlotte. Thank you for suggesting that."

She and Isaac might as well collaborate, and to be honest, Charlotte didn't mind the thought of spending more time with him. As Chai and Jace continued chatting about their project, however, Charlotte couldn't completely ignore her sharp twinge of jealousy.

Before now, Charlotte wouldn't even have considered not working with Chai. Almost from the moment they became roommates, they were inseparable, and Charlotte had assumed that would always be the case.

Furthermore, Charlotte couldn't help remembering that she was the one who met Jace first in her Global Cultures class. Chai and Jace probably wouldn't even be friends if Charlotte hadn't introduced them last year. Though she would never say it out loud, she always considered herself to be the glue that held their trio together.

Apparently, they didn't really need her after all.

CHAPTER 17

THE LOOMING LEVITON appeared to float nearly twelve feet above the ground. Resting on only a few minimal supports, the building seemed to defy gravity when seen from most angles. Through the viewer, however, the supports completely disappeared, providing the illusion that the building was levitating entirely. Aesthetically, the cylindrical steel-gray facade failed to inspire, but with the undoubtedly impressive effect, it was widely regarded as one of Winton Latham's greatest architectural accomplishments.

Charlotte and Isaac climbed the stairs, which also hovered above the ground, and upon entering the classroom found themselves on what appeared to be the command deck of a spacecraft, overlooking a planet resembling Earth.

Dr. Vosima, their Tech Innovations Design Lab professor, did have a flair for the dramatic.

"Welcome, my tech innovation designers!" he bellowed as the students filed into the spacecraft. "For you explorers new to my realm, I am Dr. Vosima. Pleased to have you joining us. For the rest of you, welcome back!"

Dr. Vosima's inclusive introduction couldn't mask the evident division between the students and the two present androids. Charlotte's classmates gawked at Isaac and Denton with a mixture of caution and awe. Unaffected by the tension in the room, Dr. Vosima pressed onward as the spacecraft approached the nearby planet.

"Much as I would like to believe that you remember all of my lessons from last year, the unfortunate tradition of a summer break often renders students forgetful." His white curls bobbed mischievously as he paced around the front of the room. "Given that, I thought we'd jog your memories with a little challenge and a bit of fun."

The students eyed each other. They knew from experience that Dr. Vosima's definition of fun did not always match their own.

On cue, their spacecraft lurched, and sirens reverberated through the room.

"Emergency life systems online. Oxygen levels stable for T minus five minutes." A calm, feminine voice broke through the sirens.

Charlotte's pulse sped up. She knew, rationally, that they would not actually run out of oxygen, but her overly empathetic nature pulled her emotional awareness deep into these fictional situations. This *could* happen to astronauts - *had* happened, in fact, decades before Charlotte's birth, on one of the first manned ships to Mars.

The students sprang into action. Similar in many ways to enigma matches, Dr. Vosima's puzzle challenges were his signature teaching strategy. He designed them himself as a formative assessment of his students' critical thinking and collaborative skills.

Athena, a natural leader in high-intensity situations, spoke first and directed her classmates. "You - figure out what's causing the system to malfunction. You - search for emergency supplies. You -" she pointed at Beckett and Charlotte. "Use the androids to see if we're missing anything. I'm going to try to land."

Beckett, ignoring Athena's directive, moved with the group exploring the ship. Charlotte turned to Isaac and Denton.

Isaac jumped right in. "The planet appears to have a habitable atmosphere. If it is inhabited by intelligent life forms, then they may be able to provide assistance."

"Okay, great. See if you can find the communication panel. Denton, any thoughts?" Charlotte asked.

He shrugged, his shoulders jerking up and falling back down. "Oxygen levels will not affect me. As this is a closed-loop simulation, action is futile."

Charlotte didn't know how to address this, so she left him and joined Isaac. "Any luck?"

He shook his head. "No one is acknowledging receipt of the distress messages I have sent in 6,124 verbal languages as well as 103 code-based signals."

"Emergency life systems online. Oxygen levels stable for T minus three minutes."

Charlotte paused to think, but her concern that the oxygen already seemed a little thin distracted her. She knew this was psychosomatic, but her breathing became labored nonetheless. With relief, she felt the ship accelerate forward as Athena directed the spacecraft toward the surface. The planet loomed larger in the observation screen when suddenly - pop!

Darkness enveloped Charlotte for a long moment. With a jarring brightness, the white-walled classroom reasserted itself, all evidence of the spacecraft gone.

Athena, still grasping an imagined steering portal, stared at Dr. Vosima, who seemed a bit unsettled as well. "Did we...did we solve it?"

"In a way," he said, slowly turning to Denton, who had remained in the same spot since the start of class. "Would you like to explain your strategy, Denton?"

"I inferred that the shared goal was to remove the humans from the increasingly dangerous situation on the spacecraft. While one method involved finding a solution within the virtual scenario, I identified the code running the simulation and analyzed the class's statistical expectation of success. When their chances dipped below fifty percent, I terminated the program."

Athena glowered. "That's cheating. We were almost there!"

"That's an interesting assertion, Athena. Class, any thoughts?"

When no other students responded, Isaac spoke up. "Cheating implies the violation of rules or a social contract. As no rules were established at the beginning of the challenge, cheating was not possible in that sense. Perhaps there is a social contract in which students are expected to remain within the constraints of a simulation presented by a professor?"

Most of Charlotte's classmates nodded, but she didn't agree. "Maybe none of us ever thought to look for a solution outside of the assumed parameters. Maybe because we know we wouldn't have the skills to make that work."

Dr. Vosima smiled sagely. "In my experience, you don't know what skills you do or don't have until you try. I will admit that this isn't exactly how I intended today's class to proceed, but that is part of the joy of teaching. I look forward to receiving your reflections on today's exercise, especially given the surprising resolution."

He paused, and the sparse classroom transformed to a bright

co-working space, complete with virtual whiteboards. Transitioning to the rest of the lesson, Dr. Vosima said, "In some ways, this is a wonderful segue into the theme for our design work. This semester, you will be designing technology for exploration. We started class with a rather traditional definition of exploration - space travel - and while that is certainly a realm you can explore (pun intended)," he chuckled at his own joke, "I present this example as a metaphor rather than as a definition. One of the hallmarks of intelligent life is an insatiable urge to explore new lands, new facts, new societies, new ways of existing as our best selves, new methods of perceiving the world around us. Explorations are driven by curiosity and need, by self-preservation and self-actualization, by collective achievements and tragedies."

Though one of the oldest professors on campus, Dr. Vosima bounded around the room with his usual youthful energy. "By the end of class today, you will all submit three inventive proposals related to exploration. And of course, remember that we are a community-centered design campus. Your ideas, therefore, must have a clear and direct benefit to members of our local, national, or global community. We will use your proposals as a starting point for narrowing down areas of focus and creating specific design principles. I encourage you to work with your peers today and begin to consider whose interests might align with yours this semester. Questions?" His eyes briefly rested on each student. "Well, I will be circulating to stretch your thinking. The countdown starts now!"

Charlotte and Isaac moved to one of the whiteboards. No one else joined them. As she observed her classmates clustered throughout the room, Charlotte felt grateful for Isaac's presence. An android partner was still a partner.

Heading toward another group, Beckett left Denton on the far side of the room as the only student standing alone.

"Why aren't you working with Denton?" Charlotte asked as Beckett passed her.

"We don't have to babysit them, Charlotte. They're machines. Just because you've adopted yours like a little pet doesn't mean that Denton and I have to be together every minute." Beckett elevated his voice as usual, drawing a few sniggers from nearby students.

Charlotte's cheeks flushed. If Chai were here, Beckett would be in for it, but Charlotte could never think of a proper retort in time. Luckily, today she didn't need a response.

Through the viewerspace, Dr. Vosima transmitted his voice to only Charlotte and Beckett. "If I were picking groupmates, I wouldn't discount our newest students. You may find that Charlotte has made the wiser decision, Beckett."

Dr. Vosima's eyes were sharper than usual, even from across the room, and Beckett kept any further comments to himself. Charlotte heard him mumble a brief "yes, sir," but he made no move to include Denton.

Charlotte hesitated. While she couldn't blame Beckett for being less than enamored with his android, she remembered what Isaac had said about Denton's empathy level. It wasn't his fault that he was created this way.

Knowing she was making the right, albeit distasteful, decision, she invited Denton to join their group. They began to brainstorm some preliminary ideas, and after shooting down Charlotte's contributions as primitive, Denton suggested that they explore how humans have managed to use such a small percentage of their cognitive capacity despite more than two hundred thousand years of evolutionary advancement.

As Beckett smirked at her from across the room, Charlotte realized that trying to work with Denton may have been a mistake.

Chapter 18

"HUNGRY TONIGHT, JACE?" Chai laughed as Jace sat down across from her and Charlotte. The two heaping plates he placed on the table were impressive, even for his prodigious appetite.

"Ha, very funny. This one's for Isaac. I picked the finest selection the Mod has to offer." Jace scanned the room, today a sweeping open-air pavilion, and wrinkled his brow. "Wait, where is he?"

"I don't know," Charlotte said. "I expected him to join us for dinner, but after class, he got a message and said he had to go. It's weird because Dr. Menta said the androids would be fully integrated now, and I thought that included meals."

"Gavin!" Jace's face lit up as his roommate approached without a plate. "I already got you dinner, man. Picked up your favorites."

"Thanks." Gavin surveyed the plate and shrugged. "These aren't exactly my favorites, but I appreciate it."

"No android with you either?" Chai asked.

"No. After class, Eli said he had to go. By the looks of it, all of the androids got pulled away tonight. Not surprising, given how things went today."

"What do you mean?" Charlotte asked. "I didn't hear about any problems."

"The androids in our classes were fine," Chai affirmed. "Quiet but okay."

"I think the other bio-ad majors were mostly disappointed they weren't more exciting," Jace added.

"Charlotte, you had a front-row seat to the most interesting part, I think." Gavin took a bite before continuing. "Everyone already knows about Denton hacking Dr. Vosima's simulation. I overheard Dr. Vosima tell Dr. Picartz that he can't figure out how Denton did it. Having a student who can outsmart our best professors is probably concerning for them."

Jace said, "I also heard that one of the first-year androids kind of went silent in one class and didn't move or talk for a long time, which must have been pretty creepy."

"That does sound a bit weird," Charlotte said, "and Denton's actions were definitely surprising, but you really think that was enough to get them banned from dinner? It doesn't seem that serious."

Gavin glanced at a nearby table, where Athena was speaking animatedly to a group with somber faces. They couldn't hear everything she was saying, but the word "androids" did float their way a few times. "From what I hear, some people are making it out to be more serious than it is," Gavin said.

Charlotte shook her head. "I don't understand why Athena is so against the androids."

Gavin shrugged and said, "Probably she's upset about not being chosen as a guide."

"What?" Charlotte asked. "She said she was offered a spot, and she turned it down."

Jace and Gavin shared a look. "That's not the word on the street," Jace said.

"I heard she practically begged her advisor to get her in," Gavin added.

Uncomfortable with the level of gossip they were descending into, Charlotte frowned. Was it possible that Athena really wasn't chosen for the program? "Okay, if that's true, I guess it could explain Athena's attitude, but it doesn't explain why other people are being so dramatic. It seems like we should at least give the androids a chance."

"You're right. I mean, I understand being a little nervous around them," Chai admitted, "but meeting Isaac was cool. He seems like the best android by far." She looked apologetically at Gavin. "No offense. We haven't met Eli yet."

"None taken. I hope to make the introductions soon." He turned to Charlotte. "You and Isaac still hitting it off?"

"Um, yeah. It seems like he got some pleasant personality features, so he's easy to talk to. I'm glad you and I got good partners."

"Cheers to that." Gavin raised his water bottle in a mock toast and then cleared his throat. "So Charlotte, do you, um, want to go to the viewerflik tonight?"

On most Fridays, the school presented viewerfliks at the Gem. Though students could stream immersive movies through their own viewers, Charlotte enjoyed the communal experience. She loved the vintage 2-D movie nights the best, but this was not a popular opinion. Despite many debates on the topic, Chai and Jace, like most of their classmates, still couldn't appreciate what was charming about watching a film on a large, flat screen.

"Yes," Charlotte said. "We're planning to go."

"Oh, okay. Cool. Yeah, let's all go. I'll sit with you guys. And girls." The tops of Gavin's ears reddened inexplicably.

"Of course, dude." Jace changed the conversation to share graphic details of their embryonic experience in Creation of Life; medical things always made Charlotte a bit queasy, so she half-listened as her mind wandered to Isaac. She thought that he would probably enjoy a viewerflik, and she wished the androids could join them tonight.

After dinner, Chai and Charlotte decided to drop by their room first and promised to meet the boys at the Gem soon. Once out of earshot, Chai linked her arm through Charlotte's.

"So what do you think?" Chai asked with a playful gleam in her eye.

"About what?"

"About Gavin!"

"What about Gavin?"

"Charlotte! He asked you out!"

"What? When?" Charlotte scrunched her eyebrows at Chai's outlandish idea.

"When he asked if you wanted to go to the viewerflik!"

"He asked all of us."

"No, silly. He asked you. Then you made it a group thing."

"But we were planning to go as a group." This whole conversation was making Charlotte's head spin.

"True." Chai stopped and looked at Charlotte directly. "You really had no idea he was flirting with you?"

"Do I look like I had any idea?"

Chai laughed as they continued toward their dorm. "No, you don't. But now that you do, what do you think?"

Charlotte took a moment to consider. With his white-blond hair spiked up haphazardly around his face and his thin runner's limbs, Gavin had never struck her as being particularly attractive. But she had to admit that his single-dimpled smile was kind of cute, and his hazel eyes were always kind. And the thought of him noticing her out of all of the girls in the school did bring a certain warm, lightheaded rush. Still, she didn't feel the spark of attraction that she had felt with other crushes. But then, nothing had ever happened with those boys, so maybe this feeling was a better sign?

"I really don't know, Chai. I guess I've always thought of him as Jace's roommate. And as our friend."

"Sometimes friendship is the first step to a relationship. From what I hear, anyway."

"Okay, Ms. Relationship Expert. Who are you crushing on?"

"Eh. Nobody's really catching my eye." The way she avoided Charlotte's gaze, however, suggested that this might not be true. "But we're not talking about me. We're talking about you and Gavin, who would make an excellent couple."

"Yeah, maybe." Drawn into Chai's enthusiasm, Charlotte resolved to keep an open mind. Later, when Chai subtly nudged Charlotte to sit next to Gavin, rather than between her and Jace, she didn't resist.

As if sensing the girls' earlier conversation, Gavin was suddenly shy, and they spoke little before the feature started. Once the comedic movie opened, however, Gavin's laughter bubbled up at the same times as Charlotte's, and he leaned over occasionally to whisper additional jokes in her ear. Though they edged closer together by the end of the show, Charlotte kept some distance, ensuring that they remained firmly in friendly territory.

After all, she and Gavin were just friends. For now.

CHAPTER 19

EXACTLY AT 10AM, Charlotte and Marissa arrived at Norby Cafe, their favorite brunch spot in Ternion. Students were free to visit the microcity on weekends, and the sisters established a tradition of monthly brunches early last year. Sometimes Chai or one of Marissa's friends would join them, but as a late riser, Chai harbored little desire for a weekend meal before noon, and Charlotte occasionally preferred catching up with her sister alone.

They chose a table near the stream running through the middle of the cafe, and Charlotte breathed in the scent of the late-blooming flowers hanging from the surrounding trellises. Without looking at the menu, Charlotte and Marissa placed their twin orders: seasonal French toast and cafe mochas, large.

Though Marissa seemed happy to be there, Charlotte couldn't help noticing the dark circles shadowing her sister's eyes. "How have things been?" she asked gently.

Marissa sighed through a tired smile. "Good. Busy. This week was a little nuts. We've had some new high-priority projects pop up, so I'll be back in the lab this afternoon. As always."

"Anything I can help with?" Charlotte didn't like the fatigue stooping Marissa's shoulders. Her sister had always pushed herself hard, had always struggled to balance her work and her own well-being, but Charlotte worried that this was a new level, even for Marissa.

"Thanks, but I've got this. We both know you have plenty to keep you busy. The professors only go easy for the first couple of days."

"That's true." Charlotte provided a colorful summary of her first classes, leaving room for Marissa to reminisce, mostly about her enduring affection for Dr. Cariciarra.

Charlotte treaded carefully with details about the androids. Despite Marissa's initial reaction after the keynote, she had been supportive since learning that Charlotte was selected as a guide. They hadn't spoken about it much, given Marissa's current schedule, but Marissa seemed to make an effort to maintain a positive outlook about the program. Even with the encouraging messages, though, Charlotte still sensed a slight wariness from her sister. With this in mind, Charlotte presented Denton's behavior in Dr. Vosima's class as a lighthearted, creative solution to the simulated challenge.

Marissa's eyebrows shot up. "He was able to bypass the simulation for everyone in the room?"

"Well, yeah."

"In other words, he hacked all of your viewers, including Dr. Vosima's?"

Charlotte hadn't thought of it like that. "He was just trying to solve the simulation, like we all were."

Marissa sipped her mocha and lowered the intensity of her tone. "It does make sense that they would approach problems differently." She took another sip, thinking. "But it sounds like your interactions with Isaac have all been positive?"

"Definitely." Charlotte tried to sound firm but not too enthusiastic. "Like I said, even Chai and Jace like him. From what I've seen, he got the best personality sequence."

"Have you talked to Mom and Dad about him?"

Charlotte shook her head. "I tried to view them several times, but I've only gotten a few messages. You?"

"Same. They're usually better about keeping in touch. This project must really be a beast. I wonder -"

At that moment, their parents' faces appeared in their viewerspace. Startled by the coincidence, the girls accepted the request, and their parents' full bodies materialized, visible only through the sisters' viewers. Also seated, they seemed to join Marissa and Charlotte at their table.

"Oh Marissa, Charlotte." Their mother clasped her hands in front of her mouth as she looked at her daughters with misty eyes. "I've missed you two so much."

"Hi, girls," their dad said warmly.

"Mom, Dad! We've missed you, too." Charlotte fought the urge to hug them. A hug through the viewer always provided more disappointment than comfort. She instead reveled in seeing them, relieved that they looked rested. Like Marissa, her parents had a tendency to work themselves to exhaustion, but to be honest, they appeared to be doing better than ever. Charlotte's concern over not hearing from them in so long floated away in the face of their smiles.

Marissa, however, was less affected. "We've been trying to reach you."

"We know, Rissa." With a sigh, their father said, "We're sorry that we've been so out of touch. This project has been much more demanding than any of us expected."

Her disapproval noted, Marissa relented slightly. "I know

how that goes. I'm glad we get to talk now, at least."

"I am too, sweetheart. In fact, we have some excellent news."

Their parents shared an ecstatic smile as their mom said, "Our work is wrapping up soon, which means we'll be back for good by the holidays. We just can't wait to be home with you. We never would have accepted this assignment if we knew it would take us away for so long."

"Really? You're coming home?" Charlotte asked, barely hoping to believe it. When Cognation first assigned them to a top-secret project at an undisclosed location, their parents had expected to be allowed short trips home, but that had not happened in over six months. Last time they'd spoken, there had been no end in sight for the project.

"That's right. We thought we might celebrate the holidays back home on the North Shore," their dad added. "How does that sound?"

"That sounds awesome!" Charlotte loved holidays at their old house, and she couldn't wait to see her parents again for real.

Even Marissa seemed lighter from this news. "That sounds really nice, Dad."

"We're counting down the days, girls." Their mom took a wobbly breath and blinked back the tears shining in her eyes. Exhaling, she changed the subject. "How are things with you two? Tell us everything."

Marissa shared first, offering a few more details about her work than earlier but also downplaying the exhaustion that Charlotte hoped their parents could see.

When they moved onto Charlotte's classes and initial experiences with the androids, their parents positively beamed. "We are so proud of you," her dad said. "We knew you'd be picked. We weren't sure if the program would launch this year, of course. And as Denton's actions show, this technology isn't en-tirely predictable, but it sounds like things are off to a fairly successful start."

"Wait." Marissa's demeanor clouded again. "You knew about the androids?"

Their parents hesitated. "Officially, no. But unofficially, we might have heard some bits and pieces."

"It seems like very few people knew about it, either officially or unofficially," Marissa said.

Their mother responded calmly, ignoring the edge in Marissa's voice. "You know how the company is with their special projects, Rissa. One day, you'll understand when you're in charge of projects like this."

Marissa nodded, the corner of her mouth edging into a frown. "We'll see."

They chatted for a few moments more before their dad reluctantly wrapped up their conversation. "We'd love to stay with you longer, but the lab calls, I'm afraid."

"We'll talk to you again soon," their mom promised, her eyes moistening again.

"We love you," their parents said in unison.

Their faces disappeared before Charlotte and Marissa could finish saying, "We love you, too."

With their parents gone, the patio felt lonelier than before, and the sisters finished their breakfasts mostly in silence. Marissa was still in a mood, and Charlotte had learned long ago not to bother her in these situations.

"Charlotte." Marissa looked over her shoulder though no other patrons were sitting near them. "I think you should record your interactions with Isaac."

This was not what Charlotte expected to hear. "What? Why?"

"Just to be safe. I think, I mean, it might be helpful at some point."

"I thought you supported this program. That's what you said earlier."

"I know. I just…my gut is telling me that you need to be cautious."

"Well, I'll need to talk to Dr. Menta about this first."

"No!" Marissa's tone startled Charlotte, and her sister quickly composed herself. "It's best if you do this without telling anyone. Including Isaac. And Dr. Menta."

Marissa's calm assertiveness made Charlotte's skin tingle. "Marissa, what's going on?"

Her sister leaned in and lowered her voice. "Probably nothing, Char. Probably I'm just being paranoid. You know how I get." She hesitated, picking her next words carefully. "It's just that no one I work with had any idea that Cognation had android technology this advanced. We know even the senior members of our team weren't clued in. Something doesn't add up. We're just not sure what."

"I'll be breaking the rules if I record Isaac secretly." Charlotte was not a rule breaker. Neither, she thought, was her sister.

"I know. I'm sorry to ask you to do this. Don't worry. If you get caught, I'll tell Dr. Menta or anyone else that I made you do it."

"Then *you* will get in trouble, Rissa."

"It's worth the risk to me."

Marissa never pressured Charlotte to do anything, especially not something that could land them both in serious trouble. But Marissa's concern was palpable, in her voice and in her anxious expression. Charlotte wished their parents were still here; their enthusiasm from afar had done little to assuage Marissa's worries.

"Okay, okay." Charlotte didn't see any other way out of this conversation. "I'll record our interactions."

In the moment, Charlotte felt grateful for the relief that softened Marissa's eyes. Lowering her own eyes to the coffee grounds left in the bottom of her mug, she hoped that Marissa couldn't read the guilt on her face.

Charlotte had never lied to her sister before, but she could not record Isaac on Marissa's whim.

CHAPTER 20

MONDAY'S CLASSES PASSED without incident, and to Charlotte's delight, Isaac agreed to accompany her to dinner.

"Sweet! I was hoping you'd be here," Jace said to Isaac as he and Charlotte reached their table. Jace placed a heaping plate, identical to Friday's, in front of his test subject.

"Thank you, Jace. As I believe I mentioned, however, I do not need to consume food as humans do."

"Trust me, Isaac. Food is one of the great pleasures of life. You need to learn what you like."

Cautiously, daintily almost, Isaac proceeded to taste the countless delectables under Chai, Charlotte, and Jace's fascinated gazes. They had never before witnessed someone trying food for the first time.

Isaac, though, turned out to be an underwhelming subject. His face remained agreeably neutral as he worked through garlic mashed potatoes, macaroni and cheese, various synthetic meats, avocado tacos, braised vegetables, buttered cornbread, spicy curries - to name only a few of the dishes Jace selected. "They are very pleasant," he concluded after tasting everything.

"Which one's your favorite?" Chai asked.

"Because they have all been prepared to appeal to a human palate, they all taste equally enjoyable. Therefore, I do not have a favorite."

"Well, you haven't tried dessert yet." Chai slid a second full plate in front of him, and Isaac repeated the process with the same result, much to the girls' dismay. Even a sip of ginger beer, the friends' dinner drink of choice, failed to arouse an exceptional response.

A similar follow-up tasting experiment with Eli produced the same outcome; clearly, choosing favorites was a concept the androids needed to work on.

What Isaac and Eli lacked in personal preferences, though, they more than made up for in their affability and willingness to engage in any exploit the group of friends dreamed up over the following weeks. They zip lined with Jace, Charlotte, and Eli from Lepus (Chai, of course, sat that one out), let Chai take samples of their hair and nails, climbed trees on demand, and responded to endless strings of questions - at least, the questions they were at liberty to answer.

"Where's your dorm?" Charlotte and her friends asked the two androids repeatedly.

"Near the edge of campus," was the most specific answer they could obtain. "Only androids are allowed to enter, so the location is immaterial."

Immaterial, perhaps, but no less fascinating. No one, it seemed, could discern the location of the androids' resting quarters; how an entire building hosting ten androids could remain hidden on campus grew into a legendary conundrum. The students knew only that the androids headed toward the Abyss at the end of the day and emerged sometimes from that direction and other times from the aerotram at the main entrance before classes commenced each morning.

Despite their mysterious home, Isaac and the other androids increasingly folded into the fabric of life at the Academy. With unspoken familiarity, Charlotte and Isaac walked between classes together and worked alongside each other during flex time. Gavin and Eli could often be seen jogging around campus in tandem, their matching runner's strides giving the illusion that they could almost be brothers. At meals, Chai and Jace would immediately ask about Isaac and Eli on the rare occasions that they didn't accompany Charlotte and Gavin to the Mod.

A few of the other androids seemed to have formed similar bonds with their human peers. Harper and Grayton became nearly inseparable, always deep in the throes of artistic exploration, and the entire cohort of first years regularly flocked around their year's androids, Adon and Kelvin. Most of the androids assimilated seamlessly into the social culture of the school, and as the first weeks of the school year flew by, even students like Athena grew begrudgingly accustomed to the androids' presence.

Despite their lack of emotional capacity, the androids generally appeared to enjoy the company of humans; unfortunately, the same could not be said for Denton. While Charlotte and Isaac had continued working with him in class, he spent his unscheduled time largely away from other students. Repeated invitations from Charlotte and Isaac had failed to elicit any interest from Denton in joining their group for non-academic activities. Rarely seen with Beckett, Denton either disappeared to the android dorms immediately after class or gathered with a couple of other androids who seemed to be more comfortable among themselves. Though ostensibly integrated with the student body, these few androids nearly always clustered together, often staring at one another without speaking, which they apparently found preferable to the company of human students.

"Isaac, do you know why Denton and some of the other androids don't want to spend time with any of us?" This question had been on Charlotte's mind for a while.

"From what I can tell, the amount of time allocated to human interaction is a function of our personality sequences. Some of us, like myself and Eli, prioritize human relationships and value the insights we gain about what it means to be human. Others, like Denton, have other priorities."

Charlotte appreciated Isaac's direct answer, but she had difficulty reconciling his logical assessment with Eli's expressed excitement about being Gavin's jogging partner or with Isaac's subtle but seemingly genuine happiness upon greeting her each day.

"Why would Cognation create androids who aren't interested in interacting with humans?" This contradiction had bothered her about Denton from the beginning. At face value, Dr. Menta's explanation of testing different personality types made sense, but how could creating antisocial androids be useful for Dr. Menta's research?

"I do not know," Isaac admitted. "However, it is likely that the researchers could not fully predict the outcome of each combination of personality markers." When Charlotte didn't respond, he added, "I do know that I am glad to have a personality sequence that makes me inclined to spend more time with you."

That, like so many of Isaac's comments, made Charlotte smile. "Me too."

Though Denton wasn't really her android to worry about, Charlotte couldn't dismiss her curiosity about his behavior and how it fit into the program's goals. For reasons she couldn't quite articulate, her wonderings about Cognation's work with the androids encouraged her to investigate further into the company's past. Since the first week of school, she had read through Dr. Coggins' first two journals, but they provided few insights. She hoped to find more interesting details in his later volumes, so she visited the library alcove again, this time with Isaac.

"What are you looking for?" he asked.

"I don't know." She explained how something felt incomplete about the information available on the viewernet regarding the inception of the Alliance and the founding of Cognation. "I'm not sure what I hope to find, though. And it's taking forever. I don't know what people did when they had to rely on paper books. I've only skimmed the first two journals, and so far, I don't think I've found anything useful. Clearly, Dr. Coggins was a copious notetaker, so there has to be something interesting somewhere." She waved her hand along the wall of journals and pulled the next few volumes out and onto the table in the center of the room.

As she began reviewing the pages of the third volume, she noticed Isaac perusing the two journals she had reshelved. By the time she reached page ten, he came over to glance at the journal in her hands.

"At your current reading speed, getting through these journals will take three months, two days, and five hours. I could read all of the volumes in less than one hour. Completing data analysis scripts will take additional time, but once my systems organize the patterns, we could review them together."

"Seriously?" Charlotte's jaw dropped. She couldn't believe she hadn't thought of asking for Isaac's help. "That would be great!" She had considered trying to digitize the journals through her viewer, but even that would have taken quite a while. She handed the next journal over to Isaac and watched with awe, and perhaps a touch of jealousy, as he efficiently worked through countless volumes.

While she queued up the next books, Charlotte smiled to herself, grateful to have Isaac here as a partner in her work. When she mentioned the journals to Chai and Jace earlier, they had been only mildly interested, and though she knew they would have come with her if she asked, they would not have done so with such enthusiasm.

As she watched Isaac run his hands over the pages while he read, Charlotte felt her developing fondness for him start to calm her nerves from the past few weeks. Though Marissa's concerns and the antisocial tendencies of some of the androids weighed on her mind, none of that mattered when Charlotte and Isaac were together.

Isaac, she acknowledged to herself, wasn't just an android to her; he was her friend.

CHAPTER 21

AS THE SEMESTER'S workload ramped up, the Academy faculty made sure that students didn't get bogged down with all work and no play. Encouraging a much-needed mind break, the faculty declared an upcoming Saturday to be a work-free day. All academic files on students' viewers were subsequently locked down. While some extra-studious individuals found ways to work around that, Charlotte and her friends didn't need any extra nudges to take a break.

"Time to launch Operation Gigglebot!" Like a kid on his birthday, Jace arrived at Charlotte and Chai's room bright and early - well, early by Chai's standards. Knowing that sweets were the best way to lure Chai out of bed, he brought three chocolate muffins and mochas.

The seed for this operation planted itself in their minds a few days ago when the androids' limited understanding of humor became painfully apparent. At dinner, Gavin recounted an unfortunate ride he'd taken on the zip line from Lepus that had resulted in a rather regrettable underclothes situation. An exuberant and detailed storyteller, Gavin soon had Chai, Jace, and Charlotte nearly in tears.

In the midst of their giggling, unnatural chuckles from each end of the table brought their laughter to an abrupt stop. "Ha. Ha. Ha. Ha." Isaac and Eli exhaled awkwardly through their smiles, ending a few beats after the rest of the table had grown silent.

As soon as Isaac and Eli stopped, the others broke out into another laughing fit, ten times more boisterous than before. This time, the androids did not join in, instead watching closely as the four students regained control of their breathing and wiped the tears from their eyes.

Eli exchanged a look with Isaac before speaking. "Could you please clarify what this second bout of laughter arose from?"

Gavin gaped at him. "It's not obvious?"

"It could have been a renewed reaction to your story, or it may have resulted from the laughter contributed by me and Isaac."

"Dude," Jace said. "It was definitely because of your laughter, if you can call it that. You two sounded like a pair of depressed robotic clowns."

"Wait." Charlotte wracked her brain, trying to remember if she had heard any of the androids laugh. "Do you understand humor?"

Isaac nodded. "Of course. Humor is a quality which appeals to a sense of the ludicrous or absurdly incongruous, in other words, a funny or amusing quality."

"No, no. I know you know the *definition* of humor, but do you *understand* humor? Like, did you really think Gavin's story was funny? Or were you just laughing because we were?"

"Laughing along with the group seemed to be the socially appropriate action," Isaac admitted, and Eli agreed.

Charlotte smiled conspiratorially at her friends. Teaching androids to laugh - *really* laugh - just became their new mission.

Over the past few days, Jace and Gavin, self-proclaimed comedic experts, had spearheaded the effort to gather three hours of the funniest standup clips available on the viewernet. With input from Charlotte and Chai, the boys stitched together an elegant compilation spanning comedic tastes and styles. This morning, while Gavin went on a run, Jace wanted to review the choices with the girls and add some backup clips as well. By the time the three of them left for the vieweroom they had reserved at the Gem, they possessed an excellent set that they were confident would accomplish their goal.

They arrived to find Gavin, Isaac, and Eli already there. Gavin had even initiated Jace's program to virtually transform the room into a comedy club, complete with a small, elevated stage in front of a dark red brick wall.

"Excellent!" Jace said when they entered the space. Charlotte had to admit that the bar along the side of the room was the perfect touch.

"Hey." Gavin smiled at Charlotte and gestured to the seat beside him. "You can sit here if you want."

"Oh, sure." She had been about to follow Chai, but she took the seat Gavin offered.

Standing in front of them, Jace clasped his hands together, commencing their proceedings with mock formality. "Thank you all for joining me here today. Isaac and Eli, I sincerely hope that you enjoy the presentation we have put together for you. As you know, our objective is to find out what type of humor can make you laugh - *really* laugh. Therefore, the only rule, for all of us, is that no fake laughter will be permitted." After receiving a nod of acknowledgment from the group, Jace took his seat next to Chai and started the captures.

At first, the four humans held their attention on the androids, but Charlotte got the feeling that this could be counterproductive.

She messaged the other three. *Maybe we should try to enjoy the comedy? It might be hard for Isaac and Eli to get into it if we're staring at them.* Jace flashed her a thumbs up, and they all relaxed a bit, only sneaking an occasional glance at their test subjects.

Though Charlotte already heard many of these jokes, most of them still made her laugh, especially with Gavin laughing beside her. He had an unencumbered way of laughing, almost giggling, that she found infectious. Next to Gavin, however, Isaac and Eli did not appear to be similarly affected - at least, not at first.

About halfway through the set, Isaac and Eli each let out a small chuckle at the end of a joke about robotic technology. Charlotte's eyes narrowed; were Isaac and Eli just faking again? As the comedy set continued, the androids' laughter increased, gradually matching the natural, irregular cadence of the rest of the laughter in the room.

When the last joke concluded, they all sat in silence for a moment. Finally, with hope in his eyes, Jace turned to Isaac and Eli. "So, was that real laughter?"

Isaac paused. "I believe that yes is the most accurate answer."

"Meaning what?" Gavin asked.

Eli explained. "We did not laugh during the first part of the comedy set because our neural networks were analyzing the inputs of the jokes and the laughter from the four of you to create classifiers to determine what is considered funny within this context."

"During the second part of the set," Isaac continued, "those classifiers sparked a laughter response whenever they detected a humorous input. Through iterative refinement, our processors then became more adept at detecting humor in later jokes."

Jace's shoulders slumped a bit. "That doesn't exactly sound like a real appreciation of humor. You just laughed at whatever jokes your data told you were funny?"

Charlotte disagreed. "I don't know, Jace. Is it that different from how we internalize humor? We've been socialized to think certain things are funny. The comedians' words have to fit certain conditions for us to respond by laughing."

"Charlotte is correct," Isaac said. "When preparing for today, Eli and I modeled our classifier creation based on how humans develop a sense of humor. The timeline may be different, but the process is analogous."

"But why didn't you have a humor algorithm before today?" Gavin asked

Eli shrugged. "We had not determined that as an objective, so our neural networks did not analyze our sensory inputs through the lens of humor."

Chai spoke slowly, almost to herself. "So you're able to identify new objectives. And your responses to those objectives are shaped by the sensory inputs you experience."

It wasn't exactly a question, but Isaac answered anyway. "That is correct."

Chai frowned, but Gavin looked eagerly at the androids. "What were your favorite jokes from this set?"

Eli scrunched up his eyes in thought, an expression that mirrored Gavin's thinking face. "I cannot identify a favorite joke. However, I found that one-liners elicited the greatest laughter response from me."

"I would prioritize the anecdotal and observational comedy," Isaac said. "The context included within the stories provided more opportunities to identify humor."

"How could the two of you have different responses to the

same inputs?" Chai asked shrewdly.

Without hesitation, Isaac said, "We identified that one of the problems with our reaction to your humorous dinner conversation was our synchronous laughter; therefore, we ensured that our evolving classifiers, while based on the same assumptions, would not be identical. This was not difficult, as our differing personalities and experiences provided unique contextual foundations."

"So...this was sort of a success?" Jace asked hesitantly.

"Dude." Gavin bumped his fist into Jace's shoulder. "I would say this was a total success. We helped Eli and Isaac develop a very refined sense of humor. We are basically pioneers of android laughter algorithms. There could be a real market opportunity here."

Charlotte rolled her eyes, but before she could respond, Isaac surprised them all by laughing.

"My apologies," he said, looking at their astonished faces. "I thought Gavin's assertion that he had any involvement in our classifier development was a joke."

Charlotte laughed. "Isaac just might be the funniest one among us."

"Man, tough crowd," Gavin said with a wry smile. "We might have been too successful for our own good. But let's continue this discussion over dinner. I'm starving!"

The six of them walked over toward the Mod as they continued debating the merits of their experiment. Charlotte agreed that it was definitely a success; inwardly, she admitted that her favorite part was the sound of Isaac's laugh - deep, warm, and just uniquely Isaac.

She decided to keep that reflection to herself.

CHAPTER 22

WALKING BESIDE ISAAC, Charlotte entered Tech Ethics with her usual apprehension. Though Dr. Picartz's first-day hacking stunt remained a one-time occurrence, she nevertheless kept her guard up whenever stepping into the Treetop. Taking a seat next to Chai and Jace, she could sense their elevated tension as well.

With a characteristic flourish and twirl of his cane, Dr. Picartz called the class to attention. "Today, as some of you may be happy to know, we are revisiting the topic of viewer hacking." The students, with the exception of Isaac and Denton, took in a sharp, collective breath. "Relax, relax. I got the message that my unique theatrics weren't exactly appreciated. Pity. We could be having so much more fun."

Deep in thought, he circled the room for a moment before snapping back to the students. "In any case, we have a new hack gaining steam across the viewernet, and it is a particularly nasty one. Cognation is of course working on a network-wide defense, but our task today is to work out some personal defense strategies. In defending against a viewer hack, remind me what we want to consider."

Unsurprisingly, Athena spoke up first. "The key is to recognize that you are being hacked and to then regain control of your viewerspace."

"Excellent. In today's exercise, you of course already know that you will be hacked, but pay attention to additional clues that give the hack away. In most cases, these programs lack elegance. A slight change in quality, an awkward sensation, the uncanny feeling of being in a dream - begin attuning yourself to these signatures." As Dr. Picartz continued, details materialized in their viewers. "You are now receiving your pairings for today. They are not negotiable. When I say start, Partner A will engage the hack against Partner B, who will have ten minutes to work on a counter hack. Partner A, observe your partner's progress, but do not intervene. This hack has been configured in a safe manner for us to practice with, so I repeat: *do not attempt to alter the program.* After the ten minutes are up, your roles will switch. Your manual override phrases, as you know, will not work as a counter hack, so my name will be your signal to use if at any time you would like your partner to stop."

Charlotte expected to be paired with Isaac, so she was startled to see his name listed next to Jace's. She found her own name disappointingly paired with Beckett's.

"One final note, Mr. Templeton." In a fluid motion, Dr. Picartz spun his cane through the air, ending with the base a mere two inches from Jace's face. "For the purposes of this exercise, leave your viewer glasses on. In the real world, of course, your first defense would be to remove them." Jace nodded wordlessly.

Dr. Picartz surveyed the class with his piercing eyes. "Any questions?" After a momentary pause in the silence, he waved his cane once more, prompting them to find their places.

Charlotte walked over to Beckett, and they greeted each other cordially. Her recent limited communication with her parents made her sympathetic to Beckett's plight as the child of politicians working on both sides of the Atlantic, and she had resolved earlier this semester to extend more patience toward him. But then, in his uniquely provoking manner, he said, "Hope you can keep up with me. Too bad your android pet can't help you now," and any kindness she felt toward him dissipated. He was the one who would be lucky to keep up with her.

Dr. Picartz rapped the floor three times with his cane. "You may begin."

As Partner A, Charlotte initiated the hack against Beckett. In her viewer, she could see a minimized version of Beckett's perspective along with the telemetry from his viewerspace. At first, nothing appeared to be amiss. Subtly, though, the colors started to darken, and shapes distorted. The sunlight coming in through the windows faded away, and everyone else, with the exception of Charlotte, appeared to leave the room.

From her backend access, she could see his actions as he attempted to regain control. Cutting power to the network, reworking his graphics input - nothing he tried worked. Given the frustration on their classmates' faces, no one was having much success.

"Are you messing with this, Charlotte?"

"What? No!" *Not a bad idea, though,* she thought to herself. "The hack is blocking you automatically. Maybe try to restore factory settings?"

"I don't need your help!" His growing irritation indicated otherwise, but Charlotte held her tongue.

"You have one minute left," she reminded him as the timer started blinking red in her viewer.

A high-pitched shriek interrupted their concentration. "I told you to STOP!" Athena's voice, devoid of its usual haughty confidence, reverberated throughout the room. Dr. Picartz jumped to his feet and instantly disabled all of their viewers. Wide-eyed, the students stared at Athena, cowering against the back wall. Denton, impassive as ever, stood across from her.

Dr. Picartz asked Athena some questions, out of earshot of the other students, but she could barely mumble responses. An uncomfortable hush permeated the class. No one had ever seen Athena spooked like this.

"Denton, grant me access to the last ten minutes of your viewer record," Dr. Picartz instructed without his usual dramatic flair. For a terrible moment, it seemed as though Denton might not honor that request, but finally, he offered a subtle nod.

Though the students couldn't see what Dr. Picartz viewed, his increasingly distressed expression brought a feeling of dread over Charlotte. She looked at Isaac questioningly, but he only shook his head.

"Denton, as Partner A, what were your instructions?" Dr. Picartz looked at the android as one might look at an unpredictable animal.

"Instructions for Partner A were to engage the hack, monitor Partner B's progress, and not intervene."

"And did you follow those instructions?"

"No."

Everyone, except for Isaac, gasped at Denton's brazen admission.

"Please explain your actions."

"Within the first minute, I deduced that Athena would easily be able to defend against the hack given the allotted time. Therefore, I deemed it in her best interest to increase the difficulty of the hack in order to further strengthen her abilities in a way that the original exercise would not."

"I thought you weren't supposed to be able to hurt humans!"

Pri, now sitting next to Athena in an effort to comfort her, snapped at Denton.

"Like all androids, I am bound by the Benevolence Principle. In contributing to Athena's long-term skill development, my actions rested within the principle's constraints."

Denton's logic conflicted with the obvious evidence that whatever he did to Athena's viewer had left her visibly shaken. Dr. Picartz started to say something, possibly along those lines, but he stopped himself, instead saying only, "Denton, please go to Dr. Menta's office."

Denton turned and left the room without glancing at Athena, much less apologizing. By the time he was gone, Athena stood up, having regained most of her composure.

Dr. Picartz turned back to her. "Athena, I am deeply sorry for Denton's behavior. You may be excused for the rest of class."

She cut him off. "I'm fine, Dr. Picartz. I don't need to leave. It's the androids who are causing the problems. I won't be working with any of these faulty machines again, and my parents will be hearing about this." Her defiant words almost masked the shakiness remaining in her voice as she looked pointedly at Isaac. Charlotte's cheeks flushed; Isaac didn't do anything wrong.

"I understand, Athena. I will schedule a meeting for us to debrief this with your advisor as well." Dr. Picartz paired Athena with Jace, subtly asking Isaac to move to the side of the room, where he remained for the duration of class.

The students completed the exercise more somberly than before, and Dr. Picartz mercifully released them a little early. As she left the room with Isaac and their friends, Charlotte felt the weight of Athena's glare.

"That was crazy," Jace said, more subdued than usual, once they reached the ground outside the Treetop.

"He shouldn't have been able to do that," Chai said.

Isaac nodded. "On Denton's behalf, I apologize. I do not expect that this will happen again."

"I should hope not," Chai replied sharply while avoiding eye contact with Isaac.

Charlotte didn't know what to say, but Jace shrugged off the awkward moment. "I guess we'll see you guys later," he said before heading off with Chai to their next class.

Charlotte and Isaac walked toward a study pod in silence while Charlotte tried to process her thoughts. Marissa's words of warning came suddenly back to her, though she tried to push them away.

Charlotte trusted Isaac. She did. But Athena's shrieks continued to echo in her mind, pulling her toward Marissa's paranoia. Maybe it couldn't hurt to record her time with Isaac. If she didn't do anything with the captures, then it almost wasn't breaking the rules, or Isaac's trust, at all. With only a slight confidence that she was making the right choice, Charlotte discreetly programmed her viewer to capture all future interactions with any of the androids.

She hoped this would turn out to be an unnecessary precaution.

CHAPTER 23

"I FOUND SOME interesting patterns in Dr. Coggins' journals."

"Hmm?" Charlotte broke out of her thoughts to look at Isaac, who had already repeated himself twice. "What did you say?"

"I mentioned that there are some interesting findings in Dr. Coggins' journals. Given your distracted state, however, this may not be the most advantageous time to review my analysis. I can ascertain that there is something else on your mind. Would you like to discuss it?"

Charlotte sighed. Anyone else telling her that she was too distracted would have irritated her immensely, but Isaac's directness, untainted by any ego or ill will, somehow came across as endearing. Besides, she *was* distracted. Denton's treatment of Athena left Charlotte unnerved, and she wished that she and Isaac hadn't agreed to work with Denton for Design Lab. The fact that he would be joining them any minute made her jumpy.

She looked over her shoulder through the transparent globe encapsulating their study pod. Dotted throughout campus, the study pods allowed students to work simultaneously within nature but without interference from the elements. On a foggy fall day, this pod, one of Charlotte's favorites, provided a sooth-ing spot nestled among the trees; from the edge of anxiety, however, Charlotte could see that it was also both isolated and exposed.

As though he could read her mind, Isaac said, "I received a message from Dr. Menta that Denton will not be joining us to-day."

"Oh!" Her intense relief showed on her face before she had a chance to temper it.

"You are relieved."

"No. Well, yes."

"You would feel uncomfortable in Denton's presence because of what happened between him and Athena."

"Yes."

He paused for a moment, processing. "What part of Denton's actions made you the most uncomfortable?"

Charlotte was unclear about why she needed to spell this out, but she decided to humor him. "He disregarded Dr. Picartz's directions."

"Correct. I have observed, however, that many students dis-regard instructions in one way or another. Jace, for example, occasionally arrives to class a minute late despite being in-structed to arrive on time."

"That's different. The instruction about not intervening with the hack was provided to keep us safe. That's a more important rule."

"From your perspective, then, Denton compromised Athena's safety."

Charlotte was losing patience with this line of conversation. "Yes, Isaac. Obviously, he compromised her safety. I've never seen Athena that terrified, and it wasn't right for Denton to do that to her."

"That is a fair point, and I am not arguing against it. I am only wondering what would have happened if a human partner had acted in the same manner."

This question threw Charlotte off. "What do you mean?"

"For example, if Beckett had been paired with Athena and had similarly manipulated the exercise, would Athena have been similarly distressed? Afterward, would you consequently feel uncomfortable about being in Beckett's presence?"

Charlotte started to say yes, then stopped. She realized that she wasn't sure, but she also recognized the flaw in this line of reasoning.

"Beckett wouldn't have done that."

"From what I have observed about Beckett's behavior, it stands to reason that he might."

"Even if he wanted to, Beckett wouldn't have the skills to manipulate her viewer. He could barely defend against the hack himself."

"For the sake of argument, let us suppose that he did have the skills."

"I don't know, Isaac. I would at least be suspicious of him, and yeah, I probably wouldn't want to be around him. But I don't know if this is a good example. I already don't love being around Beckett." Suddenly frustrated that she couldn't read more from Isaac's subtle facial expressions, she looked at him. "What are you getting at with this?"

"I am trying to identify what caused the greater discomfort: Denton's actions themselves or the fact that they were enacted by an android."

Charlotte tried to replay the class in her head, imagining how she would have felt if Athena's fear and anger had been directed against a human student. Would she have reacted differently? "I don't know, Isaac." That was the most honest answer she could give.

"This is perhaps an interesting design question. Through the Android Inception Program, we are all exploring a world in which androids and humans interact within the same physical space but not within the same social boundaries. Androids have principles, and humans have laws, but these rules are not entirely equivalent." Isaac paused to gauge Charlotte's reaction. After she slowly nodded, he continued, "Given identical scenarios and identical choices, what is the difference between an artificially intelligent being carrying out those actions versus a human carrying out those actions? What are the consequences of this perceived difference, and how can they be addressed to facilitate a more productive integration of androids into human spaces?"

"You're right!" Charlotte brightened as she considered Isaac's ideas. His fascinating questions aligned nicely with the design focus they had been exploring regarding android integration. "In other words, conscious and unconscious bias against androids may affect the way humans react to them. We could test that first, to see if our theory holds any water, and then based on the results, we could design interventions to help humans recognize their bias."

Charlotte's growing excitement chipped away at her fear of Denton. From this angle, she could see his actions more objectively. "It also works the other way. Denton incorrectly believed that pushing Athena cognitively was the right decision. He holds a bias toward intellectual achievement at the exclusion of emotional well-being. This research could perhaps also help androids work through their misconceptions about humans."

"That is an excellent point." Isaac smiled at her, and unless Charlotte was imagining things, his smile was becoming a bit more natural every day.

The hours that afternoon flew by as they developed a proposal. They would dig into research from previous centuries when race and gender bias were still prevalent, and they would develop an experiment to assess the current level of bias at the Academy. Though by far the most ambitious work she'd ever attempted, Charlotte was energized and, more than anything, grateful to be working alongside Isaac.

Charlotte's stomach grumbled loudly, drawing Isaac's attention. He looked at her with concern. "It would appear that you require food in the immediate future."

She laughed. "Yeah, I think it's probably dinnertime. Let's wrap up here."

As they left the study pod, something nagged at the back of her mind. She took a quick mental inventory of their work. They had ended in a good spot, and they had a plan. So what was bothering her?

"Shoot!" She reflexively smacked Isaac on the arm. "We didn't get to talk about Dr. Coggins' journals. I'm sorry!"

He looked down at her quizzically. "There is no need to apologize. I will share my preliminary analysis with you now so that you may review it at your leisure. Though they are personal journals, his writing style is unusually convoluted, so my full analysis is taking longer than anticipated."

"Interesting. Maybe he never intended for his journals to have an audience."

"If he did not want anyone to read his thoughts, then it would have been prudent not to write them down."

"I can't argue with that, Isaac. But perhaps prudence wasn't Dr. Coggins' strong suit."

CHAPTER 24

FOR THE THIRD time, Dr. Menta asked Charlotte a similar question during their check-in the following day. "You have always felt comfortable around Isaac?"

"Yes. I'm completely comfortable around him. And around the other androids, for that matter." Charlotte's conversation with Isaac the day before had helped her see Denton's behavior in a new light, but Dr. Menta's line of questioning worried her. "Is something wrong? Is the Android Inception Program in danger? Because of what happened in Tech Ethics?"

"Not at all. These questions are a routine part of our research. And while yesterday's events were unfortunate, they will not disrupt the program. Of course, the school's top priority is our students' well-being, and we want to make sure that we're covering all of our bases. I have followed up with Athena, and Denton will certainly be monitored more closely from now on." Dr. Menta paused, registering Charlotte's expression. "Is there something else you'd like to ask me?"

Charlotte squirmed, unsure about how to put her thoughts

into words. "Well, it seems that Denton's unique personality sequence has led him to…have some difficulties when interacting with other students."

"Yes."

She hoped Dr. Menta would pick up the thread, but in the ensuing silence, Charlotte continued, "So did you predict this? If the purpose was a smooth integration, then I'm confused about why you would intentionally create an android who is, well, more difficult to get along with."

Nodding thoughtfully, Dr. Menta smiled, seemingly pleased with Charlotte's thoughts. "Why do you think our purpose for the program was a smooth integration?"

"But." Charlotte faltered. "Isn't that the purpose?"

"Yes and no. As I mentioned earlier, we would never do anything to compromise students' safety. Please understand that on a personality spectrum, Denton still falls firmly on the side of benevolence. However, an entirely seamless integration with effortlessly pleasant androids would not provide us with complete data on how humans interact with artificially intelligent beings. Interestingly, some people find an android as amiable as Isaac more difficult to work with than a more direct one like Denton. Our purpose, therefore, has been to analyze how the students and faculty navigate their interactions with the androids, and vice versa."

Charlotte nodded, flushing slightly with the embarrassment of her faulty assumptions.

After a pause, Dr. Menta changed the subject. "I've heard that you, Isaac, and Denton are collaborating on your design project?"

"Yes."

"How did Denton come to be in your group?"

Charlotte hesitated, not wanting to rat Beckett out, much as he might deserve it. "Well, it seemed like Beckett already had a group, and it didn't feel right to leave Denton alone."

"Would you prefer to be working only with Isaac?"

"I don't know if I would say that." But she also wouldn't *not* say that, and Dr. Menta apparently caught the subtext.

"I think, moving forward, that it might be best for you and Isaac to continue alone. Given Denton's recent actions, we may be adjusting his schedule, and I would hate for that to interfere with your work. Is that acceptable?"

"Yes, thank you." Charlotte smiled while trying to conceal the depths of her relief.

"Excellent. I will communicate with Dr. Vosima and Denton about the change. I think we're done for today, unless you have anything else to share?"

For a brief moment, Charlotte thought of the secret captures she was now storing in her viewer, but she shook her head. "No, nothing I can think of."

Jace and I have to work late tonight, so we can't make it to dinner. Miss you!! See you later at home :)

Charlotte frowned at Chai's message as she and Isaac walked toward the Mod. Dinner was one of the few times left for all of them to hang out together, and Chai and Jace were starting to make a habit of working through it. Charlotte knew that many of their experiments depended on their physical presence in the Boulder biology labs, but she hoped this wouldn't continue for much longer.

With a quick pang of spite that she immediately regretted, she noticed Chai and Jace were missing a gourmet dining night. This might teach them not to skip dinner.

Though food at the Academy was always top-notch, gourmet nights took the students' palates to a whole new level.

Throughout the year, Cognation hired a handful of up-and-coming chefs to showcase their creations for students and staff. Tonight's elegant Italian offerings wafted through the Mod, which had arranged itself into a spacious Mediterranean plaza. Charlotte did actually feel bad that Chai and Jace had to miss this.

Trying in vain to find Gavin and Eli, Charlotte led Isaac to an empty table, and they sat across from each other. They had eaten meals alone together before, but Charlotte suddenly felt weird about it, perhaps due to the more formal setting and Athena's disapproving gaze from across the room.

Rather than the usual cafeteria-style service, bustling auto-carts efficiently served up the gourmet meals, and a gorgeous caprese appetizer soon appeared before them. The non-humanoid carts, with their boxy silver frames and mechanical arms, in no way resembled Isaac, but seeing them serve Isaac still made Charlotte pause. A vision of similar mechanics lurking below Isaac's skin flashed across her mind.

"Is everything okay?" Isaac asked.

"Yes." Charlotte smiled and cleared her expression. She envied Isaac, who never had to worry about unintentionally wearing his thoughts on his face. Or worry about anything at all, in fact.

They ate in silence for a moment. Charlotte knew she was being completely ridiculous, but she couldn't think of a single thing to say. She had no reason to feel unsettled right now, but dwelling on this fact only made the awkwardness worse.

Was it her imagination, or were several people glaring in Isaac's direction? Word of Denton's behavior in Tech Ethics had spread quickly, breeding an unexpected level of aversion to the androids from some of her classmates. None of the other androids appeared to be in the Mod at this time, which left Charlotte feeling even more in the spotlight. Though usually a slow eater, she anxiously picked up her pace.

Once the robots delivered the gorgonzola and butternut squash ravioli, Isaac broke the silence. "Would now be an opportune time to discuss Dr. Coggins' journals, or would you prefer a more conversational topic, like the weather?"

"The journals!" Why hadn't Charlotte thought to bring them up? "This is a perfect time to talk about the journals."

"What were your thoughts on my preliminary analysis?"

"Um," Charlotte mumbled through her bite of pasta. "I only had a chance to glance at it very briefly…"

"That is understandable." In their viewerspace, Isaac pulled up an intricate map of graphs and charts. "As I mentioned, I have not found anything conclusively valuable, but I will walk you through my organization so far. I started by running the text through independent algorithms, which mostly resulted in surface-level patterns. Now, I am working on different combinations to identify underlying patterns and hidden clues."

As Isaac identified each method, the graphs rearranged themselves in front of Charlotte; she struggled to keep up with both Isaac's information and the visual data. "With an association classifier, I have mapped connections between the most common topics referenced. In addition, I have run a dimensionality reduction analysis, as the most frequent topics are not always the most significant. Given the fact that the last journal entry is dated one year, two months, and three days before Dr. Coggins' death, I am also working on a regression analysis to predict what he might have written about, had he continued to write."

"Perhaps he did complete more journals, and they're just not here," Charlotte suggested.

Isaac brought his hand to his chin, thoughtfully. "That is possible. The other curiosity I noticed is that his forty-second volume was not with the collection. I originally thought it was the only missing volume, but perhaps there are others."

"Maybe. But why wouldn't the library have the complete set?" Setting aside the mystery of a missing journal, Charlotte took a moment to flip through the graphs as she interpreted the data. Several of the categories and associations were expected - the Alliance and Cognation were linked in every data set as were virtual reality and the viewernet - but a few surprises stood out.

"Cats? Isaac, why are there so many data points about cats?"

"Dr. Coggins evidently owned a number of cats throughout his life. In researching pet culture, I have learned that humans can become very attached to their mammalian companions, at times even ascribing human-like personalities to them. Dr. Coggins appears to fall into that category. He speaks of one cat in particular, Marvin, almost as though he were a person. Furthermore, there is a strong association between Marvin and the library, and I am working to better understand the connection there."

"Huh. I understand being really attached to your pets. I mean, I loved my family's cat. But journaling about it? That seems odd, especially for someone like Dr. Coggins. You'd think he would have had enough other things on his mind. Maybe I'll read over some of those passages."

"That is an excellent plan. Because my analysis is being done on a purely statistical level, your human interpretation will be invaluable in refining the connections."

"Thanks, Isaac." They continued chatting about the journals through the tiramisu course, and by the end of dinner, Charlotte couldn't remember why she had been so worried about having a meal alone with Isaac in the first place.

CHAPTER 25

AFTER A PARTICULARLY intriguing Philosophy of Reality period, Charlotte shivered on the walk to one of the larger study pods, where she, Gavin, and their android partners planned to meet Chai and Jace for some "chworking," as Jace liked to describe their chill working sessions.

That morning's uncharacteristic burst of late autumn sunshine had made Charlotte overly optimistic about the weather, leaving her unprepared for the mist that now shrouded the forest. "I want to grab a heavier sweater," Charlotte said. "I'll meet you guys there."

Gavin started to speak, but Isaac beat him to it. "I will walk with you."

"Cool, thanks." Charlotte smiled at Gavin and Eli. "See you soon."

Gavin hesitated but then nodded. "Sure, we'll see you there."

As Charlotte and Isaac walked toward Lyra, she looked at his thin black shirt. "You don't get cold?"

"My skin is equipped with sensory inputs, so I can determine that this time today is 0.5 degrees Celsius cooler than yesterday.

I have observed that humans, when excessively cold or hot, cannot concentrate on anything else; however, I have a higher tolerance for temperature variation."

"So you can compartmentalize it?"

"Yes."

"That would be super useful. As a mere human, I must rely on the comfort of a sweater." With a wry smile, she left Isaac at her favorite bench under one of her dorm's curving petals. "I'll just be a minute."

Upon entering the lobby, Charlotte spotted Jace on the far side of the courtyard. He seemed to be talking to someone concealed behind a pillar. Just as Charlotte started to call out to him, she saw him lean forward, and whoa! If Charlotte wasn't mistaken, Jace was kissing someone.

Jace. Was. Kissing. Someone. She couldn't *wait* to tell Chai!

Charlotte stepped out of sight and surreptitiously craned her neck in an effort to identify the mystery girl. On first glance, it looked like - she squinted and blinked - no, it *was*. But it couldn't be.

Jace wasn't just kissing someone.

Jace was kissing Chai.

Jace and Chai? Chai and Jace.

Did this mean they were dating?

It was the only logical explanation for what she had witnessed, but shouldn't Charlotte have known? Why wouldn't they tell her? Tears stinging the corners of her eyes, she stared at her best friends, the people she thought she knew best in the world, as they walked away together.

A hand touched her arm, and she jumped, startled to see Isaac right behind her. Great. He had witnessed the whole thing, including her stupid near-crying reaction. He started to speak, but she avoided eye contact and brushed him off.

"I don't want to talk about it." She ran up to her room and willed herself into a calmer state by trying to channel Isaac's compartmentalization powers. By the time she met Isaac downstairs, her outward emotions were more or less under control. Still, she could barely meet Isaac's gaze, and he granted her unspoken request for space as they walked silently to the study pod.

When greeting her friends, Charlotte bristled as Chai and Jace acted perfectly normal, despite the fact that they were kissing only moments before, despite the fact that they'd been lying to her for who knows how long.

Why would they lie? Is this the real reason they'd been "working" through dinner so often? Should Charlotte be this upset?

How could Chai not tell her?

This question, more than any other, stung. Charlotte and Chai shared everything. Chai knew about all of Charlotte's crushes (well, all except her initial attraction to Isaac, which didn't count). Charlotte thought she knew about all of Chai's romantic interests as well. Sure, they hadn't talked about any of Chai's crushes recently, but Charlotte assumed there weren't any.

"Hey, are you okay?" Chai's concerned look brought Charlotte back to the present.

"Oh, yeah." Charlotte tried to smile naturally. "Just a lot on my mind."

"Ugh. Tell me about it! We're facing some serious roadblocks on our experiments. I'm worried we're not making enough progress."

"We'll be fine," Jace said, patting Chai's hand in a way that

Charlotte wouldn't have thought twice about before this afternoon. Now that she considered it, though, maybe there had been some signs of a budding romance. On top of everything, she could now also feel like an idiot for not noticing the clues.

Isaac's eyes bounced between Charlotte, Chai, and Jace in a rhythmic, almost hypnotic pattern. *Please stop,* Charlotte mouthed to him when she caught his gaze.

He paused his conspicuous glancing but then started a new topic of conversation. "We covered some interesting points in Philosophy of Reality today regarding whether or not we can ever truly know another person."

"Huh," Jace said. "I think you can know people pretty well."

"Dr. Pythema, one of the most prodigious researchers on this topic, spent years trying to understand the perspective of other people, and even she was not entirely successful."

Now Charlotte worried about Isaac's motives for this discussion. "I don't think we need to rehash this, Isaac. More than half of us were in the class, and we're all trying to do some work here."

"That's okay," Gavin said. "It is interesting."

Isaac continued, "Understanding another person is especially complicated by humans' propensity for duplicity. When people are dishonest with even those close to them, it can be very difficult to discern whether you know the actual person or the persona created by them."

"Wow, this is getting even deeper than class," Gavin said.

Isaac looked pointedly at Chai and Jace. "Given these thoughts, does anyone have anything to share?"

"Isaac!" Charlotte didn't want to do this now, not in front of Gavin, not when she felt her emotions so close to bubbling over the surface. Chai and Jace exchanged a look more of bewilderment than guilt. Out of the corner of her eye, she saw Gavin raise his eyebrows at Jace, who shrugged.

"Gavin and I found a challenging new trail today." Eli expertly changed the subject, mitigating some of the awkwardness Charlotte's outburst had caused. If she weren't so frustrated, she would have been impressed by Eli's sophisticated social awareness, but she said little until they all eventually got to work.

Back in their room later that night, Charlotte considered how to make Chai divulge her secret.

"So…you and Jace have been spending a lot of time together on your design work. Is it going well? Aside from the roadblocks you mentioned?"

"Yeah, it is. I mean, it's a lot more work than I expected, but that's second year, right?"

"Right." Charlotte nonchalantly added, "And working with Jace has been good?"

Chai paused in the middle of organizing her shower caddy. "Definitely. It's been great. Really great, actually." Charlotte held her breath, waiting for Chai to say more. "How about your project?"

Charlotte tried not to let her disappointment show. "Oh, it's been good. Really interesting."

"Cool." Chai hesitated, and Charlotte's hope returned. Maybe this would be the moment of truth. "And it doesn't bother you? To be working so much with Isaac?"

"What?" That came out of left field. Charlotte knew Chai was uncomfortable around Denton, but that didn't explain why she would question Charlotte's work with Isaac. "No, I like partnering with him. I thought you liked being around him, too."

"Yeah, sure. I was just asking." Chai smiled weakly, letting the conversation drop. "Shower time for me."

Charlotte kept a smile on her face until the door shut behind Chai. How long was her best friend planning to lie to her? And what was with the sudden concern about Isaac? Refusing to let the moisture in her eyes spill into tears, she changed into pajamas and climbed into bed.

I apologize for any distress I caused earlier, Charlotte. It will not happen again.

Isaac's message popped up unexpectedly, and Charlotte's pulse quickened at his name. Aside from occasionally confirming meeting times and locations, they were not in the habit of sending messages.

It's okay. I'm sorry I overreacted.

Am I correct in assuming that you are upset because of your own romantic attraction to Jace?

Charlotte's eyes widened. *What? No!*

Then do you have a romantic interest in Chai?

Charlotte shook her head. Isaac clearly still had some things to learn about human relationships.

No, Isaac. I'm friends with Jace and Chai. No romantic interest here. It's more complicated than that. She paused, trying to distill her feelings into a message that he would understand. *Best friends usually confide in each other about things like this. I had no idea that Chai and Jace liked each other that way, and I'm upset because they didn't tell me.*

Understood. Am I correct in interpreting that you did not feel ready to talk about it earlier?

Yeah. I knew I might get emotional, and I didn't want that to happen in front of everyone. A part of me also wants to respect their privacy. I expected Chai to say something once we got to our room, but she didn't. I think I might wait until she brings it up.

It felt good to entrust Isaac with her feelings, but he didn't respond for a few minutes. She was considering whether or not to say something else when his next message came through.

You are a good friend, Charlotte.

She smiled. Whether he meant she was a good friend to Chai and Jace or a good friend to him wasn't clear, but she would take it in either case.

Thanks, Isaac. You're a good friend, too.

CHAPTER 26

"WHERE'S ISAAC?"

"I don't know," Charlotte answered Jace. "It doesn't seem like Denton's here either. That's odd."

"Maybe the androids have a separate meeting?" Chai offered as the three took their seats.

Are you coming to Tech Ethics? Charlotte quickly messaged Isaac, but he failed to respond before Dr. Picartz locked their viewers for class. With his perfect internal clock, Isaac never arrived anywhere late, but Charlotte saved a spot next to her anyway.

Never wasting a moment, Dr. Picartz got right down to business. "Today, we will consider a topic that is perhaps overdue: how to respond to concerns about android integration."

Charlotte frowned. They were discussing the android program on a day when the androids were conspicuously absent from class? "Is this why Isaac and Denton aren't here?" Her whisper to Chai came out louder than she intended, and Dr. Picartz turned to face her.

"I'm sure you're not the only one with this question, so I am happy to answer it, despite the interruption. For anyone who didn't hear, Ms. Blythe commented on the absence of Isaac and Denton. Because our topics today, and for the rest of the semester, will intersect with some concerns that have been raised about the androids on campus, Dr. Menta and the faculty have determined that it would be best to move them to a separate Tech Ethics course. Isaac and Denton will therefore no longer be joining this section."

The students nodded, as though it were normal, acceptable, to segregate students at the Academy. Unmoored, Charlotte wondered briefly if she were in another one of Dr. Picartz's viewer hacks.

"That's not fair." Charlotte surprised everyone, including herself, by speaking up. In the face of Dr. Picartz's annoyed expression, she tried to level her tone. "It doesn't seem ethical to discriminate against the androids because a few students are concerned."

Beckett's clipped laughter rang out. "You can't discriminate against a machine, Charlotte."

"Let's not forget that some of us are rightfully concerned to be around such dangerous technology," Athena added with a dramatic sigh that almost covered the smirk beneath it.

"Isaac isn't dangerous. You're just-"

Dr. Picartz flicked his cane, signaling them to stop. "This is jumping a bit ahead in my lesson, but I am of course always ready to adapt. Our question for the moment is whether or not it is ethical to remove androids from a class in response to student concerns. Here are some facts to consider. One: A student in this class felt unsafe following an interaction with an android. Two: Aside from that incident, students have had largely positive interactions with androids. Three: Androids were welcomed into this school as students. Four: Androids can identify and understand emotions, but they do not feel emotions as humans do. Please organize yourselves into groups and plan your arguments."

The room transformed into colorful thirds: yellow for "ethical to remove androids," blue for "not ethical," and green for "it depends."

Expecting Chai and Jace to follow, Charlotte immediately moved toward the blue section. Once she got there, though, she turned to find them hovering near the border between the green and blue spaces. After a moment's hesitation, they took a step closer to the "it depends" section. Catching Charlotte's eye, Chai shrugged and mouthed, *Sorry*. Charlotte smiled weakly and pushed down her disappointment. This wasn't kindergarten; she didn't always have to agree with her best friends. Still, she wondered how they could support android segregation after spending so much time with Eli and Isaac.

Turning back to the blue group, Charlotte noticed with a sinking stomach that only she and Pri occupied the space. The vast majority of their class made up the yellow group, with a few others joining Chai and Jace in between.

Smiling, Pri pulled two chairs forward, and Charlotte's frustration turned to gratitude as she realized how easily she could have been the sole person on this side. Charlotte wouldn't have expected Pri to join her, given that she was usually friendly with Athena.

Reading her mind, Pri said, "You're probably surprised I'm here, but I think it was really brave of you to speak up earlier."

"Thank you." Charlotte tried to convey her true appreciation with those two words. "A segregation policy just doesn't feel right."

"I agree. I didn't like what Denton did to Athena, of course, but it's not fair to judge the entire group on one person's - one android's - actions. I've worked with some of them in my other classes, and they've been generally pleasant."

Charlotte nodded. "Denton has an abrasive personality; that's undeniable. But I've spent a lot of time with Isaac and Eli, and they're both really kind."

"Right. I think that's a good starting point. Everyone is talking about the androids collectively, but they have individual personalities. Treating people as a category rather than as individuals is practically the definition of discrimination, and I don't see why that wouldn't transfer to androids."

Using that idea as their anchoring concept, they built up their argument and researched the precedents from earlier eras, including the sweeping Equal Rights Amendment that protected civil rights for people of all genders. Pri had a sharp mind for debate, and Charlotte became so deeply engrossed in fleshing out their final ideas that she almost didn't notice Beckett and Athena passing by them on their way to ask Dr. Picartz a question.

"It's so kind of you to take this side, Pri. It would have been a shame to see Charlotte have to argue by herself." Athena's sugary voice oozed over them.

Calmly, Pri said, "I believe in this argument, Athena."

"Oh." Athena was taken aback for a moment, but she recovered quickly. "In that case, I look forward to hearing your ideas."

As they moved away, Beckett leaned over to Athena, and his poorly covered whisper reached Charlotte and Pri. "Looks like the android lover club has a new member."

Charlotte's cheeks reddened, but Pri brushed the comment off. "Don't worry about him. He's just bothered because the androids knocked his popularity down a few notches."

"Opening statements in two minutes." Dr. Picartz's time check snapped Charlotte back into focus, and she and Pri reviewed their arguments one more time before Dr. Picartz called on Pri to start the debate.

"How we treat others, including technological beings, shines a light on our humanity. The way that we are speaking about androids today, as a monolithic group, defined only by their status as androids, reflects the worst of human nature. Furthermore, removing all androids from these discussions feeds into a troubling historical trend of segregation that our ancestors fought hard to dismantle. We cannot let our advancements into the future push us instead into the past." Pri sat down modestly, allowing only a hint of a smile in response to Charlotte's thumbs-up.

For a brief moment, Charlotte thought that this debate might help her classmates consider a different perspective; unfortunately, that soon proved to not be the case, at least not for Beckett.

"We believe that how we treat humans is the most important reflection of our humanity. The *human* students must be the Academy's first priority - a priority, I'm afraid, that has been sadly neglected in the name of science. If we don't feel safe, then how can we learn? I know that we may not all be best friends, but I for one am appalled by my classmates' callous indifference to the suffering of one of our own." Beckett gestured toward Athena, who adopted a wounded expression. "Surely real emotions, from real humans, are more important than esoteric principles?"

This was the problem with sequestering the androids. Athena, directly in front of her classmates, would receive much more empathy than the abstract idea of nonhuman peers. Charlotte barely heard the third group's opening statement as her anger flared against Denton. This was his fault. If he hadn't spooked Athena, then they wouldn't be in this situation.

Charlotte and Pri held their own as the debate swung back to them, but Charlotte still wished Isaac were there to support their case.

"Who do you care more about, Charlotte? Athena or Isaac? It's that simple." Beckett's question, completely disconnected from the line of reasoning they'd been debating, left Charlotte speechless.

Any answer she thought of seemed wrong. "It's not that simple," was the best response she had.

"I think we have our answer then. So much for loyalty to the human race," Beckett sniggered.

Charlotte tried to ignore the disgusted looks from some of her peers, but she hadn't been prepared for this level of animosity. Wishing for a quick end to the class, she let Pri conclude their arguments.

After what seemed like an eternity, Dr. Picartz brought the debate to a close and assigned a reflection. Keeping her eyes toward the ground, Charlotte slipped on her jacket. She attempted to push away her festering frustration, but the brief apology Chai and Jace offered as they filed out of class couldn't quite make up for the fact that they had failed to support her.

Charlotte wondered if this philosophical misalignment, even more than Chai and Jace's secret romance, might splinter their friendship beyond repair.

CHAPTER 27

CHARLOTTE STUDIED ISAAC as they worked in their favorite study pod and tried to identify any signs that his eviction from Tech Ethics bothered him. Not surprisingly, he seemed annoyingly unperturbed.

She sighed in an effort to release the residual stress from the debate. Isaac glanced her way, but, apparently sensing that she didn't want to talk, he said nothing. His interpretation of nonverbal clues was improving.

Putting aside all distracting thoughts, Charlotte focused on the task at hand, and the hours flew by as she and Isaac continued their effortless collaboration. When they wrapped up their design work for the day, Isaac revisited the topic of Dr. Coggins' journals, and Charlotte tried not to feel chastised. With so many other things on her mind, the journals had lost their priority status; she vaguely remembered offering to glance through some of the passages, but she hadn't been able to fit that into her schedule. Isaac, however, had plenty of mental space for multitasking.

"While the journals do provide some unique personal anecdotes, most of what Dr. Coggins recorded aligns with the multitude of biographies published after his death." Obviously,

Isaac had read every book published about Cognation's founder. "What is curious, perhaps, is that unlike most of the notable figures of his time, he did not publish a memoir or autobiography. With these journals, he easily could have done so."

"Hmm." While interesting, Dr. Coggins' choice not to write a memoir hardly counted as a discovery, in Charlotte's opinion.

Isaac's brow wrinkled in a way that was becoming less, well, robotic. "I am still parsing his final journals. For some reason, his later writing became more and more obscure, which is a distinct difference from the precision in his earlier volumes. For example, in his third-to-last journal, he describes a personal project at length without providing any identifiable details. I cannot find any corroborating evidence of this type of work in any other records."

"Huh. That is weird." Charlotte thought back to her own brief experience with journaling. A new interface for viewer journals became popular when she turned ten, and she remembered recording a few entries until she learned that Marissa was secretly reading them. After that, she wrote in code for a while before that became too time consuming.

That gave her an idea. "Isaac, is it possible that Dr. Coggins was writing in code?"

"In code." Isaac paused, ostensibly to conduct a few seconds of research. "Yes, that is entirely possible. I will rerun my analysis through a decoding process to see what new insights emerge. That is an excellent hypothesis, Charlotte."

"Thanks." She smiled and tried not to look too pleased. It wasn't every day that she came up with a thought that had not occurred to Isaac first.

"In the meantime, I do believe I have found something of note in one of his earlier volumes." A digital model of the journals appeared in their viewerspace, and Isaac flipped to a page about two-thirds of the way through. He pointed Charlotte toward a passage on the bottom of the right-hand page.

Today the Humane Innovation Alliance agreed that they will not pursue artificial general intelligence until such future time that we have determined it is safe for the industry to proceed with this line of research.

Charlotte read the passage three times without understanding why Isaac highlighted this section. The Alliance's decision regarding artificial intelligence research was general knowledge. "What am I not seeing, Isaac?"

He underlined a single word, and Charlotte reread the passage.

Today the Humane Innovation Alliance agreed that <u>they</u> will not pursue artificial general intelligence until such future time that we have determined it is safe for the industry to proceed with this line of research.

"So the pronoun he used is significant?"

"I think so. Cognation Industries is part of the Humane Innovation Alliance, and in all other references to the Alliance, Dr. Coggins uses 'we,' which is a more accurate pronoun, given his inclusion in the group. This is the only time he uses 'they' when describing the Alliance."

"Okay. And you think that means…"

"It could mean that Dr. Coggins did not consider himself bound to the statute regarding artificial general intelligence."

"What?" Wide-eyed, Charlotte turned to Isaac. "You don't think he conducted research into artificial intelligence? After publicly vowing that he wouldn't?"

"From his linguistic patterns combined with the deceptive nature of leaders throughout the history of humankind, this is the most logical conclusion. It is possible that the project he references in his later journals is related though I have not yet found a conclusive link. If he were delving into this research secretly, it would provide a compelling reason for him to be cautious about what he recorded."

Charlotte nodded, but Isaac's interpretation based on one pronoun seemed shaky at best. Everything she had learned about Cognation and the Alliance made this hypothesis incredibly unlikely.

"That's a serious claim, Isaac. Dr. Coggins was known to be an ardent supporter of the Alliance's agreements. We would need a lot more evidence to disprove that."

"I agree. I will look for additional clues as I continue my analysis. I hope to discover some answers soon."

Charlotte had little doubt that Isaac would indeed get to the bottom of this mystery promptly. When he messaged her later that night, she assumed he had new evidence to share. Instead, he surprised her with an unrelated question.

Would you mind clarifying something for me? Isaac initiated their conversation, as usual. Though they didn't message every single night, Charlotte had grown accustomed to hearing from him on most evenings.

I can certainly try.

Are Chai and Jace dating? Aside from the kiss we observed and some indications of physical attraction, I have noted no explicit romantic signals to suggest that they are a couple.

Charlotte paused. This was an excellent question - one that she had been trying to answer herself. Charlotte kept waiting for Chai to confide in her, but if Chai did have feelings for Jace, she was doing an excellent job of keeping her crush a secret. To complicate things, Charlotte and Chai hadn't been speaking about much of anything since the Tech Ethics debate.

I really don't know. I haven't noticed any other signs either, so I'm guessing maybe not. Hoping not was probably a more honest answer, though Charlotte couldn't bring herself to admit that.

Thank you. For the moment, I will categorize their romantic partnership as inconclusive.

Charlotte didn't know what to say to that. Why was he categorizing Chai and Jace? Before she could respond, another message appeared.

Are you and Gavin dating?

Charlotte's cheeks flushed. *No. Why would you think that?*

His attentiveness to you in group settings indicates a level of interest that exceeds friendship. Furthermore, his elevated pulse and enlarged pupils signify his attraction to you.

Charlotte felt the color deepening on her face, and she was thankful not to have this conversation in person. Isaac noticed people's pulse and pupil size? What had he detected about her?

No, we're just friends. She decided that a simple, nonchalant answer was best. *Why so many questions about dating?*

In my pursuit of better understanding human adolescents, I am conducting an analysis of courting patterns.

Only Isaac could compose a sentence like that, and Charlotte laughed out loud, drawing Chai's attention from across the room. Ordinarily, Chai would have asked what was so funny, but she remained silent as she glanced at Charlotte before turning back to her work. Charlotte wondered if Chai could guess that she was messaging Isaac.

Feeling suddenly self-conscious, Charlotte concluded the conversation.

If you need any more help with your analysis, let me know. Good night, Isaac.

I will certainly do that. Good night, Charlotte.

CHAPTER 28

AS ACADEMIC DEMANDS continued to increase throughout the semester, Charlotte gradually found a new equilibrium with Chai and Jace. Though she thought about it, Charlotte never confronted them about the Tech Ethics debate or their potential secret dating life. Nothing got solved, exactly, but at least she avoided the risk of creating any larger issues.

On the bright side, Chai and Jace made a concerted effort to include Charlotte and Isaac over the following weeks as they all prepared to present their research. As often as possible, the four of them spent their flex time working together, and Charlotte appreciated Chai and Jace's comfort with Isaac, especially as tensions rose within the Academy community at large.

Many students regularly avoided the androids, and though Charlotte didn't visit the Academy's viewerboard often, Chai mentioned that anti-android rhetoric was heating up there. Despite knowing this, Charlotte didn't understand the full extent of the anti-android sentiment on campus until the tech innovations research symposium.

At the semester's midpoint, each major had an afternoon to share their research with their peers from other disciplines. In the three-hour sessions, all of the groups set up stations around the Gem. Cleared of seats, the auditorium transformed into a cavernous, woodsy space, giving teams plenty of room to spread out among the trees. The symposiums served not as times to show off, but rather as opportunities for students to participate in research conducted in other majors.

It also allowed first years to learn about the subjects they might want to pursue later on. Before coming to Cognation, Charlotte already knew that she would pursue tech innovations like her sister, but last year's symposium solidified her decision. She remembered being intimated by the inventive proposals and interactive simulations created by the older students. This year, with Isaac by her side, Charlotte hoped that her research would similarly impress some of her peers.

The tech innovations event occurred first this time, and Charlotte and Isaac were eager for feedback from a wider audience. Their station included a self-assessment regarding android bias followed by a viewer simulation that placed participants in several situations with individuals who could be either humans or androids. The true identities of the simulated characters were announced at the end of each scenario, and participants reported their reflections, which Charlotte and Isaac then compared to the physiological reactions captured by the viewer.

The results from their initial testing in Design Lab were quite instructive; even Beckett admitted that the simulation was thought-provoking. Athena, of course, refused to participate as the simulation was partially created by an android, but Charlotte didn't let that bother her. Athena's refusal was its own form of data about bias.

"I think we're ready." Charlotte smiled at Isaac after they finished double-checking their setup list. From the corner of her eye, she could see some groups scrambling in the few minutes remaining, but Charlotte and Isaac were both too organized to frantically rush around.

After the faculty ushered the rest of the students inside the Gem, Dr. Vosima, the tech innovations sponsor, called the room to attention. From her spot, Charlotte could only see the top of his curly white hair, but his voice came through her viewer clearly.

"Welcome, one and all, to our tech innovations research symposium. I know you are all familiar with the guidelines, but please be reminded that you must interact with at least six different projects in order to receive your credit for the day. Of course, you will likely have time for more than that, and I encourage you to visit as many teams as you can, both for the benefit of your peers and for your own learning. As the other professors can attest, the most successful design projects over the years improved greatly from insights gleaned across the disciplines. Feedback portals have been shared through your viewers, and your reflections are due by midnight tonight. If anyone has any questions, please don't hesitate to grab a professor. Let the fun begin!"

Chai and Jace arrived at Charlotte and Isaac's station first, followed closely by Gavin and Eli. Charlotte provided a brief overview of their bias research while Isaac shared the self-assessments and simulations. They then guided each of their friends into one of the semi-private viewing areas.

Before beginning, Eli asked, "Is it appropriate for me to participate in this research though I am myself an android?"

"Yes." Isaac explained what he and Charlotte had previously discussed. "Android bias against other androids or against humans is a possibility. Even if this is not the case, your participation will serve as an important point of comparison for our other respondents."

Once their friends began their self-assessments, all Isaac and Charlotte had to do was wait. With four other spots available,

Charlotte expected that they would receive another round of participants soon. As the minutes ticked by, however, that seemed not to be the case. Many of Charlotte's peers made eye contact with her as they passed by; then, as their gazes drifted over to Isaac, an alarming number of them changed direction abruptly.

By the time Jace had finished the research cycle, nearly thirty minutes later, not a single other student had come over to Isaac and Charlotte.

"Wow," Jace said, looking a bit more serious than usual as he stepped out to the front of their station. "That was super fascinating. I really thought I knew who the androids were in each scenario, and I was wrong almost every time. You did a really good job of tricking me." He paused and chuckled awkwardly. "Or maybe I'm just more biased than I thought." It seemed to pain him to admit this.

Charlotte shared a knowing smile with Isaac. They assigned the android and human personas in the scenarios randomly, independent of the characteristics exhibited in each scene. In other words, they weren't trying to trick anyone; rather, all of the assumptions were in the eye of the beholder. "From our research into historical race and gender bias, we learned that almost everyone is more biased than they expect, so that's not a surprise," Charlotte reassured Jace.

"Huh." His face lifted a bit. "That's good to know. In any case, your research is really interesting. I'm surprised you don't have a whole crowd here at this point."

"Yeah." Charlotte looked around. There were plenty of students milling around and waiting for other teams. "It does seem a little weird to me. No one seems to want to come over." *Not once they see Isaac,* she thought. "Would you mind mentioning to people that you liked our simulation?"

"No problem! You know how some people are; they like to get a feel for all of the options before jumping in. I think you'll have more participants than you can handle pretty soon."

"I hope so." From attending last year's symposiums, Charlotte remembered that some groups were busier than others, but something about their complete lack of foot traffic still struck her as odd.

A moment later, Chai emerged silently and pulled Charlotte to the side. "Char, this is all anonymous, right?"

"Of course." Charlotte had explained that before they started. "Is everything okay?"

"Yeah, I just...it just felt like kind of a private experiment."

Charlotte started to understand. "It is. Any type of bias reflection is really personal. There's nothing to worry about, Chai. We're not judging any of the data. Frankly, we already know that most people are biased against androids. That makes sense. The main point of this project is just trying to raise awareness about it."

Chai smiled warily. "Mission accomplished, then. I guess I better go join Jace in visiting some more teams. I'll see you after."

Once Eli and Gavin also moved on, Charlotte and Isaac spent a pretty uneventful hour as only a handful of human students, a few androids, and several professors came to their station.

"We will need more participation than this to deliver determinative conclusions," Isaac observed.

"I know." Charlotte didn't understand. Had this happened before? Surely the professors would have organized things better if they worried about some teams being excluded?

Nearly out of breath, Jace returned to their booth. "So, I've got good news and bad news. Bad news first: it turns out that someone was telling a bunch of people that participating in any of the androids' research is dangerous."

"What?" Charlotte snapped.

"The good news is that I told Dr. Vosima, and he and the other faculty members are on it. They're going to require some students to come over here, so you should be seeing an increase in your participation quite soon."

"Thanks, Jace." Charlotte tried to use her gratefulness for Jace's help to calm her anger toward the mysterious saboteur. "Do you know who started the rumors?"

He shrugged. "Want to take a guess?"

Charlotte's eyes widened. "You think it's Athena?"

"I don't know anything for sure, but it wouldn't be that surprising."

"This type of action would be consistent with her recent behavior toward androids, though that of course does not count as proof," Isaac offered. "This scenario is not at all a waste. We can include it as a tangential data point."

"You're right," Charlotte said as Jace nodded his agreement. "We're learning quite a bit about android bias today."

CHAPTER 29

AFTER A LONG string of symposiums, Charlotte was ready for a night off. More importantly, she was eager to find out what surprise Isaac had planned. A few days ago, he "requested the pleasure of her company" for tonight, but he refused to offer any details.

"Charlotte!"

As she entered the lobby, Charlotte turned to see Gavin running after her. "Hey," she said.

"Hey."

When he didn't continue, Charlotte asked, "So...what's up?"

"Oh, right." Gavin shoved his hands in his pockets and gazed over her shoulder. "I was just wondering if you wanted to hang out tonight. I know Jace and Chai are busy, so I thought, what the heck? Maybe we could watch a viewerflik or something. If you want."

A tingle ran up the back of Charlotte's neck. "That would be great, Gavin. It's just that I kind of already promised to hang out with Isaac. He has something he wants to show me. Maybe we could hang out tomorrow?" At Gavin's crestfallen expression, she stuttered on. "But I could reschedule with Isaac...or, um, you could join us…"

Gavin shook his head and started to back up. "No, that's cool…tomorrow's fine. I should probably catch up on some running tonight anyway."

"Oh, okay. I guess I'll see you tomorrow then."

"Yep. See you then."

Charlotte offered a weak smile, but Gavin had already turned and sprinted away. A part of her wished she had agreed to see Gavin tonight, but it was too late now. Groaning inwardly as she went up to her room, Charlotte told herself to snap out of it. She didn't want to cancel her already established plans with a friend, and she was still going to hang out with Gavin this weekend. This was a win-win situation. Wasn't it?

With these thoughts replaying in her head, Charlotte changed her scarf four times - no, five times - before going downstairs. It was stupid, really; at least Chai wasn't here to witness her indecision. It didn't matter what she wore, but none of her choices felt right until she selected the silky one with a blue and green braided pattern. While not her warmest scarf, it complemented her coat and her eyes, and she nodded approvingly at her reflection in the mirror.

"Hey, Isaac." She found him, with a bag over his shoulder, waiting in the exact spot where she had just spoken to Gavin.

"Hello. Thank you for agreeing to spend time with me tonight."

His formal manner, so characteristically Isaac, made her smile. "Of course. Thank you for planning a surprise."

Given the unusually clear night, she expected they might go to the observatory on campus, but Isaac steered her in the opposite direction. When they reached the base of the hill adjacent to Jace and Gavin's dorm, Charlotte stopped.

"We're not going up there, are we?" With no buildings atop

this peak, no stairs or lift existed to support their climb.

"We are," Isaac confirmed. "It is steep but well within the limits for someone of your height. I will assist you." He grabbed her hand and led her up the hillside with the confidence of an accomplished hiker; even in the dark, he effortlessly guided her through a winding path that tempered the sharp slope of their ascent.

When they reached the summit, they found a small clearing surrounded by trees stretching endlessly toward the star-studded sky. Charlotte took a moment to catch her breath and take in the view. Few spots on campus were new to her; not usually much of a climber, though, she had never made it up here. Thoroughly impressed by the majestic space, Charlotte nonetheless wished Isaac had warned her to wear something a bit warmer. Her sweat started to cool her skin beneath her light coat, and she held in a shiver.

Before she could ask how long they were going to stay there, Isaac drew her over to the tallest tree on the northern edge of the clearing. As they stared at the trunk, Isaac invited Charlotte to share his viewerspace. When she engaged her viewer, she gasped. Right before her eyes, an elegantly carved door suddenly emerged within the previously untainted bark.

Something about the pattern tugged at the corners of Charlotte's mind, but Isaac brushed his fingers over the carvings before she could get a closer look. At his touch, the door swung outward, exposing the entrance to a narrow spiral staircase.

Charlotte switched out of Isaac's viewerspace for a second, and her eyes widened as the doorway disappeared, only to reappear when she rejoined his viewerspace. "Isaac, how did you find this?"

"I have heard several students mention the myth of Winton Latham's secret spots; furthermore, Dr. Coggins even alluded to them in one of his journals. Eli and I therefore decided to discover if the stories held any merit." He swept his arm in front of him, beckoning her to go first. "As it turns out, at least three such hideaways exist."

Losing count somewhere after two hundred steps, Charlotte fervently hoped that no other climbs remained on the agenda for tonight. She had never missed an autopath so much. When she reached the top, though, she immediately knew that her burning legs were worth it.

Above the highest branches, the staircase opened onto a rustic balcony encapsulated by a transparent dome that provided an assurance of safety without obstructing the view. With the starry sky stretching in every direction above the gently waving treetops, it was one of the most beautiful places Charlotte had ever been. She stood still for several moments, adjusting to the height, the grandeur, the majesty of the landscape.

"Would you like to stay here for a while? If the height is bothersome, we can go back down."

"No, Isaac, I love it." She smiled at him, and he mirrored her grin. "I just needed a minute to take it all in."

Moving to where he stood in the center of the room, Charlotte now turned her attention to the interior. A thick, woven rug covered most of the space, with a couple of fluffy blankets folded off to the side. She sat down, cross-legged, and Isaac joined her on the floor. "The room was like this when you found it?"

He nodded. "Yes. That was part of what made me think it might be a nice place to hang out."

Charlotte stifled a laugh. Somehow Isaac could make even "hanging out" sound like a formal activity.

Isaac placed his bag in between them and pulled out two ginger beers and an assortment of chocolate snacks. "Oh, Isaac, you know me too well." She grabbed one of the drinks and handed the other to Isaac. "Cheers," she said, showing him how to clink his bottle against hers before they snacked and gazed at the stars in silence.

"Isaac, do you know the names of every star we can see?"

"I can access the names, locations, and identifying features of all known stars in the universe. However, I do not have that information currently activated."

She raised her eyebrow. "Why not?"

"I was trying to approach the scene as a poet might, not as a scientist. Sometimes beauty is easier to see when facts fall to the background."

Coming from Isaac, this reflection surprised and delighted Charlotte. "Well, that is a very poetic thing to say indeed."

"Thank you." Isaac stretched out flat on his back, and Charlotte reclined beside him, close enough that their arms nearly touched.

"What type of poetry would you want to write?"

"I have not considered that. Some would argue that any poetry created by an artificial being would not be real poetry. Without true human experience, without emotions, poetry would just be words."

"I think it would still be poetry. You have your own experience, and you can recognize emotions. I would read your poems."

"Thank you." Isaac turned toward her, and Charlotte leaned onto her hip to face him. She looked into his eyes, noting how the shape of his pupils, so strange at their first meeting, were familiar now. Like a visible birthmark, their irregular shape almost made him more human. Though logic told her that the expressive depth she saw reflected in his artificially deep brown irises was devoid of real human emotion, she could not, or

169

maybe would not, believe it.

"Are you happy, Isaac?"

He took a moment before responding. "I can infer that you would like me to say yes, but I want to give you an accurate answer. I know that tonight includes all of the elements required for happiness, and by that logic, I will categorize tonight as a happy memory."

A warm glow wrapped around her, and, suddenly bashful, she returned to her back and stared out into the night. "That's a good answer. I will categorize this as a happy memory as well."

They resumed their companionable silence and stayed that way for a while longer, two individuals, together in the universe, smiling up at the stars.

CHAPTER 30

STARTLED BY AN 8am viewer announcement, Charlotte awoke with an inexplicable feeling of dread.

All Academy students must report to the Gem at 11am. Attendance is mandatory. No exceptions.

An unplanned, schoolwide assembly on a Saturday morning was an extremely unusual occurrence. While Chai promptly fell back to sleep, Charlotte's overactive imagination kept her wide awake. What could have happened? Could this have anything to do with the androids?

To distract herself, Charlotte thought back to the night before and tried to recapture the calming comfort she had felt during the entire evening. Staying in bed, she replayed some of her favorite moments, including the unexpected hug from Isaac before they parted. While this uncharacteristic show of affection had surprised Charlotte, she had to admit that she enjoyed feeling his arms around her.

As her thoughts wandered, Charlotte's early-morning anxiety gradually evaporated. Though still curious about the assembly, she felt less worried by the time she woke Chai up and got ready to go. On their way to the Gem, the girls met up with Jace, who was oddly alone.

"Where's Gavin?" Charlotte asked. She had assumed they would be together.

Jace shrugged. "He didn't come back to our room last night, but sometimes he crashes with his running friends. I figured we'd see him at the meeting."

Charlotte had never been to a somber gathering within the central auditorium of the Gem; the yawning space, so grandiose during keynotes, now echoed with apprehension as they found their seats among the available section on the ground level. They hadn't seen Gavin on their way in, so they saved him a spot. By the time eleven o'clock struck, though, his seat remained empty.

Exactly on time, the entire faculty filed onto the stage, and a complete and total silence ensued. Seeing grave expressions from such exuberant professors as Dr. Yarrow, Dr. Anise, and Dr. Cariciarra sobered the students, who waited with a grim apprehension.

Dr. Menta entered last and walked to the center of the stage. "Thank you all for joining us here. I apologize for interrupting your Saturday." She took a breath and cleared her throat. "I'm going to get straight to the point. Last night, an incident involving one of the androids caused serious injury to an Academy student. Thankfully, your classmate is already on his way to making a full recovery, but we know that an unfortunate event like this, even without a tragic ending, is still terribly distressing. We also know that incidents like this can breed pernicious rumors. Therefore, we are here today to provide you with the facts and with any emotional support you may need."

Charlotte's eyes darted to the empty seat beside her.

"Here are the facts. At 8:45pm last night, Gavin Hooper, a second year, went trail running through the hills on the northwest side of campus." At Gavin's name, Charlotte looked at

Chai and Jace, the fear in their eyes mirroring her own. "At 9:12pm, the infirmary received an automatic distress signal from Gavin's viewer. At 9:15pm, emergency staff located Gavin lying at the base of one of the hills. He was immediately transported to the infirmary. After a thorough evaluation, it was determined that he suffered a concussion, some minor scrapes, and several broken bones in his leg; however, as I stated before, he will make a full and speedy recovery."

Hushed whispers started to swell throughout the student body, but Dr. Menta silenced the sounds with a raise of her hand. "Please let me finish. In evaluating Gavin's viewer, we discovered that it had been hacked to provide the illusion that Gavin was following a familiar trail when in fact he was running into steep, unclear terrain. By tracing the hacking markers, we determined that Denton, one of our androids, planted the program."

Charlotte's mind reeled. How could this happen? Androids couldn't harm humans; the principles were supposed to make something like this impossible. All around her, expressions of shock and alarm clouded her classmates' faces.

It took Dr. Menta longer to quell the anxious rush of chatter this time. "In light of this incident, Denton will be suspended from the Academy indefinitely. We are working to understand why this happened, but I can assure you that this was an isolated event that does not in any way involve the other androids. None of you is in any danger." Several faculty members' frowns deepened throughout Dr. Menta's speech. "Your parents have been notified, and while we encourage you to discuss this with your families, you are not permitted to publicly share any information about this incident."

Dr. Menta stepped aside to let Dr. Vosima conclude the meeting. "We know that this news is difficult to hear, and we invite you to reach out to us with any questions or concerns. Following this meeting, faculty will be distributed throughout the meeting rooms in the Gem, and their locations will be shared through your viewers. Please take the time to visit with your professors if it will be helpful to you. In your viewers, you will also find details on how to submit questions or concerns, either personally or anonymously. You have my word that every submission will be addressed. Thank you again for your attention this morning."

As the faculty began to disperse, Charlotte, Chai, and Jace looked at each other in unspoken agreement before bolting out of the Gem.

"Hey there." Gavin's lopsided grin brought a flood of relief over Charlotte as she, Chai, and Jace rushed into his room at the infirmary. They offered gentle hugs under Nurse Scrubb's watchful glance.

Aside from a few fading scratches on his arms and the thin, healing gash across his forehead, Gavin looked tired but okay - well, okay except for his left leg, trapped within the mender. An imposing contraption, the cylindrical dome surrounding his leg hummed quietly as it reconstructed his fractured bones.

"Don't worry." Gavin eyed their concerned faces. "I'll be running out of here by tomorrow."

Nurse Scrubb placed a hand on Gavin's shoulder. "You may get out of here tomorrow, but you'll be taking it easy on the running for a while, as we discussed."

"Yes, sir," Gavin said though Charlotte guessed he'd be running on his own timeframe.

The nurse left them alone with a pointed reminder that he would be just down the hall, and Jace lightly bumped his fist against Gavin's shoulder. "Dude, if you wanted the whole school to be talking about you, there were probably more fun ways to accomplish that."

"Eh. What isn't fun about rearranging my bones a bit?" The lightness of his comment couldn't hide the fact that his injuries, though curable, were still serious and could have been much worse.

"Do you remember what happened?" Chai asked.

Gavin shook his head. "I know about as much as I'm guessing you do. One minute I was running on the trail I always take, and the next minute, the ground fell away from me. When I woke up, I was here. I didn't even understand what happened until Dr. Menta visited me this morning. Part of me can't believe that Denton did it." He looked at Charlotte. "We've spent a lot of time with the androids, and I've never felt unsafe. Even around Denton. He's unpleasant, sure, but I always got the feeling he didn't care about humans one way or another."

"You're right." Charlotte nodded, thankful to give voice to some of the thoughts that had been bothering her since the announcement. "Denton mostly disregards humans. An act like this requires at least an interest in humans, albeit a dark one."

"Well, he did do it, whether we believe it or not," Chai said sharply before turning to Jace. "Let's go track down some snacks, okay?"

Finding herself alone with Gavin, Charlotte smiled shyly, suddenly unsure of what to say.

"I guess we won't be able to hang out tonight." Gavin broke the silence, looking more upset about that than about his injuries.

"Raincheck for next weekend?"

He grinned. "That would be nice."

Charlotte fidgeted. "Look, Gavin, I'm really sorry that we

didn't hang out last night. If we had...I mean, this wouldn't have..."

"Hey." He wrapped his hand around hers. "It's not your fault. Even if we had hung out, I probably still would have gone for a run before or after, so the same thing could have happened. Don't put this on yourself."

Looking at their intertwined fingers, Charlotte tried and failed not to think of Isaac holding her hand last night. "Here you are, making me feel better, when I should be the one doing that for you. I'm just really glad you're okay."

"Me too." Gavin held on for a moment longer, letting go only when Chai and Jace came back into the room. Noticing Jace's eyebrows wagging in Gavin's direction, Charlotte slipped her hands into her pockets.

For the rest of the visit, Charlotte tried to focus on her friends, even as part of her mind drifted back to Isaac.

CHAPTER 31

"ISAAC HASN'T ANSWERED my messages all day. I hope he's all right." Though the faculty clearly named Denton as the only culpable android, a nagging worry wouldn't leave Charlotte's mind.

What if this incident led Dr. Menta's team to take drastic measures against the other androids? What those measures could even be remained unclear in her mind, but Denton's actions left no doubt about the fact that androids could be more dangerous than anyone realized. Gavin could have suffered more serious injuries, and the Academy couldn't let that happen again.

Chai didn't respond to Charlotte's comment. Charlotte knew she heard her, but Chai remained focused on setting out their take-away meals on their tiny corner table. The infirmary staff allowed one friend to stay with Gavin through the evening, so with promises to see him as soon as he returned to campus tomorrow, the girls had left Jace with him for the night. Not wanting to field a million questions from their classmates, they had grabbed food from the Mod to eat in their room.

As the silence wrapped around them, though, Charlotte

wondered if eating alone had been the best idea.

Chai seemed okay in the infirmary, but maybe she was taking Gavin's injuries harder than Charlotte realized. "Hey." Charlotte placed a hand on Chai's arm. "I know you're worried, but Gavin's going to be okay. He was practically good as new when we left. With the nurses to wait on them, I wouldn't be surprised if Jace and Gavin tried to stay there another night."

Charlotte's feeble attempt at a joke failed to catch a smile. "I'm not worried about Gavin, Charlotte." Chai chewed slowly before adding, almost under her breath, "I'm worried about you."

Pausing mid-bite, Charlotte asked, "What do you mean?"

Chai bit her lip, as if wishing she could take her words back. "I'm worried about how much time you're spending with Isaac."

Charlotte's brow furrowed in confusion. "Isaac and I are working on a lot of projects. Of course we're spending time together. That's the whole point of the android guide program."

"So last night? Was that for your projects?"

Her words hit Charlotte like a slap in the face.

When she didn't respond, Chai said, "It just seems like sometimes you care about Isaac more than your friends. More than Gavin."

"Gavin has nothing to do with this, Chai." Charlotte struggled to keep her tone even. "And Isaac *is* my friend. *Our* friend, I thought."

"Isaac is a machine, Charlotte. Don't forget that."

"I'm not forgetting that, Chai. And if you don't care for spending time with a *machine*, then why have you and Jace been inviting us to join you for so many work sessions?"

Chai shook her head. "I thought that was obvious. We're worried about you spending time alone with him."

"What?" This revelation changed everything about the past

few weeks. Apparently Chai and Jace were willing to lie about much more than their relationship.

Perhaps sensing Charlotte's wounded emotions, Chai lowered her voice. "We don't know if it's good for you to be alone with him, so we thought it might be best if we all spent more time together. Gavin agrees. He was really hurt that you blew him off yesterday because you had plans with Isaac. Come on, Charlotte."

"Wow." Charlotte willed herself to hold back the tears stinging her eyes. "This is just great. So you've been ganging up on me? Behind my back? Judging me for trying to do a good job with the android program? How can I even defend myself when I don't know that everybody's got a problem with me?"

Also on the verge of tears, Chai replied, "We don't have a problem with you, Charlotte. We care about you. We've been worried."

"Lying to me is an interesting way to show you care."

"Charlotte, we weren't lying, we just didn't know how to-"

"Really? You haven't lied to me about anything this semester?"

Chai's confused expression almost stopped Charlotte from going further, but she had already held onto this secret for too long.

"How long have you and Jace been dating?" Chai's eyes widened, and Charlotte could see her trying to formulate an excuse. "Don't try to deny it. Just don't. I saw the two of you kissing a while ago."

Chai remained silent for a long moment before she said softly, "We were going to tell you. We talked a lot over the summer, and then, when we got back to school, things were different between us. We weren't sure for a long time if we even wanted to date, and we weren't sure how you'd react. We didn't want to screw up our friendship."

On another day, in another conversation, this explanation might have made sense to Charlotte, but in that instant, she only heard confirmation that her best friends had been lying to her for months.

"Well, I guess that plan backfired."

Chai couldn't seem to meet Charlotte's gaze. "I don't know what else to say, Charlotte."

It wasn't an apology. It wasn't an acknowledgement that they had betrayed her trust. It wasn't enough for Charlotte to want to smooth things over. "Maybe there isn't anything else to say right now."

So that was that. They pushed food around on their plates for a few more moments of silence. Charlotte knew that letting this fight linger unresolved was a mistake, but she couldn't be the one to fix it. Not when Chai had been lying to her and judging her for so long.

Without another word spoken between them, Chai left for the shower, and Charlotte climbed into bed.

Meet me by the hammocks tomorrow at 9am.

Sending the message to Isaac brought Charlotte a sliver of comfort, enough to slow the tears trickling toward her pillow. She replayed her capture from their private observatory, and the peaceful expanse of the stars calmed her further.

By the time Chai returned with the start of an apology on her lips, Charlotte had already fallen asleep.

CHAPTER 32

CAREFUL NOT TO wake Chai, Charlotte slipped out of their room silently the next morning. She knew that the longer they let their anger fester, the worse things would become between them, but the only person she wanted to see right now was Isaac.

On her way to meet him, Charlotte watched a capture sent by her parents late last night. She wished she had woken up when they viewed her; it seemed like forever since they had actually spoken.

"Charlotte, sweetie." Hearing the familiar concern in her mother's voice nearly brought Charlotte to tears. "The Academy told us what happened, and we wanted to make sure you're okay. They assured us that no students are in danger, but honey, it's so hard to be this far away from you."

Her mother bit her lip, and her father continued, "We want you to know that Dr. Menta had only glowing things to say about you and the work you're doing with your android partner. Char, we are so proud of you, but we care about your safety above everything else." He paused, on the verge of saying more, but her mother rested her hand on his arm.

"We'll call again soon, sweetie. We love you." They blew her a kiss, and the capture ended, for some reason leaving Charlotte sadder than before. At least she would see her parents soon. Knowing that the end of their secret project was approaching made their sporadic communication more bearable for now.

Approaching the hammocks at a quarter to nine, Charlotte was surprised to see Isaac already waiting for her in the morning mist. How did he know that she would be early? When he saw her, his eyes brightened, and his mouth curved into the smile that she was starting to believe he reserved just for her. Without thinking, Charlotte ran the rest of the way and, nearly crashing into him, wrapped her arms around his body. A beat later, his arms returned the embrace.

Reluctantly, she pulled away after a moment, and they settled into the same hammocks they had chosen on the first day they met.

"I'm so glad you're here, Isaac." She fought to keep the tremble out of her voice. "I was worried they wouldn't let you come to campus. Because of what Denton did."

"At this point, our actions have not been restricted." He paused. "I expected that you might not want to see me because of what happened to Gavin."

"No!" She smiled at him and reached forward to grasp his hand. "I know you would never hurt anybody."

He cocked his head, and his eyes searched for something in hers. "Based on what the faculty has alleged about Denton, your assessment is a somewhat illogical conclusion."

"I don't care what they say about Denton. I know you. You're not anything like him."

The shadow of a frown tugged at his lips. "Aside from some distinct personality markers, I am very much like Denton."

"Not in the ways that count." Frustration flared up within

her. "Why did he do it, Isaac? Why would Denton want to hurt Gavin? I know he doesn't seem to like humans that much, but this doesn't make any sense. What did Denton gain from this? What's going to happen to him now?"

"I do not know what is going to happen to Denton. He has been removed from our presence, and I have not been able to contact him." He stared at her for a moment, and she could tell that he was calculating, considering his next words. "You are correct, Charlotte, that it does not make sense. It does not make sense because Denton did not do anything wrong."

As though struck by an electric spark, Charlotte pulled her hands back. "How could you say this wasn't wrong?"

"What happened to Gavin was of course wrong, but Denton was not the one to cause Gavin harm. The markers tying the hack to Denton were fabricated."

Charlotte gaped at him. "That sounds crazy, Isaac. Who could even do that?"

He shook his head. "I have not been able to conclusively determine the responsible party; however, my current analysis identifies Athena as the most likely culprit."

"Isaac! That's a serious accusation. I know Athena hasn't exactly welcomed the androids, but you can't just go accusing people of things like this."

"I agree. I only shared this information with you because you asked."

This was unbelievable. "Hold on. Go back." Charlotte took a deep breath and tried to give Isaac the benefit of the doubt. "Why do you think Denton didn't do it? Dr. Menta and the faculty seem really sure."

"I do not *think* that Denton did not harm Gavin. I *know* that he did not do it."

"Okay…how? How do you know?"

Isaac's voice was a bit more hesitant than usual. "I accessed the telemetry from Gavin's viewer, and the construction of the hack is inconsistent with what Denton would develop. It is more indicative of what a human might think an android would do."

Charlotte pursed her lips, trying to hold on to her already frayed patience. "Isaac, that doesn't make any sense. How do you know what type of hack Denton would use? Androids aren't supposed to be hacking anyone."

"That is correct. Theoretically, though, a hack created by Denton would be more elegant than what I discovered. While on the surface the telemetry ties him to Gavin's viewerspace, it appears that the markers were left there intentionally to place the blame on Denton."

"Couldn't Denton have done this to fool you? Make it look like someone was framing him?"

Isaac shook his head evenly. "I have analyzed millions of scenarios, and it is nearly impossible that Denton would have done what he is accused of. As you know, the Benevolence Principle would have prevented him from harming Gavin. Even if he had figured out a way to circumvent that principle, I can determine no logical reason for why he would do so."

Charlotte closed her eyes for a moment to gather her thoughts. "Isaac, I want to believe that Denton is innocent, but I'm sorry. I can't just take your word for it, not when everyone else says Denton is guilty. This sounds like a theory, not proof that he's innocent."

"To me, the analysis I have completed does function as proof, but it is difficult for me to present the evidence in a way that you could understand."

"You think I can't understand this?" By now, her patience had evaporated entirely. "Are you kidding me?"

"I am not kidding you."

"Isaac, I understand your reasoning. You don't think Denton did this, and you're seeing the evidence in that light."

"Charlotte, that is incorrect. I analyzed the evidence and then reached the conclusion that Denton was innocent. Your words more clearly describe your own illogical human reasoning."

Though Isaac said this in a neutral tone, the sharpness of his comment stunned Charlotte nonetheless.

Noticing her expression, he attempted to soften his point. "Charlotte, I am sorry. I recognize that my last statement conveyed a patronizing tone that I did not intend. I simply meant that to me, the evidence is determinative, but I realize that this is not the case from a human perspective. I wish I could more clearly explain in a way that you would understand."

His words illuminated the chasm between them, the irreconcilable divide that, in the time she had grown to know Isaac, a part of her didn't believe existed. Charlotte had defended him as her equal, and now he refused to do the same. A wave of anger and disappointment left her speechless.

Before she could formulate her feelings into words, an urgent message from Dr. Menta came through her viewer. *Charlotte, please report to my Academy office now.*

Charlotte jumped at the terse command. Why would Dr. Menta summon her on a Sunday morning? Nervous apprehension tightened her stomach.

Eyes on the ground, Charlotte slid off her hammock and stepped away from Isaac. "I have to go see Dr. Menta for some reason. I guess I'll talk to you later."

"Charlotte." Isaac grabbed her hand lightly as he stood. "I am sorry that I have upset you. I wish I could more effectively explain why I am certain of Denton's innocence. A human would be better at this, but it is a limitation I am trying to overcome."

His earnest expression chipped away at the edges of her annoyance. "I know, Isaac. We'll figure it out."

Isaac walked with her toward Dr. Menta's office, but neither of them spoke. Charlotte hoped he wouldn't be able to guess her thoughts; without further explanation, she had to believe that he was wrong. Some telemetry markers - which she thought Denton easily could have faked - just weren't enough. What Charlotte couldn't figure out, though, was why Isaac would try to defend Denton and, even worse, blame Athena.

And if Isaac couldn't explain why he was so confident about this, then what else was he keeping from Charlotte?

CHAPTER 33

WHEN SHE ENTERED Dr. Menta's building, Charlotte felt her chest constrict. She must have done something wrong to warrant this unprecedented meeting, but she had no idea what that something might have been.

Worse, distinct loneliness crept in alongside her anticipated guilt. After their silent walk, Isaac had offered to wait for her. On any other day, Charlotte would have accepted this gesture, but for the first time, she didn't welcome the thought of seeing him again. Politely, yet distantly, she told him that waiting for her wouldn't be necessary.

As Charlotte stepped onto the autopath winding upstairs, muffled voices floated down to her. At first, she caught only errant words, but the voices, as well as her trepidation, grew clearer with each foot she climbed.

"This program was supposed to demonstrate that the androids were docile and harmless. First, we had a traumatized girl, next a boy with a broken leg, and now this?"

At the sound of Dr. Kindred's voice, clipped and sharp, Charlotte grabbed the handrail, pausing the path. Dr. Kindred? Why was he here?

Though softer, Dr. Menta's voice still reached Charlotte. "We're trying to figure out what's behind Denton's actions. As you know, his sequence appears to house a powerful anomaly, a part that we can't access."

Charlotte released enough pressure on the handrail that the path resumed its upward spiral, albeit at a snail's pace. What was this anomaly? Less than eager to interrupt their tense conversation, she wracked her brain, trying and failing to figure out why they would want to talk to her.

"The androids are ours, Rosalind, and it is imperative that they remain under our control. Particularly Denton. If what we suspect is true, then without him, this whole program is for nothing."

"Denton is still under our control, Victor. You can trust me on that. I know these androids better than anyone."

Pausing in the doorway, Charlotte cleared her throat. "Um, hi. Dr. Kindred. Dr. Menta." She did her best to seem unaware of their conversation. "You wanted to see me?"

"Yes, Charlotte. Please take a seat." Dr. Menta gestured to the wingback chair across from her desk. Dr. Kindred remained standing beside her.

Looking up at Dr. Menta's kind but reserved smile and Dr. Kindred's scowl, Charlotte still couldn't guess what this meeting might be about.

"Charlotte," Dr. Menta started, "we knew that working closely with the androids this semester might present some challenges. Some emotional challenges, among others. Given recent events, we wanted to check in and see if you are doing all right."

"Yeah, I'm fine." She searched for the subtext in Dr. Menta's words. "Is this because of what happened to Gavin? I was worried about him, of course, but he seems to be doing okay."

"Yes, Gavin was released this morning, and we're all glad that he made such a quick recovery." Dr. Menta paused and leaned forward before continuing, "We didn't call you to talk about only that, though. We wanted to ask how things are going with Isaac."

"Oh. Things are good." Charlotte kept her face neutral. Part of her wanted to share Isaac's theory of Denton's innocence, but she didn't know what repercussions that could bring.

"Too good, perhaps?" Dr. Kindred, speaking for the first time since Charlotte arrived, startled her.

Charlotte's brow furrowed. "I'm sorry, what do you mean?"

Dr. Menta threw an exasperated look at Dr. Kindred and continued with a kinder tone, "We're talking about this, Charlotte." Dr. Menta pulled up a capture in their shared viewerspace.

Charlotte's hands flew to her mouth as she watched Isaac wrap his arms around her under the moonlight. Someone must have been spying on them that night, and her stomach sank with the knowledge that her private evening with Isaac was no longer theirs alone. Cheeks burning under Dr. Kindred's disapproving gaze, Charlotte kept her own eyes pointed toward the floor.

"Where did you get that?" Her voice barely reached a whisper.

"It was shared across the Academy's viewerboard this morning, I'm afraid," Dr. Menta answered gently. "We've been monitoring for any mention of the androids."

Charlotte bit the inside of her cheek, willing her tears back. She understood what this capture looked like. Anyone who didn't know Isaac was an android would see a boy and a girl who were close, possibly closer than friends. Everyone seeing this, though, did know Isaac was an android. They would see a pathetic girl allowing herself to be hugged by a machine. Even as the flush of embarrassment gripped her tightly, she refused to acknowledge her distress out loud.

Charlotte looked up, feigning confusion. "So is there a problem? I come from a hugging family. My friends and I hug all the time. I didn't realize there was a rule against hugging an android."

"There's not." Dr. Menta sighed. "Charlotte, you have formed a remarkably close bond with Isaac, and that has undoubtedly contributed to the success you have had together in your projects. We just want to make sure that it's not negatively affecting you in any way."

Less empathetically, Dr. Kindred added, "As you are no doubt aware, not all of your classmates view the androids favorably, and, especially so soon after Gavin's injury, such an intimate display may spark further concerns for us to deal with."

Bristling at the notion that she may have done something wrong, Charlotte said, "It seems like the real person causing the problems is whoever spied on me and Isaac and then decided to share this capture."

Dr. Menta nodded. "We are working to find that person, Charlotte. Do you have any idea who might have taken it?"

Isaac's earlier comments about Athena sprung to Charlotte's mind. Athena had been the most vocal opponent of the androids, and she and Charlotte weren't exactly best friends. Still, Charlotte couldn't bring herself to accuse Athena on nothing more than a feeling. "No, I don't," Charlotte answered slowly.

"If that changes, please let us know," Dr. Menta said. "In the meantime, the capture has now been removed from the viewerboard, though I'm afraid that a number of students saw it before we became aware. This was a gross invasion of your privacy, and I do apologize that this happened."

"Thank you," Charlotte said, pointedly looking only at Dr. Menta.

"Well," Dr. Kindred said matter-of-factly, "given your increasing personal attachment to Isaac, we are wondering if it might be prudent for you to discontinue your work with him for this semester."

"What? No!" Charlotte stood from her seat. "Please. This is getting really blown out of proportion. Isaac and I have a good working relationship. That's all. I thought we were supposed to interact with them as regular students, and that's what I've been doing. As a result, our projects are going really well. If I had to abandon that work…that would set me back for this whole semester, and I don't think I deserve that. Please."

Dr. Menta looked at Dr. Kindred, who, after a long pause, offered a faint nod. Dr. Menta turned to Charlotte. "You're right. We will allow you to continue your work with Isaac. But Charlotte, this entire weekend has shown me that encouraging students to spend so much time socially with androids was perhaps premature. For the foreseeable future, therefore, androids will be interacting with students during classes and flex periods only. That should give you ample time to complete your projects together."

"Thank you." Charlotte knew she should keep it at that, but she couldn't help herself. "I respect that you make the rules, but I don't think segregating the androids is necessary or fair."

Dr. Kindred raised his eyebrows. "Your opinion is noted."

"Thank you, Charlotte." Dr. Menta attempted to smooth over

the moment with a smile. "That will be all for now. We will check in again this week."

Without another word, Charlotte left and practically flew down the spiral path. Bursting out of the front door, she took a deep breath of autumn air.

"Isaac?" she called softly, hoping, though not expecting, that he would still be there. The ensuing silence provided her answer.

As her mind raced to process her spinning emotions, she wondered if perhaps Chai, Dr. Menta, and Dr. Kindred were right. Had she been spending too much time with Isaac? Did she really want to be a person who turned to an android for emotional support? Aside from that, how dare someone share a capture of a private memory that, until this morning, had been a happy one.

Tangled up with the furious embarrassment of the past hour, Charlotte barely made it to the hollow of a nearby tree before she burst into tears.

CHAPTER 34

IN AN INSTANT, Marissa appraised her sister's blotchy, tear-stained cheeks and immediately pulled her in for a hug. "What's wrong?"

Too drained for words, Charlotte simply shook her head and sank into Marissa's couch. Several more messages popped up from Chai and Jace, but Charlotte disregarded them, just as she had been ignoring them on her way to Marissa's.

"Okay." Marissa allowed her a few quiet minutes before joining Charlotte on the couch with two mugs of hot chocolate. "I need you to talk to me, Char."

The sisterly concern in Marissa's voice opened Charlotte's floodgates, and Charlotte spilled everything that had happened over the past forty-eight hours, starting with her guilt over deciding to hang out with Isaac instead of Gavin, weaving through her fight with Chai, and ending with her knowledge that the whole Academy probably viewed her as a machine-loving freak. Reacting only with a raised eyebrow or a slight widening of her eyes - especially during the part about Gavin's injury - Marissa let Charlotte speak without interruptions.

"I didn't think I was doing anything wrong, Marissa." Charlotte stared into the depths of her mug, as though some answers might be swirling at the bottom.

"You didn't do anything wrong." Marissa pulled the corner of her bottom lip under her teeth. "So Gavin is okay?"

"Yes, Dr. Menta said he was released this morning." Charlotte looked at Marissa, who had her thinking face on. "What?"

Marissa shook her head. "It's nothing. I just wish you didn't have to go through all of this. I wish I could do something to help."

Charlotte smiled weakly through her sniffles. "This is helping." Though Marissa's expression had cleared, Charlotte knew there was something her sister wasn't saying. "Please, Marissa. What is it?"

Marissa chose her words carefully. "I'm just surprised, frankly. Denton should not have been able to hurt a student. The fact that he did opens up a whole host of questions about what else the androids are capable of. What's worse, I didn't hear anything about this at Cognation. They're doing an awfully good job at keeping these things a secret."

As Marissa's expression clouded, Charlotte wondered what her sister would think of Isaac's theory. "Isaac doesn't believe Denton did it. He said a human student might have framed him."

Marissa's eyes snapped up toward Charlotte's. "Really? Why?"

"Something about the markers in the telemetry of Gavin's sequence. I don't even know how he accessed that." She tried to temper the frustration creeping back into her voice as she also told Marissa what she overheard between Dr. Menta and Dr.

Kindred. "What do you think they meant by an anomaly in Denton's sequence? And why is Denton so important to the program?"

"I have no idea." Marissa paused to think, caught up in the intrigue of the situation. "But I'm definitely going to try to find out."

Ordinarily, a mystery like this would have piqued Charlotte's interest as well, but she couldn't garner more than a mild interest at the moment.

Marissa picked up on her sister's dejection. "You're worried about your friends. And about what your peers will think about you now."

Charlotte nodded, almost imperceptibly.

"Charlotte, people have an instinctual aversion to things they don't understand. Chai doesn't understand your connection to Isaac. It's likely that your classmates don't either. But that doesn't mean they're right."

"I don't understand it." Only once the words were spoken out loud did Charlotte realize they were true. "I know he's a machine, something Cognation created and sequenced. But the more time I spend with him, the more he becomes…just Isaac. I don't know why other people can't see that."

Marissa spoke carefully. "It's natural to have some reciprocal feelings toward affective technologies, Charlotte. It's always been that way. But given what happened to Gavin, I have to ask: do you have any concerns about Isaac hurting you?"

"No, Marissa," she said. "He would never try to hurt me. We enjoy working together. He's…he's my friend."

Charlotte knew she wasn't explaining herself well, but in Marissa's eyes, she saw a level of understanding. "Okay. If you're comfortable with your connection to Isaac and the work you're doing together, then that's all that matters. I wouldn't worry about your classmates. I know as well as anyone how thoughtlessly cruel teenagers can be."

Something in her tone told Charlotte that Marissa did know what this felt like, but before Charlotte could ask her to explain, a knock interrupted them. Marissa opened the door to reveal Chai and Jace standing there, outwardly nervous. Charlotte stood but didn't move toward them.

Marissa ushered them in, and Chai spoke first. "Hey. We thought you might be here." She glanced at Jace for support before turning back to Charlotte. "I hope it's okay we showed up."

"Gavin wanted to join us," Jace added, "but he's still not supposed to walk too much."

"Of course it's okay." Marissa answered after the silence stretched over them for a moment. "I actually have to, uh, take care of something, so I'll be in the other room if you need me." She retreated to her bedroom, leaving the three of them to untangle the twisted threads of their friendship.

"I'm guessing you saw the capture," Charlotte said eventually, getting the worst out of the way.

They nodded, with perhaps a touch of pity, and Jace said quickly, "But don't worry, we've been telling everyone it's not what it looks like."

"What does it look like?" Charlotte knew she shouldn't challenge him, not when it seemed like he wanted to help, but she couldn't stop herself.

Stuttering, Jace walked his comment back. "N-nothing. I mean, I guess...some people might say it looked like you were flirting or something, but you were just hugging a friend."

Chai chimed in, surprising Charlotte with the intensity of her support. "We've told everyone how nice Isaac and Eli are and how we enjoy spending time with them, too. Basically, anyone making a big deal out of this is just dumb. You know we've got your back on this."

"Is that true?" Charlotte asked slowly. "It hasn't felt like you've really had my back this semester."

Chai sighed as her eyes moistened. "You're right. I'm sorry, Charlotte. We know we haven't been the greatest friends recently, and we're really, really sorry.

"Yeah," Jace said, looking equally upset. "We didn't mean to lie to you. It just kind of happened. And then the longer we kept things a secret, the harder it got to come clean. I didn't tell Gavin either, for what it's worth."

"Believe it or not, we were trying to protect your feelings," Chai added softly. "But I get that all we did was make things worse."

In their apologies, Charlotte caught a glimpse of what their friendship used to be. "I appreciate that. And I'm sorry if I did anything to make you feel like you couldn't tell me."

They looked at each other, all three unsure about how to move forward until Charlotte asked, "Can we try to be honest from now on?"

"Of course!" With a sigh of relief, Chai smiled through her sniffles and straightened with mock formality. "Charlotte, Jace and I would like to ask for your blessing upon our courtship."

Charlotte laughed for what felt like the first time in ages. "Blessing granted." In a more serious tone, she added, "I am happy for you, you know."

"Thanks, Char. You're the best." Jace pulled Charlotte and Chai into a group hug, cementing their unspoken forgiveness.

Charlotte desperately wanted to hold onto this moment, but she had to ask another question as they moved apart. "Did you mean it earlier? When you said that you enjoy spending time with Isaac and Eli?"

Jace nodded but Chai paused before responding. "It's true for Jace. For me - I want to mean it. There have been times when I've enjoyed being around them. But it's hard for me to look at them as other students. And then everything with Denton...The honest answer is that they make me uncomfortable. But I'm trying to get past that. Jace and I have talked about it a lot, and that's helping. And seeing you interact with Isaac helps, too."

"Okay." Charlotte wasn't sure what to say. She and Chai had never disagreed about something so important, and she didn't know how to bridge this gap.

"I'm trying, Char. I hope that's enough."

Charlotte smiled weakly. "Of course." It wasn't enough, but it would have to do for now.

"I don't suppose there are any refreshments around here?" Jace asked, eyeing Charlotte's mug.

Charlotte and Chai laughed as Jace's insatiable appetite broke the tension; over snacks in Marissa's kitchen, the natural rhythm of their trio gradually emerged. The afternoon away from campus provided a much-needed retreat, and for the first time in a while, Charlotte's mind didn't wander to when she would see Isaac next.

CHAPTER 35

HOURS LATER, CHARLOTTE braced herself as they approached the Mod for dinner. She would have preferred to remain in the cocoon of Marissa's apartment, but Chai and Jace promised her they would shut down any and all annoyances. As they entered the building, today arranged in an elegant spiral, Charlotte nearly laughed at Chai beside her. Chai's game face was no joke, and Charlotte almost felt bad for anyone who dared to cross her path.

As expected, their entrance drew Beckett and Athena like magnets.

"Oh, Charlotte." Beckett's mock surprise didn't fool anyone. "Athena and I were just having an interesting debate about whether hugging an android felt more like hugging a person or like hugging a statue. Maybe you can clear it up for us? Or perhaps you don't kiss and tell." Though they both smirked, Athena's refusal to make eye contact with Charlotte suggested some reluctance at being pulled into his conversation.

Charlotte paled at the comment, but Chai threw her retort at Beckett. "Dude. I would much rather hug an android than so much as touch you. And don't think for a second that I'm the only one who feels that way." Refusing to give him time to respond, Chai pulled Charlotte and Jace away. "If you'll excuse us, we're going to get some food."

Charlotte appreciated Chai's protection, but part of her wondered if Chai would actually hug an android. She tried not to dwell on that thought.

Once out of earshot, Chai rolled her eyes. "That should be the worst of it, I expect. Beckett's losing his edge."

Weirdly, that did prove to be the worst of it. While Charlotte caught a few furtive glances and snickers, she appeared to attract only a slight amount of extra attention. Scrolling through the Academy's viewerboard, Chai soon discovered why.

"Wow. Look at this." In the viewerspace, Chai pulled up several captures of Harper with Grayton, her android partner. Charlotte nearly gasped at their intimate beauty. Though none of the captures included physical contact, they nonetheless exuded close companionship: a smile across a shared meal, heads bent toward each other over a flower, backs resting against different sides of the same tree.

Scanning the comments, Jace said, "They're part of an art installation that Harper's working on with Grayton."

"When did she share them?" Charlotte asked.

"It looks like this afternoon." Jace paused. "A few hours after the capture of you surfaced."

That explained it. Harper's artistic expressions were way more provocative than an ordinary hug. *Thank you so much*, Charlotte messaged Harper, hoping she knew how much she appreciated this gesture.

Dinner concluded quickly and uneventfully. Jace left early to take a meal back to Gavin, and Chai and Charlotte treated themselves to extra dessert before a leisurely walk back to their room. Tentatively testing the waters, Charlotte even managed to coax a few details from Chai about her experiences as Jace's girlfriend so far; Chai's beaming smile told her most of what she wanted to know.

Over the next couple of weeks, Academy life settled into a new normal, one in which androids made an appearance during classes and structured flex time but otherwise retreated to their dorm. Neither Gavin nor any of the other guides complained about the androids' removal from social events on campus; rather, they seemed to accept that Dr. Menta had every right to adjust the androids' schedule. When Charlotte considered discussing this with Gavin, she remembered his fallen expression after she chose to spend that fateful evening with Isaac, and she decided to keep her concerns to herself.

Despite Harper's humanizing captures, a general undercurrent of distrust for the androids persisted, thanks to Denton, who still carried the blame for Gavin's injuries and had yet to return from Cognation's suspension. Occasionally, Chai would mention an outlandish rumor shared on the viewerboard - the latest one claimed that Denton was trying to kill Dr. Menta and the other researchers - but after receiving little more than a lukewarm response from Charlotte during these conversations, Chai stopped bringing it up.

Charlotte and Isaac also established a new equilibrium within the altered schedule. They didn't speak about their argument over Denton or about their captured hug; Charlotte wasn't even sure if Isaac knew that the end of their evening together had been put on display for the school. They continued to make progress on their projects, and if Isaac noticed Charlotte's careful avoidance of any physical contact or the more distant tone she adopted during their conversations, he did not comment on them.

Whenever Charlotte felt the impulse to brush her hand

against Isaac's or send him a late-night message, she told herself that maintaining her distance would ultimately strengthen their professional collaboration. This flimsy logic almost convinced her, but she never managed to completely talk herself out of missing Isaac when he wasn't with her. When they were together, she searched his face for signs that he might have missed her; the lack of such evidence was most effective in helping to keep her feelings in check.

Less time with Isaac did allow her more time to focus on her other friends, including Gavin. Ever since Chai and Jace officially became a couple, Gavin had established himself as a regular member of their group. While Charlotte appreciated that his presence saved her from third-wheel status, it also lent a de facto double-date undercurrent to much of their time together.

The more time she spent with Gavin, though, the less she viewed this as a problem. She liked him, didn't she? She did, of course. He had a quirky sense of humor, and he was kind. Furthermore, their growing friendship helped her give Chai and Jace some space; knowing that they would welcome some alone time, Charlotte and Gavin often made plans just for themselves.

Gavin and Charlotte fell into a natural rhythm of walking with each other before and after classes, and they shared most meals together. He even got her to join a couple of intramural enigma matches; by no means a star player, she still solved a few key logic puzzle challenges and even found herself thinking more seriously about joining a team in the spring.

By an unspoken agreement, Charlotte and Gavin flirted across the line separating friendship from something more. While she enjoyed their flirtatious banter and definitely looked forward to seeing Gavin each day, Charlotte was careful not to cross the boundary before she figured out for sure if she wanted to.

Finding herself alone one afternoon before meeting up with Gavin, Charlotte wandered into the library. She planned to take care of some work in the alcove she had come to consider her own. Upon entering the room, though, she stopped. An uncanny sensation raised the hairs on the back of her neck. On first glance, everything appeared to be in order, but Charlotte stepped forward to scan the book spines more carefully, trying to identify what was out of place.

The journals.

Pulling out the book resting where Dr. Coggins' first journal used to live, Charlotte instead discovered a title about the origins of machine learning. A quick examination of the rest of the books in that section confirmed Charlotte's suspicion.

Without hesitation, she messaged Isaac. *The journals are gone.*

CHAPTER 36

WHAT JOURNALS?

Isaac's question first angered and then confused Charlotte. Coming from a human, this response might have carried a passive aggressive undercurrent or signaled a genuine forgetfulness. Coming from Isaac, though, neither of these explanations made sense. Maybe he was hiding something? Perhaps he removed the journals? But how? Why? Questions swirled through her mind incessantly, each potential scenario more implausible than the last.

Never mind. We can talk about it tomorrow. They would need to resolve this in person.

The next morning, as Gavin and Charlotte stepped into Tech Integration, an unexpected tension hit them like a heat wave. On the far side of the room, Dr. Menta was already seated with the androids. All ten of the androids.

Instinctively, Charlotte looped her hand around Gavin's arm; under her fingers, she felt his muscles tighten. Next to Dr. Menta in the center of the group, Denton looked at the entering students impassively. Charlotte steered Gavin to the end of the row facing the androids; though Gavin sat next to her, his legs remained taut, ready to sprint.

The other students reacted with a similar jolt upon seeing Denton, but they took their seats silently, waiting for Dr. Menta to begin.

Once everyone arrived, Dr. Menta cleared her throat. "Before we get started, I know that we need to address the elephant in the room. First of all, I apologize for not providing advanced notice. I assure you that the faculty and I carefully considered our reasons for this. We anticipated that knowing when Denton would return to classes would only add unnecessary distress to certain students. By your skeptical expressions, I understand that most of you don't believe me. If you'd like, I would be happy to show you the data behind this decision. You need only ask." She paused, glancing at Denton on her right. "Before I continue with today's class, Denton has something he would like to say."

Denton stood, clasped his hands together in front of his waist, and turned to face Gavin. "First, Gavin, I would like to apologize to you. I sincerely regret that my actions caused you harm, and I am pleased to see that you appear to be in good health." He opened his hands, gesturing to the class. "Second, I apologize for how my behavior affected my fellow androids and my classmates. I understand that my actions negatively impacted the harmony that this program intends to establish between androids and humans, and I undoubtedly failed to fulfill my given role. I am committed to earning back your trust, and I thank Dr. Menta for offering me this chance."

He returned to his seat, and Gavin and Charlotte exchanged a brief, confused glance. The android looked like Denton, and the timbre of the voice sounded like Denton. But the cadence of his speech, his word choice - not to mention his sentiments - did not match the Denton they knew. On the surface, it was an improvement, for sure, but Charlotte's mind stumbled, struggling to reconcile this version of Denton with the Denton she knew.

She looked across to Isaac, but his expression presented no trace of concern.

"Thank you, Denton." Dr. Menta reclaimed their attention. "I can assure all of you that the glitch in Denton's sequence that led to his earlier actions has been addressed. He is therefore incapable of bringing any further harm. However, the faculty and I understand that this assurance may not be enough for you or your parents. For that reason, Denton will only be interacting with students under the direct supervision of a faculty member. Please understand that this is an unnecessary safeguard, but as it may make some of you feel more comfortable, we have deemed it an appropriate step to take. At this time, your families and your fellow classmates are receiving an official update regarding this information. Are there any questions?"

After a short pause, Gavin surprised Charlotte by speaking up. "How exactly did you address the glitch you mentioned?"

"Excellent question, Gavin. As you may have already gathered, we altered several dimensions of Denton's personality sequence. You all know that one of the goals of this program is to study the spectrum of personalities. Unfortunately, Denton's actions demonstrated that we had left the bounds of the spectrum a bit too broad. A few of his personality measures unexpectedly conflicted with other aspects of his sequence. By making some adjustments, we were able to resolve the conflicts."

Gavin and the rest of the students nodded, as if this made sense, but Charlotte's skin crawled. When they had discussed android personality alteration at the beginning of the semester, it had been a hypothetical action. In light of the real effects of that power, though, Charlotte fought the urge to cringe. Sure, new Denton seemed to be much more amiable than old Denton, but who, then, was the real Denton?

Preoccupied by these thoughts and anxious to talk to Isaac

about Denton's mysterious return, Charlotte lent only part of her attention to that day's coursework.

"Charlotte." At the end of the period, Dr. Menta called her over. "You seemed a little quiet during the discussions today. Is everything all right?"

"Oh, yes." Charlotte thought for a second, wondering how honest to be. "I mean, seeing Denton back startled me a little, I think, but I'm fine now." Gavin caught Charlotte's eye from the door, and she offered a quick wave as he left with Eli to get to their next class on time.

"Okay." Something in Dr. Menta's guarded smile told Charlotte that she knew there was more to her thoughts. "We can discuss this further during our next check-in."

"Sure, sounds great," Charlotte responded, barely realizing how distracted she sounded. Taking Dr. Menta's terse nod as her cue to leave, Charlotte turned to Isaac and inclined her head toward the door. They cut through the trees in the direction of their preferred study pod, but once out of sight of Dr. Menta's building, Charlotte stopped abruptly to face Isaac.

"Isaac, we have to talk."

"Yes, conversing is a necessary element of our collaborative partnership. I thought that had already been established as a shared assumption."

Charlotte sighed, louder than she intended. "That's not what I mean. We need to talk about Denton."

Isaac's head tilted quizzically. "I am unclear on what you would like me to say about him."

"What do you think about the new Denton?"

"I do not understand what you mean by the new Denton."

Charlotte searched Isaac's eyes for any insight into his

thoughts. "Well, he's quite a bit different from who he was before."

"Yes, his personality has been altered, as Dr. Menta explained, but that was a necessary part of correcting his glitch."

"Okay…but doesn't this bother you? The fact that he took responsibility for hurting Gavin?"

Isaac's brow furrowed. "Accepting responsibility was a necessary first step for Denton to rebuild trust. Why would that bother me?"

Her voice rising, Charlotte snapped, "Because you told me that Denton was innocent! That's why this should bother you. I don't understand why you're acting like this."

Isaac spoke slowly now, as one might speak to a child. "Charlotte, I never told you that Denton was innocent. All of the evidence supports Denton's culpability, and I know I did not make an assertion in opposition to that evidence."

Charlotte took a deep breath as the ground threatened to wobble beneath her. "Isaac, that's just not true."

CHAPTER 37

FEELING SUDDENLY EXPOSED, Charlotte placed a finger in front of her lips and pulled Isaac toward a thicker patch of trees. She scanned their surroundings for any signs of a spy and set an alarm on her viewer to indicate anyone approaching from a distance.

"Okay. I need you to be completely honest with me. You are saying that you always believed Denton was responsible for Gavin's fall?"

"That is correct."

"Why did you tell me he was innocent?"

"I never told you that, Charlotte." Isaac cocked his head. "Perhaps you are confused?"

"I. Am. Not. Confused." To be fair, the thought had occurred to Charlotte, but she fought against it. "Wait! There's an easy way to prove this. Isaac, pull up your capture from the morning we met by the hammocks after Gavin got hurt."

Charlotte watched as her likeness appeared in their viewerspace, from Isaac's perspective. Seeing herself hug Isaac brought a pang of nostalgia, but she pushed that feeling to the back of her mind.

She heard herself say, *I know Denton doesn't seem to like humans that much, but this doesn't make any sense. What did Denton gain from this? What's going to happen to him now?*

Isaac responded, *I do not know what is going to happen to him now. He has been removed from our presence, and I have not been able to contact him. You are correct, Charlotte, that it does not make sense, and this is likely due to the imbalance of his personality sequence. As when he inappropriately tested Athena in Tech Ethics, his ambivalence toward humans seems to be interacting with the rest of his programming.*

"No, no, no." Charlotte's hands flew to her face, and she shook her head vigorously. "Isaac, stop." Their digital bodies froze. She looked directly into Isaac's eyes and saw the reflection of her own distressed expression. "Isaac, that didn't happen." Charlotte took a deep breath, willing herself to think clearly. She snapped her fingers. Isaac's capture wasn't the only record of that day.

She took control of their viewerspace. This time, Isaac's likeness appeared from Charlotte's perspective. She moved the capture forward until she said, *What's going to happen to him now?*

Isaac responded, *I do not know what is going to happen to him. He has been removed from our presence, and I have not been able to contact him. You are correct, Charlotte, that it does not make sense. It does not make sense because Denton did not do anything wrong.*

She let the conversation continue, watching Isaac's face as he observed himself saying that he *knew* Denton was innocent, that he suspected Athena, and that the telemetry from Gavin's viewerspace provided proof. She paused the capture.

Isaac's eyes flitted from left to right, as if reading a script. His features compressed, conveying confusion as he looked at her. "Charlotte, I have no record of your version of this conversation, and I do not recall finding evidence to contradict Denton's guilt. I can determine no logical reason for the discrepancy."

Charlotte started pacing, and Isaac tracked her with his eyes. "Isaac, I think it's pretty clear." When he failed to respond, she threw her hands up. "Someone obviously altered your memory. I didn't know that was possible."

From the way Isaac's forehead crinkled, Charlotte guessed that he didn't know this either. He spoke cautiously. "I have not been explicitly told that it would be possible, but given that our recorded experiences are stored in much the same way that your captures are stored in your viewer, it would stand to reason that alteration would be feasible."

"But who would do this? And why?"

"To my knowledge, only Dr. Menta and her team have administrative access to our sequences, but I do not know why they would make this change."

Another thought came to Charlotte. "I messaged you last night about Dr. Coggins' journals. Do you remember reading them? And talking about them?"

"I know that Dr. Coggins was the founder of Cognation and is largely credited for organizing the Humane Innovation Alliance. I do not recall, however, reading or discussing any journals."

Charlotte groaned in frustration. "Why would someone take those memories?"

As she scrolled through her captures, Charlotte realized with a sinking feeling that she didn't start recording Isaac until after they visited the library. Still, she had their conversations about the cats and the pronoun discrepancy, and she played those for him. When they reviewed Isaac's captures of those days, their discussions included no mention of the journals, further proving that someone had tampered with his memory.

"Isaac, you were doing more analysis on the journals to sort out a code Dr. Coggins had used for some type of secret project. Do you have any record of that?"

He shook his head. Charlotte searched their shared records to see if perhaps he had sent her more of his work, but aside from the summary of his initial findings, she came up with nothing. She kicked herself for not talking with Isaac about this sooner.

"Okay." Charlotte drummed her fingers together while she thought. "Let's lay this out logically. We know that someone is altering your captures. To do that, someone must be reviewing your captures in detail. So much for anonymizing the data." She pursed her lips. "Is there a way for you to store any records secretly?"

"Yes, I have the technical capabilities to do that. It would require creating an encrypted copy, making it appear to be innocuous information, and then altering the accessible captures to include only details about our official coursework." Isaac paused. "However, I will not be able to do that."

Not understanding, Charlotte squinted at him. "What do you mean? You just said you could."

"No. I said that I have the technical capabilities required. Unfortunately, these actions would violate the Benevolence Principle."

"How?"

"The Benevolence Principle prohibits me from acting in a way that might harm humans and that doesn't fall within the bounds of benevolent actions."

"Isaac, how would keeping some information private harm

humans?"

"I was created for humans to learn about androids. If I am not forthcoming about my experiences, then that may hinder their research; if Dr. Kindred were to learn that Cognation does not know what is happening with their androids, then people may lose their positions. That would be harm."

Charlotte turned over his explanation in her mind; this must be the default programming, for androids to first think of the humans who created them. Humans, however, were quite a large group. "Isaac, I think that if you continue sharing your full captures, then some harm may come to me. Clearly, if someone would go to these lengths to change your memory, then it's possible that someone would also try to change my memories in some way. When you think about it from this perspective, keeping some of our conversations private will serve to protect me. Plus, doesn't the Insurance Principle come into play? If Denton really was framed, shouldn't you try to protect him?"

Isaac nodded slowly. "Those are logical points. If I can tie my actions to protecting you and Denton, while not directly causing harm to any other humans or androids, then that logic should enable me to encrypt and hide our private conversations."

Charlotte let out a breath she didn't know she was holding. "Okay. That's a good start. I'll increase the security on my captures, too."

The slight relief that these decisions brought to Charlotte dissipated as her mind drew a blank for next steps. "Is there anything else we can do, Isaac?"

He remained silent for a long minute. "In my analysis of similar situations, both fictitious and factual, it seems that we need to gather more information without drawing attention to ourselves. In many situations, sleuths also reach out to a trusted mentor; however, I am afraid that Dr. Menta may no longer fall into that category, so we should be cautious during our interactions with her and with any other members of the faculty. For my part, I can make some discreet inquiries within the android cohort. You, perhaps, can reach out to some of our friends for additional perspectives and ideas. In the meantime, it is imperative that we act as though nothing is out of the ordinary."

Charlotte forced a wry smile on her face. Nothing about this year had been ordinary. "When you put it that way, Isaac, I guess it doesn't seem that hard."

CHAPTER 38

IT WOULD, OF course, prove to be very hard; at least, acting as though everything were normal turned out to be quite challenging for Charlotte.

"Hey, I was thinking maybe we could all take a walk after dinner?" Charlotte offered the suggestion to her friends ever so casually that night.

"Why? It's freezing out." Freezing was an exaggeration for the late autumn chill, but Chai was always cold.

"I'll go with you," Gavin said, unsurprisingly.

"Great!" Charlotte paused to pull back her overly enthusiastic tone. "But, well, maybe we could all go just for a little bit?"

Jace set down his fork. "What's wrong, Charlotte?"

"Nothing's wrong. I just…thought we could all talk about some things." Aware of their proximity to their classmates and the possibility of being overheard in the Mod, Charlotte didn't want to say more.

"Okay," Jace said slowly, exchanging a bewildered glance with Chai and Gavin. After a few final bites, they all followed Charlotte outside.

"So what's this about?" Chai asked once they had stepped

into the already dark evening.

"Um…let's walk a little first." At a brisk pace, Charlotte led them deeper into the forest and didn't stop until she reached their octopus tree haven. She held her finger to her lips and scanned the surrounding area; once convinced they were alone, she beckoned them around the lowest branch.

"Charlotte, this is getting really weird. Why do we have to be in the woods at night to talk?" Chai's impatience clipped her words.

"Because I didn't want anyone to overhear us." With her voice soft, Charlotte summarized what she and Isaac discovered earlier, starting with Denton's transformation and ending with Isaac's altered memory about Denton and the journals.

She waited for the horrific significance of this realization to wash over their faces, but instead, her three friends only glanced at each other, seemingly unsure if Charlotte had more to reveal.

"All right." Jace processed his thoughts out loud. "So, Denton is now a much nicer android, and that's a problem?"

"It's a problem that he's *so* different." Charlotte fought to keep her exasperation under control.

"It was a bit disconcerting to see Denton acting so uncharacteristically," Gavin admitted. "And it was even weirder to see that the other androids were completely unaffected by his change in personality."

"Yes!" Smiling at him gratefully, Charlotte pressed on. "It's likely that Cognation wiped all of the androids' memories. That is a much bigger problem than Denton's personality. The androids' captures are supposedly being used in research, but if they're falsifying the records, then who knows what else they might be lying about."

"I can see where you're going with that." Chai spoke as though sorting out the wild claims of a child. "But isn't that a bit of a leap? I mean, they had to deal with the Denton situation, for obvious safety reasons." She gestured toward Gavin. "And maybe they knew that would be harder if Isaac still thought Denton was innocent or if the androids were bothered by the personality change. This might have been a one-time thing."

"But what if Denton *is* innocent?"

Chai's eyes widened. "You would take Isaac's word over Dr. Menta's? Over the entire faculty?"

Maybe, Charlotte thought to herself. "I'm not sure," she said out loud. "But putting this whole situation aside, why wipe Isaac's memory about Dr. Coggins' journals? Why remove the journals from the library?"

Gavin frowned. "That part is odd. Cognation has always supported freedom of information, so this type of censorship does smell funny."

"Okay, fine." Chai shrugged. "But even if all of this is some kind of crazy conspiracy, it's not like we can do anything about it."

"Yeah, probably not," Jace said, but Charlotte heard a slight reluctance beneath his words.

"Hello." The unexpected greeting, coming from two figures who appeared out of nowhere, drew instinctive shrieks from Chai and Charlotte.

"Isaac? Eli?" Charlotte's racing heart rate slowed once she saw their familiar faces.

"What are you doing here?" Chai asked. "How did you find us?"

"We have advanced geolocating skills," Eli answered. Judging by Chai's expression, she did not like this explanation, so

Eli changed the subject quickly. "And Isaac wanted to tell Charlotte something we discovered."

"I shared our earlier conversation with Eli," Isaac said to Charlotte. "Have you discussed the situation with your friends?"

She nodded. "We're all more or less on the same page. What do you need to tell us?" The fact that he felt the need to find her now, on campus, when androids were supposed to remain in their dorm, worried her.

"Here." He pulled up a message in front of them: *Help me, Isaac. I am alone.*

They all stared at it blankly. Even Charlotte had no idea why this was important.

"I received this cryptic message tonight from Denton. As we were all in our dorm, I decided to respond to him in person, since the brevity of the message indicated some distress. When I went to his room, though, Denton expressed ignorance regarding the message I had received."

Though interesting, this hardly seemed worth a late-night visit to Charlotte. "So, he lied to you? Or forgot he sent it?"

"I considered both of those options. However, we reviewed his message history, and there was no record of a message sent. Furthermore, because I visited his room less than a minute after I received the message, it is improbable that someone would have had time to alter his records in that brief window."

"Okay." Gavin tried to puzzle through this information. "Then someone else sent you the message?"

"That is an excellent deduction, Gavin. I considered that as well; however, I did not only identify the sender by the content of the message. When androids communicate digitally with each other, our messages are attached to unique markers. This message carried Denton's marker, which to my knowledge, means it could only have come from him."

"This is like one of those riddles I used to read to my siblings," Jace said. "If you know that Denton did send the message, but you also know that Denton *didn't* send the message, then..."

"Then there are two Dentons?" As though reading each other's minds, Charlotte and Chai presented this unlikely thought in unison.

Inconceivably, Isaac's bobbing head confirmed their conclusion. "That is correct."

CHAPTER 39

"TWO DENTONS?" GAVIN raised his eyebrows. "What does that even mean?"

"It means that Dr. Menta did not alter Denton's personality, as she said. Rather, she inserted an entirely separate sequence into Denton's body." Eli's matter-of-fact explanation stunned the group into silence.

"So then…where is Denton's original sequence? In a different body?" Charlotte asked after a moment.

Isaac shook his head. "Using his identity marker, I was able to track Denton's signal to one of Cognation's laboratories. Given that, on top of the complications that might be created by two physical manifestations of Denton, he is most likely contained in a different type of hardware within the lab. Furthermore, the evidence suggests that his current housing is both immobile and non-sensory."

"In other words," Jace tried to translate, "real Denton has been disembodied and is now trapped in a box while fake Denton has taken over his body?"

Eli and Gavin nodded.

"Not to be rude, but is it, like, that different for your sequences to be uploaded into a different type of hardware?" Chai asked tentatively.

"Unfortunately, yes." Isaac thought for a moment before explaining. "Because our sequences are designed to incorporate sensory inputs, depriving us of our intended senses could theoretically cause extreme damage to our neural networks."

"In other words," Eli continued, "Denton's current status is likely analogous to solitary confinement in a very small, pitch black, completely silent cell."

"The likelihood that this is causing distress for Denton is corroborated by the second message I received from him."

Isaac projected the message in front of them: *Herbie's fate may soon be my own.*

"Who's Herbie?" Gavin voiced the question on everyone's mind.

"Herbie is a robot from a twentieth-century science fiction story. At the end of the tale, a human character enforces an 'insoluble dilemma' upon Herbie, thrusting him into an irrevocable state of insanity. Denton and I discussed this story during a conversation about the theoretical capability to torture an android, given that we do not perceive pain in the human sense. Though Denton deemed a story this old to be exceedingly simple, his opinion was that it came closer than any other representation to pure artificial torture."

Charlotte squirmed, horrified both by Isaac's conversation with Denton and by the implications of the cryptic message. She noticed a similar discomfort rippling through her friends. "We have to get him out." The words tumbled from Charlotte's mouth before she fully thought them through, but if Denton was being tortured, in Cognation's own labs, then they had to save him, right?

"Given the evidence, that would be my recommended course of action," Isaac affirmed.

"But." Chai's eyes flicked over Isaac and Eli before returning to Charlotte. "But surely Dr. Menta had a reason for this. I mean, maybe she realized that Denton was really dangerous, perhaps capable of doing more harm than what happened to Gavin."

"But Isaac thought Denton was innocent. What if he was framed?" Charlotte glanced at Isaac. "I didn't think your theory made sense at first, but after everything that's happened, I don't know. Maybe you were right."

Chai pursed her lips, and Charlotte couldn't blame her. Even to Charlotte, that explanation sounded weak, so she tried a different tactic. "Okay, let's say Denton did cause Gavin's injuries. Gavin recovered, thankfully." She placed her hand on his arm briefly, lest her next comment sound insensitive. "And it could have been worse, but it wasn't. Does that situation really warrant Denton being trapped away? Taken out of his body? Tortured?"

Chai winced at this last question, but she replied, "If he has the potential to be extremely dangerous, then maybe."

A retort sprung to Charlotte's lips, but Jace stepped in first and turned to Isaac. "Hypothetically speaking, how would you rescue Denton?"

"Without an extra body available, we would need to first download his sequence onto separate hardware not controlled by Cognation. Completing that would constitute success at this point."

"Isaac and Eli, I understand your loyalty to your fellow androids, and I do hope that Denton isn't feeling any pain or whatever." Chai paused, glancing between Charlotte, Jace, and

Gavin. "But I don't get how this involves any of us."

"It does not have to," Isaac said thoughtfully. "Charlotte was the one to draw my attention to my altered records; therefore, I felt as though I should share this information." He turned to Charlotte. "If I have misunderstood your desire to be involved in this discussion, then I apologize. Eli and I can proceed alone if that is your preference."

"It's not." Charlotte threw a look at Chai.

"Speak for yourself," Chai said, her exasperation building. "You can't really be serious about this. Isaac is talking about stealing intellectual property from Cognation. Come on." She turned to Isaac and Eli. "Isn't this impossible, anyway? Won't the principles stop you from stealing?"

Isaac said, "We have considered that. In a normal situation, yes, the Benevolence Principle would prohibit us from breaking Cognation rules. Given the circumstances, however, we believe that inaction may endanger not only Denton but perhaps other humans as well."

"I don't recall Dr. Menta saying you could interpret the principles however you like," Chai replied while starting to move away.

Trying to get them back on track, Charlotte reached toward her best friend. "Hold on, Chai. I know this is a lot, but let's just talk about it."

Chai shrugged off Charlotte's hand. "Look, I can't be involved in this. I don't think you should either. I'm sorry, but this is crazy. If you stepped back for a minute, I think you'd see that, too."

"I know this sounds crazy. But I don't think ignoring this situation is right." The two girls stared at each other in silence for a long moment.

"Maybe we have different definitions about what's right." Chai grabbed Jace's hand. "I think it's best if we go."

Charlotte could see the struggle on Jace's face, but she already knew how this would play out. Jace had chosen his side, and she really couldn't blame him for leaving with Chai.

Once her supposed best friends were out of earshot, Charlotte looked at Gavin. "I want to help Isaac and Eli get Denton. I understand Chai's perspective, and I know that this may be a bad idea. I won't blame you if you want to step out as well."

Gavin shrugged with his lopsided grin. "It sounds like an interesting challenge to me. Plus, we signed on to help our android partners achieve their goals this semester, so if Eli's in, then I'm in, too." He rubbed his palms together. "What's the plan?"

Isaac pulled up a map of Cognation's campus and zoomed into the building that also housed Dr. Menta's Cognation office. "We will first need to acquire some hardware that can hold Denton's sequence. We then must gain access to this building, connect our hardware to the mainframe, and transfer Denton onto our receptacle."

Some of Charlotte's earlier conviction waned as the intricate building map hovered before them. "We'll never get past security."

"Security is not the most serious problem," Eli said. "For anything on a digital system, Isaac and I can most likely make some alterations. Furthermore, our dorm connects to Cognation's campus through a tunnel, which will provide a more direct route to the building."

"Our biggest problems," Isaac explained, "will be finding the appropriate hardware and avoiding human detection. This building is almost always staffed, and androids or students walking on the Cognation campus without an appointment may draw some attention."

Charlotte bit her lip. Now that they were thinking through the details, this was seeming more and more like a foolhardy plan. What if they got caught? What if she got thrown out of school? What would this mean for her parents' jobs? What about for Marissa?

Gavin snapped his fingers, bringing Charlotte back to the present. "What about during the pitch?"

It took her a second to understand what he meant, but then it dawned on her. "That's brilliant, Gavin!" Like the keynote, the winter pitch was attended by nearly the entire Cognation community. "Almost everybody will be at the Gem. That would probably be our best shot."

"The pitch is three weeks away." Isaac paused, ostensibly running some calculations. "That should provide sufficient time for us to locate hardware and create a plan with a statistical chance of success."

"Speaking of time," Gavin said, "it's getting pretty late. We should probably head back to our dorms now." He looped his arm through Charlotte's, and she saw Isaac's gaze dart down to their interlocked elbows.

Displaying no other reaction, Isaac said, "That is an excellent point. We can continue our planning tomorrow. Good night, Gavin. Good night, Charlotte."

With that, Isaac and Eli strode off in the direction of the Abyss.

CHAPTER 40

THIS WAS AN impossible plan. Charlotte and Gavin shared that thought as they stared at each other across the study pod table.

Luckily, androids were excellent planners.

"We mapped out a few scenarios last night. We determined that it may be best to select a course of action and reverse engineer the required steps." At the blink of an eye, Isaac filled the room with a complex, interconnected concept web. By a few scenarios, Isaac evidently meant over a hundred options.

Gavin ran his palm through his disheveled hair. "Um, I think we're going to need you two to simplify this for us a bit."

"Certainly." Mirroring Gavin's motion, Eli tousled his own hair before beginning to eliminate less feasible options. "Having all four of us rescue Denton is impractical and unnecessary; therefore, splitting up is likely best. Sending a pair to get Denton and leaving a pair at the pitch will help the rescuers avoid detection and will enable the remaining partners to implement an additional diversion at the pitch if necessary."

"Okay." Charlotte's eyes bounced between the numerous remaining options. "So who goes where?"

"As Denton has established direct contact with me, I believe I should be one of the members to break into the lab." Isaac looked at the group as they all nodded.

"Would Eli go with you then?" Gavin asked.

Isaac highlighted a few of the scenarios with their attached analytics. "Unfortunately, while Eli and I as a team bring some benefits, together we have what you might call an Achilles heel. If we were to be discovered, we could easily be deactivated. We therefore believe it is most prudent to maintain our human-android partnerships." The highlighted options disappeared.

"But that means Charlotte has to break into the lab with you? I don't like that." Gavin's concerned look, probably meant to be endearing, instead struck Charlotte as patronizing.

"Why not? You think you would be better at breaking in than I would?"

"No, I'm not saying that-"

Eli jumped in. "Due to Gavin's running abilities, he would on some level be the better option. However, we have determined that it would be less suspicious for us to remain with our assigned partners. Furthermore, if things do not turn out well, Charlotte's familial connections to the company could provide her with more protection than Gavin might be afforded."

Those were fair points, Charlotte supposed, but it would have been nice to get some mention of her own merits as well. "Okay, so it's decided? Isaac and I will sneak off to Cognation while Eli and Gavin remain at the pitch to support with the diversion?" Isaac and Eli nodded in unison; Gavin reluctantly agreed.

Another thought came to Charlotte. "Marissa might be able to help us as well. She probably won't love the idea of us sneaking into the lab, but I know she wouldn't be okay with what's happening to Denton."

Isaac and Eli exchanged a look before Isaac tentatively disagreed. "We have observed several recent instances of Marissa working privately with Dr. Menta. Given the likelihood that Dr. Menta orchestrated the incarceration of Denton's sequence, it is quite possible that Marissa may be involved as well. Acquainting her with our intentions, therefore, may pose an unnecessary risk."

"I don't believe that, Isaac."

"I understand that your intimate knowledge of Marissa's character provides additional data points. I can only infer based on what I have observed."

An uncomfortable silence permeated the room, and Charlotte knew that they would defer to her. Her gut told her that she could trust her sister, but then…another part of her admitted that Marissa had become a bit distant over the past month. She had even canceled their last brunch, which had never happened before. Maybe it would be best to keep Marissa out of their plans for now. "Okay. We don't have to tell her. But to be clear - I don't agree with your theory. And if things get out of hand, we may need her help." The rest of them nodded, and the awkwardness dissolved, at least for the moment.

Moving them back on track, Isaac rearranged the concept map, bringing some order to the chaos, though dozens of scenarios remained. "To maintain some semblance of an alibi, Charlotte and I should make an appearance at the pitch. Ideally, we could leave before or after we present, but second years present near the middle of the evening, which does not provide us with much time on either side."

"Isaac, we have to be there to present."

"You are correct that we have to present. However, we may not need to physically be there for that to happen."

Charlotte and Gavin exchanged quizzical glances. The plan was about to get interesting.

Sneaking out the next night proved to be easier than Charlotte expected. After a somewhat tense dinner, Charlotte stopped by her room alone and tucked her ring under her pillow. Though the Academy professed to track students' locations only during an emergency, Isaac and Charlotte thought it best not to have her signal show up from within the androids' dorm.

Leaving without her ring, Charlotte felt simultaneously invisible and exposed. She knew that working with Isaac within his dorm was unwise, but he said it was necessary. To keep their presentation plan as protected as possible, they needed access to computing power disconnected from the viewernet. Though all of the Academy's workstations were networked, the tech lab beneath Isaac's room housed hardware that would suffice. It didn't, unfortunately, include portable hardware they could use to rescue Denton; they were still figuring that part out.

Charlotte met up with Isaac not far from the hammocks, and they walked toward the Abyss in silence. "What if somebody sees me?" she whispered eventually.

"I tapped into the dorm's viewerspace earlier; anyone who sees you should see Eli instead."

Charlotte turned to him. "Really?" Yesterday, Isaac said he would take care of any security concerns, but Charlotte had no idea his solution would be this elaborate.

"Yes. However, it is only a visual program. If we are seen, it would be most beneficial for you not to speak."

"Okay." She followed as Isaac descended farther into the Abyss than Charlotte had ever wandered. Halfway to the depth of the valley, he turned to face the hillside behind them.

Charlotte felt Isaac activate her viewer, and a small door emerged in the unassuming hillside. Charlotte gasped. "This is the entrance to your dorm?"

"Yes. We will go straight through the atrium, down the spiral path for three floors, and to the end of the hallway on the right. Ready?"

She nodded, and the door retracted into the earth, revealing a sparse atrium, unexpectedly clinical beneath its earthy exterior. No wonder no one had discovered the dorm; it was entirely underground.

Riding down the spiral path, they reached the appropriate floor without running into any of the other androids. They walked down the hallway on the right, their footsteps echoing around them. Isaac extended his hand toward the doorknob before suddenly pausing.

"Hello." Dr. Menta's voice, coming from behind them, rooted Charlotte to her spot.

As Isaac turned, he nudged her slightly, and she turned as well, forcing herself to look Dr. Menta in the eye. Androids always maintained eye contact with humans.

"Isaac." Dr. Menta's eyes scanned Charlotte, and for a terrible moment, Charlotte was sure that Isaac's disguise had failed. "Eli."

Eli. Dr. Menta thought she was seeing Eli! Charlotte maintained an impassive expression and let Isaac speak while her insides twirled.

"Good evening, Dr. Menta."

"What are you two doing down here?"

"We wanted to use the tech lab to run data analytics for our design projects."

"And those projects are going well?"

"Yes, they are going very well."

Charlotte, practically holding her breath, wondered how long this conversation would continue.

"And you, Eli? Are your projects going well?"

Charlotte nodded, trying to look simultaneously robotic and natural. She was not prepared for this.

Dr. Menta's eyes narrowed. "You're not usually so quiet."

Charlotte panicked. If she opened her mouth, the ruse would be up. Isaac, thanks to his quick-thinking android mind, saved her.

"Eli has been researching nonverbal communication and challenging himself to communicate without words for stretches of time. I would say he is doing quite well."

Her expression smoothing, Dr. Menta nodded thoughtfully. "Interesting. Have a good evening, gentlemen."

She and Isaac were soon safe behind the door of the tech lab, and Charlotte sank into a chair.

"That was close!" Charlotte whispered.

"While running into Dr. Menta was unfortunate, it did provide a useful test case. This data point supports my hypothesis that our presentation plan will be effective."

Isaac's dispassionate confidence did little to temper Charlotte's shock at nearly being caught. As her heart rate gradually returned to normal, Charlotte realized for the first time that their theoretical plan to rescue Denton might come with some very real risks.

CHAPTER 41

THOUGH THE REST of Charlotte's time in Isaac's dorm passed without incident, sneaking back into Lyra would be more difficult than slipping out. Without her ring, Charlotte would have to ask Chai to let her back into the building. As Charlotte had ignored a few messages earlier that night, she guessed that Chai might not be so happy to hear from her roommate at 2am.

Pondering the best way to approach this, Charlotte stopped short at the sight of a shadowy figure standing near Lyra's entrance. She considered stealing around to the back of the dorm when the figure faced her.

"Marissa?" Simultaneous swells of relief and worry flooded over Charlotte. Marissa's appearance here could only mean one thing: she knew, at least in part, what Charlotte was up to. "What are you doing here?" Charlotte's feigned ignorance fell flat.

Wordlessly, Marissa held out her sister's ring, and Charlotte led them into the building. Great. Now there would be a record of her late-night return, should anyone care to look, but perhaps Marissa's presence could provide some sort of alibi.

Marissa maintained her silence until they reached Charlotte's room where, unsurprisingly, Chai sat wide-awake at their corner table. Chai's annoyed expression mirrored Marissa's, signaling to Charlotte that an apology might be a helpful way to start.

"I'm sorry it's so late. Isaac and I got a little carried away working on our project. Final crunch time, you know." Even to her own ears, this sounded a little thin, and she could tell that Marissa and Chai weren't convinced.

"I know you weren't working on your school projects, Char." Marissa didn't budge at Charlotte's apology.

"Well, we were." Technically, this was true. Their plan for Denton was directly connected to their virtual presentation for the pitch.

"That's enough, Charlotte. Chai told me everything."

Charlotte mentally reviewed what "everything" might entail; luckily, Chai had only been privy to the general plan to rescue Denton. Still, Chai shouldn't have betrayed her confidence, and anger flushed Charlotte's cheeks. "This isn't your business to tell, Chai."

"What was I supposed to do, Charlotte? I got back at midnight to find you missing, and you wouldn't respond to any of my messages. You're lucky I only reached out to Marissa. I was *worried*." Chai flung her final comment as a challenge, a reminder that Charlotte should care about how she felt.

"I'm sorry, Chai. I shouldn't have made you worry." And for a moment, putting aside the fact that Chai had abandoned her the other night, she did feel bad. "And I'm sorry you had to come out here, Marissa."

Her sister appeared unmoved. "Staying out late is one thing. But Charlotte, please tell me that you're not actually thinking about stealing an android's sequence from Cognation."

Charlotte paused, weighing her options. Ordinarily, she would confide in Marissa, but Isaac's words echoed in her mind. If Marissa were working closely with Dr. Menta, then telling her might ruin everything.

Charlotte probed the conversation forward. "Did Chai really tell you everything, Marissa? About Isaac's altered memory? And the fact that Denton's original sequence has essentially been put in solitary confinement? In torturous confinement? Perhaps without cause? Doesn't this all seem wrong to you?"

Momentary indecision flashed across Marissa's eyes. "Charlotte, there are things happening that you don't understand. I wish I could tell you more, but for now, it's best if you don't get in the middle of it."

"I understand that the androids, and their human partners, are being lied to, and I understand that Denton is being tortured. Isn't the whole point of being a tech ethicist to prevent situations like this?"

"We are doing our best to protect the androids. I need you to trust me on that."

"Mom and Dad wouldn't just sit by and let something like this happen. They would do what's right."

"Mom and Dad aren't here," Marissa snapped. In a softer tone, she added, "No one is just sitting by, but I need you to understand that this situation is more complicated than you think...it's hard to know what's right when you don't have the whole story."

The sincerity behind Marissa's words weakened Charlotte's resolve. She knew her sister, knew that she wouldn't do anything to compromise her values. But she also recognized that Marissa might not support Charlotte's decision. Telling her sister the full truth could ruin the entire plan.

When Charlotte didn't respond, Marissa pressed further. "I know that Isaac might have some ideas about what is best for Denton, but I really hope you don't let him talk you into doing anything foolish."

"He's not talking me into anything," Charlotte protested, resenting the implication that Isaac had some sort of power over her. "We did discuss trying to find Denton, hypothetically, but Isaac has since determined that it wouldn't be possible. Even if it were possible, we know it would be too risky." Though not a great actor, Charlotte made her words as believable as she could.

Marissa searched Charlotte's eyes. "So you promise that you won't try to steal Denton from his current housing?"

Charlotte swallowed. She and Marissa didn't make promises to each other that they couldn't keep, but Marissa was giving her no choice. "I promise. It does seem wrong, though, to trap Denton like this and to willfully change the androids' records. If you are trying to protect them, I hope you consider that."

"I will." Marissa glanced between Chai and Charlotte before moving to hug each of them. "I should probably let you both try to get some sleep. Chai, thank you for calling me. Charlotte, I'm glad you're okay." Hesitating on her way out, Marissa turned back. "I know this hasn't been an easy semester. One day, you'll understand more."

After Marissa left, Charlotte looked at Chai, whose relieved expression sparked a pang of guilt.

"I know you're worried about the androids, but you have to do what's best for you, Charlotte. It wouldn't have been worth risking everything. I'm glad Marissa helped you see that."

As they moved toward their beds, Charlotte just nodded silently, unwilling to lie further to her best friend.

CHAPTER 42

CHARLOTTE AWOKE THE next morning under an intense cloud of apprehension that followed her all the way to Philosophy of Reality. Her lies to Chai and Marissa, in addition to the rapidly approaching pitch, weighed on her. To make things worse, Charlotte knew that her deception might all be for nothing. If they didn't find a device to house Denton soon, they would have no choice but to abandon their entire plan.

Thankfully, stepping into Dr. Cariciarra's classroom relaxed Charlotte's muscles. With the weather growing colder, Dr. Cariciarra habitually started each period with a warm orange glow on the walls and ceiling. The soft waves of color, combined with the room's actual heat, soothed Charlotte, and she sank down onto a mat for their beginning meditation.

Today Dr. Cariciarra surprised her class with a slightly different routine than usual. "At this point in the semester, I know that clearing your minds can be especially challenging. We will therefore use this time to explore a challenge taking up mental space. This will seem counterintuitive at first as it may initially raise your stress level; however, I promise it will ultimately calm some of the anxiety you may be feeling about the upcoming pitch."

Following Dr. Cariciarra's lead, Charlotte lengthened her back, closed her eyes, and took a deep breath as the words flowed over her.

"Focus on one specific challenge you are grappling with. Choose only one concern. Thinking about your entire pitch is too general. Focus instead on one piece that is giving you trouble. Hold it in your mind."

In the ensuing silence, Charlotte focused on their hardware challenge.

"This type of meditation," Dr. Cariciarra continued, "presumes that for any unresolved challenge, the answer already rests within your untapped thoughts. Visualize your challenge in the center of a map and let your mind fill in other places, literal or metaphorical, that might illuminate an answer."

In her mind, Charlotte saw Denton, trapped in one of Cognation's labs. Taking a bird's-eye view, she zoomed out from the lab to the Cognation and Academy campuses. The answer had to be here. There were plenty of professors to ask about antiquated storage, but Charlotte worried about raising any red flags. Where could they find technology old enough to transfer data through a physical connection?

This question pulled at the periphery of Charlotte's thoughts, and it took a moment before an idea crystalized. When it did, she nearly gasped, and her eyes flickered open.

The library. That had to be the key.

"You really think the library will have what we need?" Gavin asked after class. Disappointingly, the boys had reacted to Charlotte's epiphany with more skepticism than excitement.

Charlotte persisted. "I have a hunch. Like Dr. Cariciarra said, maybe the answer was inside us."

She saw Gavin raise his eyebrow at Eli and Isaac. Thoughtfully, Isaac said, "The library is the only place I have seen technology as old as paper-based books, so it is an interesting idea. I also considered this challenge while meditating, and I determined that we would likely need to build the device. While Eli and I could theoretically do that, acquiring raw materials would create associated challenges. Starting with anything, even a piece of hardware in disrepair, would be advantageous."

They passed under the book-shaped awning and into the lobby, where Francine sat upon one of the tables. Her head remained buried in a paper book until she flipped a page and looked up to see them all staring at her.

"Hi, Francine." Charlotte smiled, hoping they weren't disturbing her.

"Hey." Francine glanced around the group when no one else spoke. "What's up?"

"Um." Charlotte adopted a nonchalant tone. "We're doing some research into storage devices that predate the viewernet. Like, something you could transfer data onto through a physical port."

"You mean like a flash drive?"

"A what?" Charlotte and Gavin asked at the same time that Eli and Isaac said, "Yes."

Francine explained, "A flash drive is a little device people used to store data on. It's pretty old tech. The cloud structure underlying the viewernet made them obsolete ages ago."

"But they still exist?" Charlotte asked.

"Hmm. I'm not sure. They were probably never used here. But if anything like that is around, it might be in the storage room one floor down. You're welcome to look. I'm actually thinking about a cataloguing project down there, something to explore the digital dark age. Who knows how much data we've lost through outdated storage. If you find anything useful, you can borrow it; just be sure to get it back before next semester."

"Of course," Gavin said. "Thanks, Francine."

Francine turned back to her book, and the other four exchanged silent smiles of victory. This, at the very least, was a good lead.

Unfortunately, the chaotic storage scene that greeted them wilted their smiles. Piles of books, hardware, furniture, artwork, and nearly all categories of junk were stacked throughout the expansive space. Most of the piles surpassed even Isaac's height.

"Yikes. I'm guessing a flash drive is relatively small?" Gavin scratched his head. "How are we going to find something like that in here?"

Isaac and Eli nodded to each other before moving to opposite ends of the room. Isaac said, "Even seemingly disorganized spaces follow some sort of organizational pattern. Eli and I will run what we observe through a classifier to narrow down our search; we will also do a material scan to identify traces of silicon, which will be found within the flash drives."

"Okay." Gavin's bewildered expression mirrored Charlotte's thoughts.

"I guess we'll just poke around over here then," she said, silently acknowledging that she and Gavin would be of little help.

Charlotte glanced through the piles of old screens and digital books while wondering why the school even had this stuff. She marveled at how many things people used to need before viewers. Thinking about that, though, also brought to mind her three pairs of viewer glasses, unused since she switched to contacts last year.

Less than five minutes later, Eli emerged from one of the stacks with two silver rectangular devices that fit inside his palm. "This is a start."

Charlotte and Gavin looked at each other with wide eyes. "Next time I lose something in my room, I'm definitely calling you guys," Gavin said.

"These appear to be low-storage flash drives," Isaac said, deflating their excitement. "We will need to combine multiple drives to contain Denton's sequence. That can be done, but two will not be enough."

Isaac and Eli returned to the other side of the room; with a better mental image of what they were looking for, Charlotte and Gavin began rummaging more earnestly in their corner. Over an hour later, though, none of them had been able to locate additional flash drives.

Isaac picked up the box containing their meager finds. Through scanning the materials, he and Eli had gathered miscellaneous connectors and chips as well as a couple of old viewer glasses that might be useful in cobbling together a suitable device, but Isaac seemed only tentatively confident in their chances of success. "These materials alone are not ideal."

"But they could work?" Charlotte asked.

"They could work, but it will be difficult to engineer enough storage capacity. If the storage is insufficient, we will run the risk of permanently damaging or even destroying Denton's sequence when we attempt the transfer."

Charlotte bit her lip. That possibility had not even occurred to her; she realized she had only been worrying about the consequences for herself.

Gavin's brow wrinkled with a new concern. "Will transferring Denton onto a device like this really make him more comfortable than he is now? Even though it's not a sensory casing?"

Nodding, Isaac said, "Our plan is to build an onboard processor and a holographic sensory application, which would allow Denton to tap into the viewerspace and simulate sensory inputs. It is not a perfect solution, but if it works, it will be much better than where he is now. We still do not believe Cognation has any spare bodies, so this remains our best option."

Shivering at the thought of lifeless android bodies, Charlotte pushed the unwelcome image from her mind.

Eli added, "It would be best to locate additional drives, as the combination process would be more straightforward and more likely to succeed. However, in the meantime, Isaac and I will have to start working with what we have."

Not seeing a better alternative for the moment - the androids had scoured the room three times - they walked upstairs to leave. As they passed Francine, she noticed the box in Isaac's hands. "I guess you found something good?"

Charlotte shrugged with a disappointed smile. "It's a start. Thanks for your help." She paused, considering whether or not to say more. "Um, Francine? This is sort of a private part of our research. It might be helpful if you didn't tell anyone about us going into the storage room."

"Sure." Francine nodded, as though that were a normal request. "What happens in the library stays in the library."

CHAPTER 43

SOMEONE MUST HAVE found out about their plan.

That was the only conclusion Charlotte could reach upon hearing Dr. Picartz's first words during their next Tech Ethics session. "Greetings. Today we will consider the ethics of ownership and control over technology, particularly in cases where the technology might be capable of independent thought processes and goals."

Ownership? Control? Even as Dr. Picartz scanned the entire room, Charlotte felt an uncanny sensation that these words were meant just for her. In her desperate effort to appear innocent, she knew her cheeks were reddening with guilt. Waiting to be called out, Charlotte held her breath and avoided eye contact with Dr. Picartz while he continued his instructions.

"To examine this topic, you will analyze Cognation's Android Inception Program policies. Working in groups, you will elevate the ethical principles behind these policies and prepare a presentation to the Humane Innovation Alliance regarding any changes you would recommend or, if you have no changes, your reasoning for why the Alliance should formalize these policies for all android development. Depending on how compelling your arguments turn out to be, you may in fact have the opportunity to present your thoughts to the Alliance. You will spend the entirety of today's class conducting a preliminary analysis and outlining your thoughts. I will check in with each group by the end of the period." He twirled his cane, the unspoken signal for them to get to work.

Charlotte took in a shallow breath, relieved that Dr. Picartz apparently did not intend to single her out. While the rational part of her brain suggested that today's topic might be nothing more than a coincidence, Charlotte knew she needed to keep her guard up.

Chai hesitated only slightly before she and Jace turned toward Charlotte to form a group. In their shared viewerspace, they pulled up the resources Dr. Picartz provided. Deciding to split up the copious amount of policies, they each began scanning and highlighting portions of interest.

"Hey, look at this." Jace enlarged a passage in front of them.

Both the hardware and software in the current models, specifically the sequences and body casings, belong exclusively to Cognation Industries. Cognation reserves the exclusive rights to direct, alter, and update the androids under the guidelines outlined in Sections I-IV. In cases of malfunction or transgression on behalf of the androids, particularly in situations that pose a direct threat to humans, Cognation reserves the exclusive rights to decommission the androids and to sequester their sequences, as discussed in Sections V-VII.

In a low voice, Jace said, "I haven't looked into those sections yet, but it seems like what they did to Denton is part of official protocol."

"I found something, too," Chai said quietly.

The current android models house artificial intelligence sequences that have the ability to adapt through their experiences with their environment and their personal interactions. Because the limits of this adaptability have not been empirically proven, the android sequences represent a Class D technology. Cognation Industries is not permitted to sell, share, or otherwise distribute any part of the sequences without explicit permission from the Humane Innovation Alliance. Furthermore, any employee or other individual found tampering with or attempting to identify or remove any sequence, in whole or part, will be prosecuted to the fullest extent of the law.

Jace swallowed and glanced at Charlotte. "That's intense. I guess maybe it's good that Isaac doesn't think he can get to Denton after all?"

"Yeah." She nodded slowly, understanding that Chai had passed on Charlotte's lie to Jace. "It's probably for the best."

In that moment, Charlotte couldn't ignore the part of her beginning to believe that it would in fact be for the best to let this go. She always knew there were risks, but seeing them in black and white gave them weight; moreover, thanks to Dr. Picartz, she could no longer claim ignorance of the seriousness of what they were contemplating.

With no guarantee of success, their plan was turning out to be even riskier than they first assumed. Though Isaac and Eli had made considerable progress on a makeshift device, they said at this point the likelihood of success hovered around 72.1%. Coming from androids, those odds were disconcerting, to say the least.

Still, Charlotte had kept relatively quiet with her concerns. She sensed Gavin struggling with their rather large margin of error, but she worried that speaking with him would only convince them both to pull away from the plan. Similarly, she hesitated to reveal her ambivalence to Isaac, lest he and Eli decided to take the entire plot upon themselves.

Charlotte tried to tell herself that it was too late to turn back, but a tremor of indecision continued to plague her. This current class period was only amplifying her anxiety.

Trying to concentrate, Charlotte pushed these thoughts to the back of her mind, but Athena and Beckett's discussion to her right provided further distraction. Beckett, as usual, was musing just a bit too loudly. "What if a human made an android do something bad? Who's at fault? The human? Or the android?"

From her peripheral vision, Charlotte saw Athena's eyes sharpen. "If the android was the one to actually cause harm, then I think the android would be culpable."

"Even if the human programmed the android to cause harm?" Beckett pressed.

Athena shrugged. "It seems like the android would still be to blame for following the program."

Charlotte frowned as this conversation propelled Isaac's earlier accusation to the front of her mind. When Isaac first suggested that Athena framed Denton, Charlotte found the theory to be ludicrous. Now, though, she reconsidered. Athena had been rather hostile toward the androids from the beginning. And as frustrated as Charlotte had been with Isaac's lack of evidence, she knew he wouldn't have shared that thought without at least some reasoning. The longer she considered it, the more it seemed to be possible. Athena's ambivalence toward the androids from the beginning, her rumored disappointment about not being a guide, her bitter grudge against Denton, her insistence that the androids be held accountable - they all could support Isaac's hypothesis.

Only one piece didn't line up. Charlotte understood why Athena would want to get back at Denton, but why would she want to hurt Gavin?

Despite this considerable cognitive load, Charlotte managed to complete her part of the assignment by the end of class. Afterwards, Chai and Jace left for their next period, and Charlotte followed Athena out of the room before pulling her aside.

"Did you frame Denton?" Charlotte whispered, wasting no

time on small talk.

Almost imperceptibly, Athena's eyes widened while the rest of her face remained impassive. "Why would I do that?"

"I don't know." Charlotte tried a different tactic. "It was just a theory. Now that I think about it, it doesn't really make any sense. I don't think you have the skills."

"Of course I have the skills!" Athena said sharply before backtracking. "Theoretically, anyway. Having the skills doesn't mean that I would do something like that."

As Athena started to walk away, Charlotte grabbed her arm slightly harder than she intended. "Why would you want to hurt Gavin?"

A momentary flicker of indecision passed over Athena's face. "No one would want to hurt Gavin. But he recovered fully, and Denton got what he deserved."

"Whether you meant to hurt Gavin or not, you have to tell Dr. Menta, Athena."

Athena pulled her arm out of Charlotte's grasp. "I don't know what you're talking about, Charlotte. If you have any proof for this conspiracy theory, please feel free to share. But don't for a minute think that I will take kindly to slander."

It's not slander if it's true, Charlotte thought. "Denton is suffering for what you did."

"Androids can't suffer, Charlotte." Athena's smirk matched her sickeningly innocent voice. "Besides, the last I saw him, Denton seemed fine. I think we're done here."

Watching Athena walk away, Charlotte mumbled a "thank you" under her breath. Whether Athena was guilty or not, she had just given Charlotte what she needed: renewed determination to rescue Denton, no matter the cost.

CHAPTER 44

SO FAR, NO one had discovered the truth about their practice sessions.

To run through the simulated heist, Charlotte and Isaac needed space, and it was Gavin who provided the ingenious solution of reserving an enigma court. Specifically engineered for the interactive enigma challenges, the court provided the ideal practice spot and the perfect cover. To any curious observer, Charlotte, Gavin, and their android partners were simply getting a head start on practicing for the spring tournament.

"Let's try it again." After countless rehearsals, Charlotte nearly had their route memorized, but she kept hoping they might reach a level of readiness that would smooth the crease lodged above Gavin's brow.

By now, Isaac and Eli had rigged together a workable drive, but it was far from foolproof, a fact that had everyone on edge. At least, it had Gavin and Charlotte on edge. The most they could do was practice the plan to perfection, a therapeutic act providing more catharsis to Charlotte than to Gavin.

Gavin and his worried frown disappeared from Charlotte's view as Isaac reactivated the simulation, commencing with their entrance to the androids' dorm. Getting to this point would be easy, they expected, so they had abandoned rehearsing it.

After the hidden door emerged from the hillside, they made their way into the building without incident, but Charlotte remained alert. Watching from beyond the program, Eli and Gavin randomized each simulation to acclimate Charlotte and Isaac to unexpected scenarios.

This round, though, no one stopped them in the dorm, and they sped through the tunnel connecting the Academy to Cognation in record time. As Isaac worked to unlock the door at the end of the passage, Gavin's voice reached them within the simulation. "Your virtual presentation isn't working. We got it pulled up for a second, but then it malfunctioned. The stage is empty, and you're up now."

Charlotte stared at Isaac. "Is that type of failure possible?"

"Yes, it is possible. Unlikely, but possible." Without wasting further time, Isaac pointed to one side of the tunnel and turned Charlotte's body to face it. "This is the audience. We will have to give the presentation from here."

Forcing a smile on her face just in time for the live capture, Charlotte ran through the presentation with Isaac, just as they had done so many times before their final recording. Gavin's updates came through their viewers. "Good...That's working...No one seems to suspect you're not there...Okay, applause is dying down, so you're free to leave the stage...And you're out of sight."

As soon as they switched their projection off, Isaac returned to the locks.

"Isaac." Charlotte knew she shouldn't break his concentration, but she couldn't help it. "I didn't know that could happen."

"That is why we practice," he responded without looking up.

While they couldn't know exactly what type of security would be in place - the locks around the labs changed regularly - Isaac had downloaded every code-breaking algorithm he could find.

"Algorithm 231." Isaac stood as the door swung forward. They had always been able to get through the locks; this wasn't terribly surprising, as Isaac designed the simulation, but Charlotte tried not to dwell on that fact.

The room housing Denton's sequence, though also underground, did not directly connect to the tunnel, so Isaac and Charlotte snuck up to the higher floors and to the back spiral path leading down to the basement lab. Isaac unlocked every barrier that stood in their way, and soon they reached Denton's prison. Completely covering the far wall, monolithic boxes hummed behind a complex array of screens dotted by blinking lights.

Delicately yet firmly, Isaac pried open the access panel running the height of the wall on the far left side, and Charlotte slid through the narrow space and wriggled behind the mainframe's wires. Pulling the drive from her pocket, she carefully connected the correct cables to the device before messaging one word to Isaac. *Ready.*

When no message returned, Charlotte relaxed slightly. No message meant that Isaac could access the device on the mainframe. She had practiced the connections so often that she could probably hook the device up in her sleep, but that didn't stop her from irrationally worrying that she would mess up. It did help, though, to recall how impressed Isaac had been on her first try. One of Marissa's coworkers had taken her behind the mainframe of a different machine last summer, and while the cables weren't identical, it provided a helpful frame of reference.

As during the other runs, Charlotte felt a bit useless while waiting for Isaac's signal to disconnect the device. Surrounded by the machine's constant hum, Charlotte pushed away absurd fears of being trapped in the confined space. After several minutes ticked away, Charlotte knew that Isaac had to be finishing the sequence transfer soon.

Suddenly, muffled voices snapped Charlotte to attention and sent a shiver down her spine. There shouldn't be anyone here. Charlotte sent a message, but Isaac didn't respond. Inching closer to the panel opening, Charlotte strained to make out the words.

Think. THINK. Charlotte desperately tried to organize her thoughts before moving further. Should she retrieve Denton's device or leave it? Charlotte started to turn back when the voices became louder, triggering an unexpected recognition that pulled her toward the opening.

"Mom? Dad?" Charlotte stepped free from the wires as she untangled her confusion. "What are you doing here?"

"We could ask you the same thing, Charlotte," her mom said firmly. "We need you to hand over what you've taken."

"But, I...you don't understand." Looking for help, Charlotte faced Isaac, but his lifeless eyes turned her blood to ice. "Isaac. Isaac!" He remained immobile as she rushed over and pulled at his arm.

Charlotte felt pressure on her own arms, and she whipped around, pushing her dad away. "What did you do?"

Without emotion, her dad said, "I deactivated him. He is no longer needed."

As Charlotte tried to process this information, she saw her mom step out from behind the mainframe. Device in hand, she said, "We have what we came for."

Before Charlotte could react, the simulation dissolved

around her. The program always ended if their chances of success approached zero.

Charlotte bit back her tears as she spun toward Isaac, who was now very much alive. "That didn't make sense. Why would my parents show up? Why would you do this?"

Assessing her heightened level of emotion, Isaac patiently said, "My program includes all known staff members of Cognation as inputs. While it is of course not probable that your parents will be on Cognation's campus on the night of the pitch, it is within the realm of possibility, statistically speaking." He glanced at Eli then back to Charlotte. "Eli also suggested that facing someone you know might be more difficult than dealing with an unfamiliar guest, so we determined that incorporating your family members in at least one of the simulations would be advantageous."

"My parents wouldn't have done that! They wouldn't want Denton to be locked up. They wouldn't deactivate you." Even as the words came out of her mouth, Charlotte heard how weak they sounded. Truthfully, she wasn't sure how her parents would react. They had always raised her to do the right thing, but they could argue that stealing Denton's sequence, no matter the situation, didn't fall under the right category after all.

Before they could continue this conversation, the door to the court opened, and all of their heads turned toward it. Heart pounding, Charlotte sighed with relief when she saw that their visitor was only Francine.

"Hey," Francine said. "I was looking for you over at Lyra, but Chai said you could be here. If you need more members on your enigma team in the spring, let me know. I might like to join."

"Um, yeah," Charlotte stuttered, thankful for their cover story. "We haven't really made an official team yet, but that would be cool." The boys nodded their assent.

"Okay, sweet." Francine smiled. "Anyway, I think I found something you might want." She reached forward, placing a small sack in Charlotte's hand.

"What's this?"

"I did some more digging after you left the library the other day, and I found a box of flash drives tucked in the corner of a smaller storage room." Charlotte peeked inside the sack to find nearly a dozen drives. "They're all labeled with different animals, so they might hold some kind of wildlife reference material? I don't know what you're doing with them, but if you find any usable data, just add it to the library's cloud. Cool?"

"Definitely! Francine, thank you so much. You have no idea how awesome this is." Charlotte struggled to adequately thank her, but Francine shrugged.

"No problem. I just wish I found them earlier. See you later."

After Francine left, Charlotte handed the drives to Isaac, who was smiling broadly.

With an equally bright grin, Eli said, "These will be extremely helpful."

Only Gavin seemed unimpressed by this turn of events. As they all walked home, Gavin pulled Charlotte aside. "It's interesting that Francine was able to find so many drives."

Charlotte searched Gavin's face. "What are you saying? This is a good thing."

He sighed. "You're probably right. It just seems like an odd coincidence."

"It could be a good omen," Charlotte suggested, pushing aside her own worries.

Gavin nodded reluctantly, without saying what Charlotte knew he was thinking.

Omens could also be bad.

CHAPTER 45

DESPITE GAVIN'S CONCERNS and Charlotte's unease, the plan moved forward.

Using the newfound drives, Isaac and Eli soon fashioned a device that they were 99.99% convinced would accommodate the transfer of Denton's sequence. With that problem solved, Charlotte found she could fool herself into believing that the entire plan's chances of success also ran that high.

She wisely did not ask Isaac and Eli for the exact statistical probability of rescuing Denton without being caught. She did not want to know.

The next several days passed by in a whirlwind as Charlotte and the rest of the students conducted final preparations before the pitch. Classes had concluded the week before, providing students with additional time to focus on their presentations; the extra time was both a blessing and a curse, as it left students no excuse for presenting anything less than perfectly refined projects.

Charlotte barely saw Chai and Jace, and when she did, they seemed too preoccupied by their own work (one of their experiments had produced some inexplicably anomalous data at the last minute) to worry much about Charlotte. For that, she was grateful. Lying by omission was much easier than lying directly.

By the evening before the pitch, Charlotte and Isaac had exhausted all of the scenarios with even a shred of possibility, and once they completed twenty successful simulations in a row, they decided that they were as ready as they would ever be. Charlotte was pleased to see that Gavin relaxed with each seamless rehearsal; it might have been her imagination, but she sensed that even Isaac and Eli were more at ease.

Of course, that was before Denton's late-night message brought their confidence crashing down.

Gathered in their study pod, the four of them had been about to call it a night when Isaac straightened suddenly and shared a message in their viewerspace.

Everything is not as it seems.

Denton's words hovered ominously in front of them.

"Isaac." Eyes wide, Charlotte looked up at him. "What does this mean? Why would Denton send this the night before the pitch?"

Isaac shrugged. "I do not know."

Though Isaac had maintained regular communication with Denton, he had been careful not to divulge anything about their rescue plot in case their messages fell under surveillance. The fact that their messages had not been discontinued suggested they were sliding under the radar, but Isaac was careful to cover his tracks.

"Did you find anything?" Isaac asked Eli.

"No. My analysis is consistent with yours. None of your messages provided any suggestion, even implicitly, about our plans."

Gavin's furrowed brow returned. "So what does this mean, then?"

"It could mean a number of things," Isaac said. "The message is too broad to determine a specific interpretation, and I cannot directly tie it to any of our prior conversations."

"Should we ask him to elaborate?" Charlotte asked.

Eli shook his head. "Denton would have had a reason for being intentionally vague. On the slim chance that his messages are being reviewed, we cannot take the risk of creating further communication records."

"This doesn't make sense," Charlotte protested. "Isaac, you know Denton the best. You really have no idea why he might send this message?"

"Well…" Isaac let his thought trail off, and Charlotte stared at him curiously. She had never heard him not complete a statement. Before she could question him again, he cleared his throat. "No, I cannot say why he would have sent me this message. Denton does, however, sometimes share errant thoughts with me. It is possible that the timing of this particular reflection is a coincidence."

Charlotte wasn't completely convinced by Isaac's response, but they didn't have time to overthink things now. The pitch was in less than twenty-four hours. "Okay. So does this change anything?" Charlotte asked the question to avoid having to answer it first.

When the androids didn't immediately respond, Gavin said what Charlotte expected he would. "I think this is a sign that we should call it off. It's the night before the pitch. There's no way this is a random coincidence."

Eli offered a cautious rebuttal. "Randomness accounts for much more than humans usually give it credit for. Assigning causal relationships to random events is a distinctly human impulse, and I do not interpret the timing of Denton's message in that way. As Isaac said, there are a number of likely interpretations behind Denton's words."

"I agree," Isaac said. "Before we received Denton's message, we were just as likely to have been compromised as we are now. While this data point may indicate a weakness in our plan, it also may not indicate that. Though it feels different, we are nevertheless in the same situation we were in twenty minutes ago."

"Like Schrodinger's cat?" Charlotte asked.

Isaac cocked his head. "Yes, in a way, our situation could be compared to Erwin Schrodinger's thought experiment."

Though Eli and Isaac clearly agreed with moving forward, Charlotte knew she was the deciding vote. The thought that they might have done all of this work for nothing turned Charlotte's stomach. From her economics course last year, she knew that considering sunk costs was a faulty way to make a decision, but she couldn't ignore how far they had come.

Charlotte locked eyes with Isaac and tried to take comfort in his logical confidence. Of course, he couldn't know for sure if they would be successful, but she also knew that he would call the plan off if he deemed the risks serious enough. In that moment, she decided that what was good enough for Isaac was good enough for her.

Until tomorrow night, she would be both right and wrong, or neither right nor wrong, depending on how she looked at it. Either way, that didn't change the fact that taking the easy route felt definitively wrong. With an apologetic shrug toward Gavin, Charlotte said, "I guess it doesn't change anything then."

They were either embarking on a noble rescue mission or making a terrible mistake.

CHAPTER 46

THE GEM BUZZED with anticipation. Every once in a while, something truly magnificent emerged from a pitch, like when Winton Latham proposed his disruptive architectural plans for the new Academy campus many years ago. This year, the inclusion of the androids especially heightened the audience's curiosity.

On this night, the students filled the ground-floor seats, behind the special guests, while the press and larger Cognation community occupied the tree-limbed balcony. Marissa would be up there somewhere, though Charlotte had not yet seen her. Family members and other interested observers could tune in by viewer; Charlotte both hoped and feared that her parents would be watching.

She and Isaac found their assigned seats, which mirrored the order of presentations. They settled in a few spots down from Eli and Gavin and two rows behind Chai and Jace. Chai caught Charlotte's eye over her shoulder, and they shared quick, encouraging smiles.

The faculty climbed onto the balconies adjacent to the corners of the stage, which gave them a view of both the presenters and the audience. Charlotte was sure she could feel Dr. Menta's gaze upon her, but she refused to look up to confirm this.

For Charlotte, time alternated between impossible slowness and incredible speed. After an interminable pause, the interior of the Gem darkened, drawing the audience's chatter into silence. Dr. Kindred, in his monochromatic grayness, appeared in a warm pool of light.

"Good evening and welcome to the annual Cognation Academy Pitch. As you know, our students have been hard at work on original design questions, and they are eager to present their research to you tonight. It will undoubtedly be an exciting ride."

Charlotte, along with the rest of the audience, was transported into the viewer preview artfully created from captures submitted by each team. The preview zoomed in and out, offering faint glimpses of topics without revealing the full stories, leaving the audience with an overwhelming sense of promise and possibility. Even Charlotte, momentarily released from her own anxiety, felt herself swept up in the magic.

The theatrics transitioned into the first years' presentations. The pitch always followed this format, with the unspoken implication that the best would be saved for last. Occasionally, a first or second year's project would outshine all others, but in general, the fourth years brought a sophistication and complexity to their work that their younger classmates simply could not match.

Though Charlotte technically watched the presentations, she would later not be able to recall a single topic. She knew only that they seemed to pass in the blink of an eye, propelling her closer to her moment of action. Her leg bounced up and down incessantly, a fact brought to her attention by Isaac resting his hand on her knee.

"Everything will be okay," he whispered, his reassuring smile doing nothing to calm her steadily increasing nerves. Charlotte tried to pretend that she too were an android, incapable of being physically affected by anything so capricious as human anxiety. It didn't work.

Against her better judgement, she placed her palm on the back of Isaac's hand and tucked her fingers below his. The smoothness of his skin and the knowledge that they were in this together helped her calm her breath and take control of her speeding heartbeat.

As the final first years concluded, Chai and Jace approached the stage, and Charlotte's nerves intensified; the end of their presentation was her cue to leave. She forced herself to focus, which turned out to be easy, given the enthralling nature of her best friends' project. Through a beautifully shot capture, they first took the audience into the world of the eastern emerald elysia and then outlined their research into transferring the chloroplast consumption process to similar organisms. Effectively transplanting the chloroplasts into different species of slugs provided the creatures with the ability to supplement their energy production with localized photosynthesis.

Astonishingly, Chai and Jace didn't stop there, instead wrapping up their presentation with an engaging simulation predicting where this research might go next - including into human fingernail cells.

"You heard it here first," Chai concluded. "Nail art of the future will do much more than sparkle in the sunshine."

Clapping louder than anyone else in the Gem, Charlotte was hit by a wave of pride tinged with regret. She expected that Chai and Jace's presentation would be amazing, but the fact that she didn't know any of the details reminded her just how out of touch the three of them had been.

Breaking into her thoughts, Isaac reached over and squeezed Charlotte's fingers lightly. It was time. Worrying about Chai and Jace would have to wait.

Being out of their seats in between presentations wasn't exactly encouraged, but it also wasn't prohibited. The faculty understood that stage fright often required last-minute bathroom trips or pep talks. Under the guise of one of these excuses, Charlotte stood from her chair and slipped into the lobby.

Trying to appear confident, she strode toward the nearest restroom, the one with a door leading to the outdoor courtyard. Once she made it outside, her first step would be complete. That small victory, surely, would help calm some of her nerves.

The door to the restroom slid open, but before it completely retracted, Charlotte caught a familiar reflection in the glass. Forcing a smile, she turned around to face her sister.

"Marissa!" Was this a coincidence? Charlotte doubted it, but she also didn't want to believe that Marissa was keeping tabs on her.

"Hey, Char. I saw you leave the auditorium, and I just wanted to make sure you were okay."

"I'm fine, thanks." If Charlotte weren't so paranoid, sisterly concern would have struck her as a perfectly reasonable explanation, but she thought she heard something more behind Marissa's words. "Just a little nervous, I guess. We're up soon. I started to feel kind of funny, so I thought I'd step out for a minute."

Marissa nodded. "I remember those days. The good news is that it gets easier by year four. And you're going to be great. You have nothing to worry about."

If only Marissa knew how wrong that was. "I know," Charlotte said. "Anyway, thanks for checking on me."

"Are you sure everything's all right?" Marissa's eyes probed Charlotte's face while also darting around the lobby. It suddenly struck Charlotte that Marissa seemed jumpier than usual.

"I'm fine. Are *you* okay?"

Marissa's eyes snapped back to meet Charlotte's gaze, and she smoothed her face into a smile. "Of course. I'm not the one doing the hard work tonight."

"Yeah, lucky you. I'll see you after the show?"

"Right." Instead of stepping back, though, Marissa grabbed Charlotte's arm. "Look, you...you don't have to do this," she stammered.

"What?" Charlotte's brow wrinkled in confusion. "Of course I have to. Everyone has to present at the pitch."

"Right. Yeah, I just meant..." Again Marissa seemed on the verge of saying something else. "I just meant that I wish I could have helped you more this semester. And...and good luck to-night."

"Thanks?" Charlotte didn't quite succeed in keeping the question mark out of her voice. Something was definitely up with Marissa, but Charlotte did not have time to dwell on it now.

For a tense moment, Charlotte wondered if Marissa would try to continue this conversation or worse, follow her into the bathroom. She didn't have a backup plan for that situation. Luckily, though, Marissa seemed to understand that Charlotte wanted some privacy, and Charlotte stepped into the restroom alone.

She waited until she heard the door slide shut behind her. There was still a chance that Marissa might wait for her; in that case, it would only take a couple of minutes before Marissa knew Charlotte had left the building.

Unable to figure out a contingency plan, Charlotte shrugged to herself and exited into the chilly, star-studded night. She desperately hoped that Marissa wouldn't unwittingly ruin everything.

CHAPTER 47

TWO MINUTES. NO, three minutes. Worse, four minutes. At the five-minute mark, Charlotte's stomach threatened to throw up.

Isaac should be here by now.

They had timed a delay for him to leave his seat and exit the building, as they didn't want to be spotted together. After sneaking out separately, they planned to meet up near the hammocks on the way to the androids' dorm.

Still no sign of him. They didn't have a plan for this.

They had assumed they would make it to this point. Well, Charlotte had assumed. Isaac had run the possibilities and determined that it was so statistically unlikely that their plot would be foiled before reaching this stage that it wasn't worth rehearsing.

Obviously, that seemed foolish now.

Should she try to contact him? That could be risky if he had been caught by someone who then tapped into his viewer. Charlotte tried to think of some clever way to communicate in code, but the mere act of sending him a message might draw attention to the fact that she wasn't in her place at the pitch.

The next two minutes were the longest in her entire life. Fear blossomed in her mind with each second that slipped away, and Charlotte sank into one of the hammocks. Should she go back? She itched to do something, *anything*, though she couldn't come up with a single solution better than uselessly sitting here.

"Ugh." Charlotte hugged her arms tightly, trying to warm herself up. She had left her coat on her seat, and her sweater, while warm, couldn't quite fight off the night's chill. Staring up at the stars between the trees, she started counting in a frantic attempt to prevent her mind from entering full panic mode.

Wait. An irregular crinkling of leaves made her lose count, and she leaned up just enough to peek one eye over the edge of the hammock. What she didn't consider until this moment was that without Isaac, she was out here alone. She had no reason to expect that anyone else might sneak up on her, but in retrospect, that seemed like a naive thought.

A faint outline began to materialize in the darkness, and Charlotte breathed a sigh of relief. Even from this distance, she recognized Isaac's measured gait. Regaining strength in her shaky knees, she stood and walked forward to meet him.

"What took so long?" Her eyes searched his face needlessly; she knew she wouldn't see any visible clues as to what happened.

In a rare moment of indecision, Isaac hesitated before shaking his head. "It is of no importance now. My delay does not change the trajectory of our plans. I believe it would be most prudent for us to discuss this later so that it does not distract us from our next steps."

Charlotte suspected that there in fact was something important behind his words, but she had to trust his judgment. "Okay. Let's go."

When they reached the hillside entry, they paused while

Isaac tapped into the security system for the dorm and deactivated it momentarily. As the system rebooted, Isaac opened the door, and they slipped in. According to Isaac, the records would show this as an anomalous power reboot, thus covering their entrance. In their preparations, Isaac had detected no surveillance within the dorm; while this at first struck them as strange, Isaac reasoned that because Cognation could access all of the androids' captures, there was little need for additional records from within the building.

Once inside, they paused again, waiting for a signal from Gavin that their presentation was complete. If they needed to remotely connect to their project, they didn't want to be in the middle of a corridor in the lab, so they had decided to use the dorm lobby as a holding space.

Thanks to Isaac's tardiness, they had barely made it here in time. As long as everything at the Gem had proceeded according to plan, Charlotte and Isaac - well, the captures of Charlotte and Isaac - should be on stage now.

Charlotte struggled to catch her breath, panic creeping around the edges of her consciousness for the second time that night. Clutching to the life raft of her adrenaline, she tried to stave off the terror of inaction.

Another human might have attempted to fill the space with awkward, rambling chatter, but Isaac maintained a deathly silence, a habit that in this moment, Charlotte found increasingly irritating.

Great work!

With a barely audible squeal, Charlotte jumped as Gavin's message popped up in their viewerspace. *Great work* meant all had gone smoothly.

With characteristic efficiency, Isaac patted her on the shoulder. "This is good. We can proceed."

Charlotte nodded and followed him to the back corner of the

building, where the doorway to the tunnel fit seamlessly into the paneled wall. She waited as Isaac engaged his lock-breaking algorithms. As she had watched him do this so many times, Charlotte should have been confident that he could open the lock, but a wave of relief still washed over her when the door swung inward after a few seconds.

Their success thus far didn't stop Charlotte's heart from speeding up as they made their way into the tunnel. When they first started practicing, Charlotte had been dismayed to learn that the passage twisted wildly; without a straight shot, they had to face the possibility that someone could be lurking around every next bend. The winding curves also prohibited them from using lights; the night vision setting through their viewers allowed them to see well enough, but the dim, discolored view added an extra layer of claustrophobia.

Isaac led the way, and Charlotte kept her right hand lightly pressed against his back. With each corner they approached, she held her breath as her certainty that they would be caught grew.

The map in the corner of her viewer tracked their progress, and when they passed the halfway point, she forced herself to calm down. If someone were going to stop them in the tunnel, surely it would have happened by now.

In the next instant, at the flip of an unseen switch, complete and total darkness consumed the tunnel, and Charlotte's fingers lost touch with the fabric of Isaac's shirt.

A hand clamped over her jaw as she opened her mouth to scream.

CHAPTER 48

A WHIMPER ESCAPED from the back of Charlotte's throat as her body froze. Simultaneously, a distant corner of her mind separated itself from the situation and rebuked her for this reaction. In a fight or flight event, she always hoped she would be a fighter.

Before she could will her muscles into action, she heard Isaac's voice near her ear and felt the hand lift away from her mouth. "It is just me. I apologize for silencing you. I do not believe anyone else is here, but I did not think it would be sensible for you to scream."

Charlotte forced herself to regain control of her body. "I'm sorry. Human reflex." She squinted and searched for an indication of him in the overwhelming darkness. "Are you sure we're alone?"

"I believe so."

"Why can't I see anything?"

"The complete lack of light indicates that our viewers have been hacked, most likely as an automatic security measure. I have never been in this tunnel unaccompanied, so it appears that I may have underestimated the protections in place."

Though Isaac delivered these details as factually as ever, Charlotte almost detected a hint of disappointment in his voice.

Her frustration mounting with each passing second, Charlotte worked through the counter hack steps they learned from Dr. Picartz. She considered removing her viewer contacts, but she knew she couldn't risk losing her viewer in the middle of their plan. "Why isn't this working?" Charlotte asked through gritted teeth. "Have you figured yours out yet?"

"Yes, I regained control one minute and twenty-eight seconds ago."

This very specific answer irritated Charlotte, but she quickly wiped the petulant look off her face. Cloaked in darkness, or so she thought, she had let her emotions run free for a moment. How wonderful to know that Isaac could see her when she thought she was invisible. "Why don't you help me, then?"

"I think you almost have it."

As usual, he was right. The world snapped back into place in front of her, and she swayed slightly as her equilibrium stabilized.

Isaac smiled at her. "I knew you did not need me. Shall we proceed?"

Charlotte nodded, hoping for no more surprises.

They continued through the tunnel with no additional impediments, and after the final curve, a door emerged in front of them. Isaac stepped forward and initiated the code-breaking algorithm; thirty-seven seconds later, the door slid open.

Charlotte sensed Isaac activating her viewer, and he nodded once their program engaged. Unsuccessful in accessing the lab's security cameras, Isaac and Charlotte had decided that disguise would be their best defense. Anyone wearing a viewer, or looking at a security capture, would see two nondescript lab techs. Anyone not wearing a viewer would see them as they were, but they deemed that a negligible risk.

Without further discussion, Isaac moved through the doorway. After a second's hesitation, Charlotte pushed her nerves aside and followed.

They crept to the end of the basement hallway, each silent step nonetheless ringing in Charlotte's ears. The building, as they expected, appeared to be deserted, but Charlotte couldn't shake the feeling that they were being watched. Trying to recall the rhythm of their practice runs, she focused on Isaac's form, confidently striding forward in front of her.

Upon reaching the spiral path to the upper floors, they pressed the manual button, allowing them to climb quietly to the main level. They crossed the lobby to the back path, and though their footsteps echoed throughout the open space, no one emerged from the darkened hallways.

Descending into the basement at the back corner of the building, Charlotte felt her pulse begin to race. Now that they were so close, all of her hesitations transformed into energetic anxiety, propelling her forward.

Only three doors stood between them and Denton's prison. At each lock, Charlotte held her breath while Isaac ran through his algorithms; each time, he arrived at the winning combination, just as they expected. The rational part of her knew that they wouldn't be in the clear until long after they returned to the Academy's campus, but once they reached their destination and shut the door behind them, Charlotte let out her breath. For the moment, at least, she could pretend that they were safe.

The cavernous room expanded before them, with floor-to-ceiling servers fanning out to fill the pentagonal space. The gentle humming of the machines formed a resonant chorus, which Charlotte found comforting after the silence of the tunnel and the deserted lab. Isaac crossed directly to the blinking control panel on the mainframe at the far end of the room; Charlotte saw, to her relief, that the mainframe exactly mirrored the one in Isaac's simulation. After Isaac popped the access panel open, Charlotte slid inside wordlessly; like partners in a well-rehearsed dance, they didn't need to speak.

Her hands trembling only slightly worse than in the practice runs, Charlotte lifted the device from her pocket and began to connect the cables to its access hub.

Ready.

The responding silence after she sent her message to Isaac indicated that the connection worked. She expected to receive Isaac's signal to remove the device in less than five minutes.

Cocooned within the humming sea of wires, Charlotte remained alert, ears straining to detect the slightest anomaly. So absorbed was she in her concentration that she didn't perceive the seconds passing by rapidly. Before she knew it, five minutes had already elapsed.

She resisted the urge to step out from behind the mainframe, as they had decided that one of them should always be within reach of the device. Unable to bear the uncertainty any longer, she settled on a message instead.

Everything okay?

His response arrived almost instantly. *I have run into a few unanticipated roadblocks, but two more minutes should be sufficient.*

Charlotte held her breath as her anxiety grew. Somehow, remaining within the five-minute mark had seemed safe. She knew her logic was irrational, but staying in this room even a moment longer than they planned struck her as a potentially catastrophic risk.

Complete.

The second she received Isaac's message, Charlotte began frantically removing the cables from the device; after a moment of fumbling, she paused and steadied her hands. While the hard part was over, it was imperative that she remove the cables carefully and replace them exactly as they were. She returned them one by one, sparing fifteen seconds at the end to review her work. Satisfied, she climbed carefully back through the panel and into the room.

Isaac offered a brief smile as he finished returning the panel to its original position. Following his lead, Charlotte remained silent. Together, they looked at the mainframe to ensure that nothing appeared to be amiss. Isaac started to walk toward the door, but Charlotte's eyes drifted to the drive resting in her hand. Though she knew this had been the plan all along, it suddenly struck her as absurd to believe that Denton's entire sequence could be captured on such a trivial device.

"Are you sure he's in there?"

Without answering, Isaac took the drive from her, and at the press of his thumb against the metal, Denton's likeness appeared in their viewerspace. "That certainly took you long enough," he said.

The ambivalent undertone in his voice convinced Charlotte that this was the original Denton. Though not exactly excited to see him, she let out a noise somewhere between a sigh and a squeak. They had really done it. Charlotte thought she had expected success, but her swift burst of elation made her realize that at least a part of her hadn't dared to believe that they could actually rescue Denton.

With a relieved grin, Charlotte nodded at Isaac. "All right. Let's get out of here."

Denton's likeness disappeared as Isaac removed his thumb. Before he could pocket the device, though, a familiar voice froze Charlotte and Isaac in their spots.

"Excellent work, you two." Dr. Menta smiled at them from across the room, where she stood in front of the door.

CHAPTER 49

IF CHARLOTTE HADN'T doubted Isaac, if she hadn't asked him to prove their success, then they could have made it out of the room seconds before Dr. Menta entered. Charlotte's mind raced to figure out a way to fix her mistake.

Before she could further complicate matters, Isaac stepped in, reminding her that to Dr. Menta, they should appear to be two nondescript lab techs. Using a different, deeper voice, he said, "Hello, Dr. Menta. We were instructed to check on the status of the servers. Everything appears to be in order, so I believe our work is done here."

"It's just me, Isaac." Dr. Menta moved toward them. "And I've taken care of the surveillance in the building. You don't have to keep up the disguise."

Charlotte looked at Isaac, in an attempt to telepathically ask him what was going on, but by the next instant, he had already deactivated their cloaking program.

"Hello, Charlotte." Dr. Menta's complete lack of surprise, lack of anger, confused Charlotte. Shouldn't Dr. Menta be upset that they broke into the lab? Aside from that brief acknowledgement, Dr. Menta spoke to Isaac as though Charlotte weren't there. "I'm glad to see that it worked. I was worried that the longer he stayed in there…well, in any case, you got him out." Glancing at the silver device nestled in Isaac's palm, she held out her own hand. "I can take him from here."

Charlotte's eyes widened as Isaac extended his arm forward. "Wait!" Charlotte's hand clamped around Isaac's wrist. "You can't make us give him to you. You're the one who trapped him in the first place!"

Dr. Menta spread her hands out calmly. "That was for his own protection, I'm afraid. I wish I could explain more, Charlotte, but there really isn't time. We should leave now before anyone misses you two at the pitch."

Isaac gently peeled Charlotte's fingers from his arm. "This is for the best, Charlotte. I promise. You will understand soon."

Lost for words, Charlotte stared at Isaac, trying to figure out if this was really his choice or if Dr. Menta was controlling him somehow. Did this mean Isaac and Dr. Menta had been working together? And lying about it?

Charlotte narrowed her eyes at Dr. Menta. None of this made sense. "If you wanted Denton out of the servers, why didn't you just take him out yourself?"

"That is complicated. Denton has proven to be a bit different from the other androids. His sequence works in ways that we're still trying to understand. The short answer is that to rescue Denton's sequence, we needed him to come to us. In other words, he had to *want* to be found. As it turned out, he only wanted to be found by Isaac."

Isaac started to reach toward Dr. Menta, but Charlotte could not let him hand Denton over. She stepped forward and snatched the device from Isaac's hand. "Isaac, I don't know what's happening to you, but I won't let you betray Denton.

This isn't who you are. She's controlling you!"

"I assure you that is not the case, Charlotte." Isaac's direct, compassionate gaze took her back to the private moments they had shared. "I know this appears to be confusing, but there are pieces you do not understand. I will explain everything later."

Dr. Menta's calm voice couldn't quite mask the layer of impatience creeping in. "I appreciate your concern, Charlotte. You, as well as your sister, demonstrate immense empathetic abilities. It's one of the reasons that you have so much potential to do this work. But the problem with empathy is that it can cloud our judgements. Right now, I need you to understand that Denton will be safest with me. Logically, you understand that you don't have all of the facts. Don't let your emotions mislead you."

Charlotte started to protest that her feelings weren't misleading her, but her rational side recognized that her emotions were in fact running quite high given these unforeseen events. She turned to Isaac for guidance. Despite the incomprehensibility of this moment, she still trusted him. Isaac nodded.

The thought of giving Denton back to Dr. Menta tightened Charlotte's chest, but she didn't know what else to do. She consoled herself with the hope that if Denton could hide in the servers, then perhaps he could also protect himself now.

Reluctantly, she placed the device into Dr. Menta's hand. The moment her fingertips brushed Dr. Menta's slightly damp palm, a movement near the door drew her gaze over Dr. Menta's shoulder, and Charlotte locked eyes with the last person she wanted to see right now.

"Well, fancy meeting you three here. Or should I say four? I trust that our hidden android is with us? At least in sequence?"

At the sound of Dr. Kindred's voice behind her, Dr. Menta's eyes widened, and Charlotte caught a trace of what she could only describe as fear. In the blink of an eye, though, Dr. Menta's expression cleared, and she turned to Dr. Kindred with a professional smile.

"Hello, Victor. We were just wrapping up here. I'm pleased to report that everything has gone according to plan."

What plan? Despite Dr. Menta's confident voice, her knuckles whitened as she clenched the device, making Charlotte wonder if Dr. Kindred's arrival truly was part of this mysterious plan. Following Isaac's lead, however, Charlotte forced her face to remain impassive.

"I am rather surprised to see you," Dr. Menta continued, her voice composed. "I thought we would be meeting up after the pitch?"

"I am surprised to see you as well. I thought Isaac was bringing the sequence to you at the Gem." Dr. Kindred moved forward slowly, and Charlotte recoiled inwardly from his patronizing smile.

"Yes, that was the initial plan, but I wanted to make sure that everything went smoothly," Dr. Menta answered in an unruffled tone.

"Indeed. That was my thought as well."

"As it turns out, we had nothing to worry about." The slightest hint of irritation seeped into Dr. Menta's voice. "Isaac successfully extracted Denton's sequence, and I was just about to transfer him to my lab."

"Excellent," Dr. Kindred responded before turning to Isaac. "Though I must say, a part of me hoped you might be a bit harder to manipulate. It's a shame. Apparently Denton is our only sequence showing any promise of superintelligence."

Charlotte fought to understand Dr. Kindred's words. Who manipulated Isaac? And why did no one seem to be that concerned about Charlotte and Isaac breaking into the lab? This illogical turn of events was starting to feel more and more like a dream. She wished for a predictable reaction from someone to bring her back to reality.

More than anything, though, she just wanted to get out of here. Dr. Menta's rigid posture suggested that Charlotte was not alone in this desire. Unfortunately, before either of them could initiate an exit plan, Isaac decided to make everything worse.

"How do you know that I am not the one manipulating you, Victor?"

CHAPTER 50

IF ISAAC'S USE of Dr. Kindred's first name bothered him, Dr. Kindred didn't show it. Instead, he smiled. "How could you manipulate me when we've been monitoring you since your inception? Did you really think you could hide anything from us?"

Dr. Kindred's words hit Charlotte like a punch in the gut, but Isaac received them impassively.

"Denton managed to."

A vein on Dr. Kindred's temple began to pulse. "That was an anomaly. I can admit that we underestimated Denton's intelligence, but that will not happen again."

"I think perhaps we should all head back to the pitch." Dr. Menta's suggestion came as a relief to Charlotte, but Dr. Kindred, hyper-focused on Isaac, didn't seem to hear her.

"It was touching, almost, to see how readily you believed that you could alter your captures without our knowledge. But that's just not how things work. You didn't consider the situation logically. Why would we give androids the option to have more privacy?"

Proving his point, Dr. Kindred pulled up a capture in their viewerspace, and Charlotte gasped at her own likeness staring back at her.

Charlotte watched herself ask, *Is there a way for you to store any records secretly?*

Isaac's likeness replied, *Yes. I can create an encrypted copy and make it appear to be innocuous information. I can then alter our captures to include only details about our official coursework.*

Charlotte swayed slightly, and she shifted her feet further apart as it occurred to her that she might faint. Everything seemed so naive in hindsight; how could they believe that Isaac's encrypted captures were private? Her cheeks burned as the full scope hit her in waves; she guessed that Dr. Kindred was probably behind Isaac's altered memories. He had the androids entirely under his control. If Dr. Kindred had been personally reviewing Isaac's records, then he likely saw everything, every interaction, every moment she and Isaac shared.

Her embarrassment, which in another situation might have crippled her, instead melted under the outrage of this injustice. Charlotte leaned forward, trying to find the words to speak out against Dr. Kindred, when she felt Isaac's hand lightly brush her own. She turned to him sharply; he caught her eyes for an instant before directing his gaze back toward the viewerspace. What did he want her to see?

She held her tongue and refocused on the captures. Dr. Kindred flipped through a number of scenes in double time, and Charlotte struggled to place them in her memory. Some she clearly recognized, such as discussions she and Isaac held about creating their pitch, but as the captures flew by, strange patterns emerged. For some reason, neither Eli nor Gavin featured in Dr. Kindred's selection, though they both had been present for much of the planning. More perplexingly, Marissa's likeness along with Dr. Menta's appeared in several conversations.

Charlotte furrowed her brow as she heard Dr. Menta persuade Isaac to contact Denton; later, Dr. Menta's likeness provided details on Denton's location and instructions for how to access the mainframe.

To Charlotte's knowledge, those conversations never happened.

The captures made it look like Dr. Menta, with help from Charlotte and Marissa, had instigated this operation and had convinced Isaac to participate. Sensing that Dr. Kindred's presentation might be a trap, Charlotte stole a look at his face, but she only saw a seemingly genuine smirk of victory that deepened her own confusion. What was happening? Where did these scenes come from?

With a wave of his hand, Dr. Kindred dissolved the captures. "I have to admit, when Dr. Menta suggested that she would be able to persuade you to find our missing sequence, I had my doubts. My ideas were a tad bit more direct. In any case, you played into our hands quite nicely." Dr. Kindred arched his eyebrows in mock pity. "Do you have anything to say for yourself now, Isaac?"

"We cannot argue with the facts in front of us." Isaac's face, as usual, belied no emotions.

The facts in front of us. With that phrase, some of the jumbled puzzle pieces within Charlotte's mind fell into place.

Dr. Kindred thought these captures were the truth.

The realization struck Charlotte like a bolt of lightning, and she almost laughed at the beauty of it. Isaac was indeed manipulating Dr. Kindred. But how did Dr. Menta and Marissa figure into this?

Before Charlotte could untangle her present reality, Dr. Kindred pressed on. "Well then, I think I've made my point. Rosalind, I will take that sequence from you now."

Casually, Dr. Menta said, "I would be happy to secure him myself, in the location we discussed."

"I appreciate your commitment, but I have decided to keep him in my private lab instead. I think that would be most prudent."

Dr. Menta's reluctance was barely perceptible. "As you wish."

No! Charlotte wanted to shout. Even without entirely understanding the situation, Charlotte knew that they must avoid handing Denton over to Dr. Kindred at all costs. Subtly and desperately, she raised her eyebrows at Isaac. Didn't they have to stop this?

With the briefest of movements, Isaac shook his head, and Charlotte remained frozen in place.

Dr. Menta extended her hand with the device resting on her palm, but Dr. Kindred paused before accepting the sequence. "Show me he's in there."

At the touch of her thumb, Denton's likeness, with his characteristically haughty demeanor, appeared before them, and Charlotte's stomach sank.

"Excellent." Dr. Kindred grinned smugly and nodded at Dr. Menta, who released her thumb, thus returning Denton to his new prison. Before anyone could make another move, Dr. Kindred plucked the device from Dr. Menta's hand and slipped it into his inner jacket pocket with the finality of a burial.

Though Charlotte hadn't betrayed Denton - not directly, not knowingly - she couldn't escape the feeling that his second captivity was nonetheless her fault.

She fiercely hoped that Dr. Kindred would leave. Her anger flared, directed not only at Dr. Kindred. Despite the incoherence of tonight's events, one thing was clear: Isaac and Dr. Menta, and possibly Marissa, had all lied to Charlotte.

As Dr. Kindred's eyes locked on hers, Charlotte realized too late that she had let her expression slip, and she quickly smoothed her wrinkled brow. Misinterpreting her emotions, Dr. Kindred spoke in what he probably intended to be a reassuring tone. "I'm sure you had some misgivings with lying about this, but don't worry." He angled his head toward Isaac. "He won't remember anything by the next time you see him. And I believe Dr. Menta communicated the importance of you and your sister keeping this between us?"

Nodding her head seemed like the only appropriate answer Charlotte could give, though inwardly she seethed at the lack of communication she had received from her mentor. *Former* mentor.

"Excellent," Dr. Kindred said. Perhaps noticing a touch of hesitation from Charlotte, he added, "Even if you did share anything, we would, of course, deny it. And we wouldn't want any slanderous accusations to get in the way of your parents' work, would we?"

Speechless, Charlotte could only shake her head.

"Indeed. I am glad to know we're on the same page. Rosalind, you and Charlotte should head back to the pitch. We wouldn't want you to miss the festivities. I hear that you, Charlotte, especially enjoy the after-pitch desserts." Dr. Kindred's suddenly congenial tone failed to soften the thinly veiled threat against her parents.

Dr. Menta took a step toward the door, but Charlotte didn't budge. "What about Isaac?"

"He'll be staying here with me," Dr. Kindred said. "As I mentioned, we need to clear his memory before he's fit to interact with anyone else."

CHAPTER 51

"NO." MOVING IN front of Isaac, Charlotte stood as a physical barrier between him and Dr. Kindred.

Genuine confusion played over Dr. Kindred's face as his eyes bounced between Dr. Menta and Charlotte. "We will wipe only his memories related to this situation. He won't remember that you manipulated him. I thought this would be good news for you."

"Charlotte." Isaac's voice made her turn. "You do not need to worry about me." He accompanied his last words with a firm squeeze of her hand. Along with the warm pressure of his fingers, she felt a surprisingly cold sensation against her palm. Charlotte cupped her hand around a smooth, flat drive; making sure to keep it out of sight, she faced Dr. Kindred again.

"I...I just hoped he'd be able to join the after-pitch celebration. I know my friends really want to say goodbye to him before break." Charlotte added a sigh for emphasis, hoping to distract Dr. Kindred as she slipped her hand - and the mysterious device - into her pocket.

Dr. Kindred exchanged a conspiratorial look with Dr. Menta. "Ah, youth. I remember when parting with friends for even a few weeks seemed like a tragedy." Despite the nostalgic expression on Dr. Kindred's face, Charlotte couldn't envision him as a young man among friends. "Unfortunately, you will have to say goodbye on their behalf."

"Okay." Uncertain about what to do, Charlotte looked at Isaac awkwardly, but he saved the moment by pulling her into a hug. For an instant, she forgot almost everything. Dr. Kindred, Dr. Menta, the uncertainty of what would happen to Isaac - all of it faded away as he held her tightly against his chest. Only Isaac's unexplained deceit remained lodged between them.

At the sound of Dr. Menta clearing her throat, Isaac pulled back, but he whispered a final message in her ear before letting go. "I am constant as the northern star. Farewell, Charlotte."

"Goodbye, Isaac," she whispered back, blinking furiously as she wondered when she would see him again.

Without looking at Dr. Kindred, Charlotte could sense his impatience with their show of affection. Not wanting him to see the wetness lingering in the corners of her eyes, she kept her gaze to the floor as she followed Dr. Menta to the hallway. Before the door slid shut behind her, Charlotte stole one last look at Isaac. To her horror, Dr. Kindred leaned toward Isaac's ear, and Isaac's head slumped, lifeless, to his chin.

"No!" Against the closed door, Charlotte's protest reached only Dr. Menta, who gently placed her hand on Charlotte's arm. The gesture, intended to be soothing, instead sent a ripple of resentment down Charlotte's spine. "You let this happen. You let him take Denton, and now you're letting him take Isaac's mind." Charlotte nearly spit her words out.

Dr. Menta didn't flinch in the face of Charlotte's anger. Instead, she lowered her voice and tightened her grip on Charlotte's arm as she pulled her toward the path to the main floor. "We can't talk about this here."

With no other choice, Charlotte accompanied Dr. Menta to the upper levels and back down to the tunnel entrance below the other corner of the lab. Almost jogging to keep up with Dr. Menta's brisk pace, Charlotte struggled to organize her questions in her mind, but all she could see was Isaac, incapacitated by nothing more than a simple phrase from Dr. Kindred.

At last, they reached the androids' dorm, and Charlotte stopped in the lobby. "I want some answers. Now."

Shaking her head, Dr. Menta held her finger up to her lips and stepped through the entrance into the moonlight. Once again with no options, Charlotte followed her into the misty forest before Dr. Menta stopped and scanned the horizon. Evidently convinced that they were alone, she faced Charlotte and held her hand up to quell the questions about to tumble from Charlotte's mouth.

"Charlotte. Before you say anything, I want to first tell you how proud I am of you. It took a lot of courage to take such a risk to help Denton and Isaac."

A few short months ago, a compliment like this from Dr. Menta would have meant everything to Charlotte, but in this moment, it only intensified her frustration. "It doesn't seem like anything I did mattered after all, does it?"

Dr. Menta took a breath. "Charlotte, you did your best to help them. No matter what happens, that means a lot. And I know you're understandably angry. I regret that I had to put you in this position." She glanced over her shoulder. "We can't be here long, so I can't explain everything. But I'll try to answer what I can."

Charlotte didn't know where to start. "Was Isaac working with you? To get Denton out?"

"Yes and no." Dr. Menta's expression tightened. "When it became clear that Denton had hidden his sequence, Dr. Kindred approached me about forcing one of the androids to find him. I convinced Dr. Kindred that the androids would never comply with that, as it conflicts with the Insurance Principle. The android would need to believe that he was saving Denton, not trapping him to turn him over to Dr. Kindred. Around that same time, Marissa told me that you and Isaac were having conversations about how Denton needed to be rescued."

Charlotte drew in her breath; Marissa told Dr. Menta that? Before she could process this fact, Dr. Menta continued, "That's when we started to formulate a plan. If Dr. Kindred could believe that Isaac was being manipulated into capturing Denton, then he wouldn't suspect that we had a different goal in mind."

"What different goal?" Charlotte asked in exasperation. "You handed Denton over to Dr. Kindred, which is exactly what he wanted!"

Dr. Menta looked at the ground and almost succeeded in concealing the tremble in her voice. "It wasn't supposed to happen like that. I was supposed to intercept and have enough time to transfer Denton off of the storage device before meeting up with Dr. Kindred after the pitch." Closing her eyes and exhaling shakily, Dr. Menta said, "I made a critical mistake. I thought that by meeting you and Isaac at the lab, I was taking enough precautions. We originally planned to have Isaac give Denton to me back at the Gem, but when he left the pitch, I let him know that I would meet the two of you at the lab, just in case."

That explained Isaac's delay, which by now felt like it had happened ages ago. But it didn't explain why Dr. Kindred now had Denton. "In case of what?"

"In case Dr. Kindred tried to get to Denton before I could." Dr. Menta shook her head. "I thought Dr. Kindred trusted me more than he evidently does. That, unfortunately, changes everything." Her last words came through quietly, directed more to herself than to Charlotte.

At the beginning of this semester, Charlotte wouldn't have believed that Dr. Menta could ever make a mistake. Now...now, with more questions than answers, she didn't know what to think. Marissa was working with Dr. Menta? And Dr. Menta was working against Dr. Kindred? But why? What was Dr. Kindred going to do with Denton?

"Why didn't anyone tell me what was going on?" The next question to come out of Charlotte's mouth, though arguably not the most significant, nonetheless hit the closest to home.

"To protect you."

Charlotte rolled her eyes at the same answer she had heard over and over from her parents and sister whenever they kept something from her. "Even Isaac lied to me." That, she realized, bothered her more than anything else.

Dr. Menta's gaze softened. "That can also be blamed on me, I'm afraid. He insisted on telling you, but I prevented him from disclosing our plan."

"You did? How?"

After a pause, Dr. Menta replied, "I am sorry to say that I used the Deactivation Principle to keep him quiet. Had Isaac shared the plan, he would have been automatically deactivated; contributing to his own deactivation would have contradicted the Insurance Principle, so he was powerless to disobey. Charlotte, there is more at stake here than you could possibly know. I thought I was doing what was best."

Though reassured to know that Isaac wanted to be honest with her, Charlotte was far from satisfied by this concerning information. Even Dr. Menta's regretful expression didn't stop Charlotte from pushing further. "What will happen to Denton?"

"I'll have to find another way to save him." Her eyes sharpened with renewed determination. "Don't worry, Charlotte. I understand things better now than I did before. I will get Denton back."

Signaling the end of the conversation, Dr. Menta started walking toward the Gem. Charlotte's hand tightened around the device in her pocket; what information did it contain? Should she tell Dr. Menta?

Charlotte's fingers tingled with indecision as she tried to predict what Isaac would want her to do. If Dr. Menta knew about Isaac's final covert act, surely she would have mentioned it. Under that assumption, Charlotte made the uneasy decision to keep the secret device to herself.

As the building came into sight, Dr. Menta stopped Charlotte one final time. "Charlotte. It is imperative that no one finds out about what happened tonight. Aside from Marissa, promise me that you won't discuss this with anyone."

"I promise," Charlotte said, hoping Dr. Menta couldn't see the lie in her eyes.

CHAPTER 52

BY THE TIME they reached the Gem's garden, Dr. Menta had transformed into another person. Smiling confidently, evidently without a care in the world, Dr. Menta bid farewell to Charlotte when they crossed the threshold. "Enjoy the rest of your evening, Charlotte."

"You too," Charlotte responded, certain that her own attempt at a smile presented more like a grimace as she stared at Dr. Menta's receding form.

The festive atrium, now ringed by lavish appetizer and dessert stations, indicated the conclusion of the pitch, and Charlotte soon lost sight of Dr. Menta in the mingling crowd. Ordinarily, the gorgeously arranged pastries would have called to Charlotte, but at that moment, the thought of a single sugary bite turned her stomach.

Pressure against her elbow made her jump, and she spun sharply, irrationally fearing that Dr. Kindred had snuck up behind her. Instead, she was met by Gavin, who wrapped her in an enthusiastic hug. After a moment, he stepped back, grinning joyfully while handing Charlotte the jacket she had left behind.

"Charlotte! I've been looking for you everywhere. It worked.

It worked! You and Isaac even got an honorable mention!" His exclamations fell flat in the face of Charlotte's harried expression, and he leaned in closer, lowering his voice. "You did get him, right? I told you to message me if anything went wrong, so I thought..." He trailed off, looking around her. "Where's Isaac?"

Charlotte faltered, the sting of their failure hitting her anew in light of Gavin's elation. "He's not here."

"What happened?" His eyes, completely serious now, pierced hers.

Her fingers brushed against the device in her pocket; she hoped it might fill in some of the holes remaining after Dr. Menta's revelations. Taking Charlotte back to her last moments with Isaac, the smooth coolness of the metal sparked a surge of panic within her, and her words tumbled out. "It's complicated. Dr. Kindred has Denton. And he's going to wipe Isaac's memory. I don't know what to do."

"Hey, we've got this." Placing his hands on Charlotte's shoulders, Gavin calmed her with his steady gaze. "What are you thinking?"

She was panicking, but she tried to string together at least a few cogent thoughts. "I'm thinking that Isaac should be here. He would know what to do next. He...he said something that seems like a clue, but I don't know what it means."

"Okay." Gavin smiled tentatively. "We can work with that. What did he say?"

Charlotte hesitated before sharing Isaac's last words with Gavin. "He said, 'I am constant as the northern star.'"

"Really?" To Charlotte's surprise, Gavin frowned not in confusion but in recognition. "That sounds familiar...hold on a sec." Charlotte watched Gavin's eyes scan from left to right as he read something in his viewer.

"What is it?" she asked.

"That's what I thought!" Gavin focused back on her. "It's a line from Shakespeare."

"Shakespeare? You mean it's poetry?"

"Yeah. It's a line of verse from *Julius Caesar*. We studied it in my ancient civilizations course. Do you know why Isaac would quote that?"

Charlotte's pulse quickened. Poetry. Stars. Isaac's message could only mean one thing.

"I know where we need to go. Find Eli and meet me outside."

Gavin sped off, and Charlotte scanned the room for her sister; to be honest, though, she wasn't sure what she wanted to say to Marissa. Unsuccessful in spotting her, Charlotte turned, finding herself face to face with Chai and Jace, who were both grinning widely.

"Hey!" Jace bumped Charlotte on the shoulder. "There you are! Your pitch was awesome. The way you and Isaac switched at the end to illuminate the audience's bias - I think everyone's minds were blown."

"Thanks." Charlotte tried, and failed, to adopt a normal tone. "Yours too. I had no idea your research had been so successful. The thought that humans could one day benefit from photosynthesis is just incredible."

Chai smiled around a cheesecake bite. "That's still quite far in the future, but thanks. We're lucky that some of our experiments came through in the end."

Jace wrinkled his brow at Charlotte as her eyes darted frantically over his shoulder. "What's wrong, Char?"

Conscious of the tenuous status of their friendship, she bit her lip and looked between him and Chai. "I'm not sure if you want to know."

"Of course we do," Jace said instantly. He looked at Chai, and Charlotte glanced away, giving them some privacy for their nonverbal conversation.

"You're right," Chai agreed uneasily. "Of course we do."

Grasping at the delicate thread holding their trio together, Charlotte leaned in and lowered her voice. "Let's go, then. We can't talk about it here." She moved outside and heard them follow her after a moment's hesitation. A few seconds later, Gavin joined them, alone.

"Where's Eli?"

He shrugged. "I couldn't find him. I didn't see any of the androids inside, actually."

This startled Charlotte. She had been so focused on Isaac and Denton that she hadn't thought about the other androids. Now she wondered if Dr. Kindred had plans to interfere with all of their sequences, but she forced herself to file this worry in the back of her mind. "Okay. I guess it's just us for now. I have somewhere safe we can talk."

Barely thirty paces away from the Gem, they froze at the sound of frantic footsteps crunching leaves behind them. Charlotte turned slowly, willing her face into a neutral expression that instantly turned to cautious surprise. "Marissa?"

Marissa, visibly relieved to see her sister, pulled Charlotte into a frantic hug. "Char, I heard what happened."

Dr. Menta must have filled you in quickly, Charlotte thought as she pulled away. She tempered her flush of anger by gripping the device in her pocket. For once, Marissa didn't know everything.

Shaking her head, Marissa said, "I don't understand how he got away. I was careful. I was keeping an eye on him. I could have sworn that he was there the whole time."

Charlotte grabbed Marissa's arm to stop her mumbling stream of words. "Who are you talking about?"

"Dr. Kindred," Marissa said, as though Charlotte should have understood. "I was supposed to make sure that he stayed at the pitch."

Charlotte didn't know what to say to this, and she eyed her sister closely. "You've been lying to me, Marissa."

After a brief pause, Marissa said, "We've both been lying."

Though Charlotte couldn't argue with that, she hesitated. Isaac had previously warned Charlotte against confiding in Marissa; then again, Isaac had been keeping secrets of his own.

Charlotte could push Marissa away and add more beads to the growing string of lies between them. Or she could tell Marissa the truth.

The distress on Marissa's face softened some of Charlotte's irritation and swayed her indecision. Charlotte knew her sister. Despite everything, she believed that Marissa cared about the androids. Refusing to live in a world in which she couldn't trust her own sister, Charlotte held both of Marissa's hands in hers. "Marissa. Can you promise me no more secrets?" She hoped trusting Marissa wasn't a mistake.

"I promise. I know I made a mistake in not telling you what was going on with Dr. Menta, and I'm sorry." She squeezed Charlotte's hands, offering a fleeting seal to her commitment. For now, that would have to be enough.

Charlotte nodded. "It's okay. I'm sorry, too. We have a lot to talk about, but we don't have time now. Come on."

With renewed urgency, Charlotte pulled Marissa to the others, and they nearly jogged up the steep hill toward the hideaway Isaac had discovered. When Charlotte opened the camouflaged door at the base of the tree, they all gasped, but

Charlotte ushered them inside. They had more pressing concerns than the marvels of campus architecture.

At the top, though, beneath the brilliant, starry sky, Charlotte paused. For a moment, the others faded away, and she saw herself here, alone with Isaac, back when she believed she could trust him completely. It seemed like a lifetime ago.

"I had no idea this was here." Marissa's astonishment brought Charlotte back to the present.

"What we talk about can't leave this room." Charlotte's tone, sharper than she intended, brought a somber mood to their gathering. "I think we'd better turn our viewers off."

They disconnected, and the encompassing night sounds, without the viewers' dampening filters, amplified around them. Like campers waiting to hear a ghost story, they settled onto the floor in a rough circle, and Charlotte considered how to start.

In a halting, jumbled rush, she outlined the highlights of what happened in the lab that evening. Trying to stitch together a coherent chain of events, she included every detail she could recall, omitting only Isaac's hug and sleight of hand.

When she finished, a thick layer of silence settled in the room. "So what do we do?" Chai asked, a hint of trepidation underlying her voice.

Charlotte wavered as her palm cupped the device in her pocket. Isaac had entrusted it to her, perhaps intending it to be seen by her eyes alone. As she looked at her friends and her sister, all waiting for her to speak, she made a decision. She couldn't do this on her own. Whatever Isaac intended, he would have to understand that.

She pulled out the device and held it in front of them. "I think Isaac might have some ideas." Charlotte pressed her thumb against the device and waited.

Nothing happened.

CHAPTER 53

ANXIOUSLY, CHARLOTTE REPOSITIONED her grip and tried again. Still nothing.

Chai cleared her throat. "Do we have to use our viewers to see it?"

Charlotte's cheeks reddened. "You're probably right." This presented a dilemma, though. As Jace repositioned his viewer glasses, Charlotte held up her hand. "Wait! It might not be safe. I don't know what message Isaac left, but we can't take any chances with someone like Dr. Kindred hacking into our viewerspace."

For a moment, they sat silently, their thoughts underscored by the softly rustling branches. Waiting for some decision, Charlotte's friends looked to her, but a rhythmic tapping drew their attention to Marissa.

"What are you doing?" Charlotte asked her sister, who, with her fingers flying across the floor, was clearly using her viewer.

Without responding, Marissa raised one index finger before continuing her solitary mission. Charlotte pursed her lips and resolved to give Marissa five more seconds. Five, four, three -

"There we go!" Marissa's triumphant exclamation was met

with raised eyebrows. "We just needed a local vieweroom. Turn on your viewers, and you'll be able to enter without getting on the network." Marissa now raised her own eyebrows at their quizzical looks. "You've never set up a local vieweroom?"

Mirroring her friends, Charlotte shook her head. "No. Why would we?"

Like a disappointed mentor, Marissa sighed. "Wow. Evidently my cohort was a little more adventurous. Let's just say we got into some things that we really didn't want the school, or our parents, to know about. Anyway, this will work. Just turn on your viewers." Marissa paused, giving them a chance to activate. "Everyone in?"

They all nodded, and Jace's eyes widened. "Dude, this is awesome. You have to show us how to do this."

Marissa offered a rueful smile. "I'll think about it."

Charlotte pointed the device toward the middle of their circle, and at the touch of her thumb, still nothing happened. Charlotte felt her face flush again. "I don't understand. This should work."

"You said Isaac's last words made you think of this place." Gavin looked around. "Do you think he left a clue here?"

"Oh!" Charlotte wished she had thought of that. "Maybe he did."

They began combing through the space. Inside the transparent dome, there weren't a lot of hiding places, and Charlotte worried that their search would be fruitless. After a moment, though, Gavin peeked under the rug, and before he set it back down, something about the pattern in the wood caught Charlotte's eye.

"Hold on," she said. "Lift that back up."

When Gavin pulled up the side of the rug, Charlotte stared

at a curious symbol etched into the floor. Everyone rushed over to join her, but they looked down uncomprehendingly.

"I don't see anything," Chai said.

"You don't?" Charlotte ran her hand over the markings and found a corner to lift up with her fingernail. Underneath the floorboard, in a narrow space, she found an additional device resting with a thin cable. Feeling a rush of appreciation for Isaac, Charlotte collected the treasures, and the group circled up again.

"Isaac must have left a marker only visible through your viewer," Marissa said. "That's brilliant."

Unsure of the cable's purpose, Charlotte pressed her thumb against the new device. Instantly, Isaac's likeness appeared, and Charlotte's heart jumped into her throat. Though the virtual figure was only a shadow of Isaac, it was better than nothing, and she waited for the message to start.

Isaac's likeness glanced around the room before meeting Charlotte's gaze. "I assume that my lack of attendance indicates I did not return with you from the lab."

Startled by the conversational tone, Charlotte squinted at him. She thought this was a capture, but his likeness appeared to be interacting with them. "No, you didn't," she said slowly. "Dr. Menta showed up and took Denton's device from us. Then Dr. Kindred came and took the device from her. I tried to stop him, but I couldn't." Charlotte lowered her eyes as she finished. "Also, Dr. Kindred deactivated you. He plans to wipe your memory."

Unfazed, Isaac nodded. "There was a 7.43% chance that events might play out that way."

Charlotte's head snapped up. "What? You never said that!"

"That information would only have increased your stress

level. Because I had established a back-up plan, it did not seem prudent to worry you unnecessarily."

Forgetting that they had an audience, Charlotte quipped, "Really? And did that work out? Considering Dr. Kindred now has Denton?"

"Given your summary of events, Dr. Kindred believes he has possession of Denton, so yes, it appears that the plan was successful."

Marissa broke in, voicing the confusion rippling through the group. "What do you mean, he *believes* he has Denton?"

"The device in Dr. Kindred's possession holds a limited simulated copy of Denton's sequence. Dr. Kindred will eventually discover this, but the copy should serve as an effective decoy for at least a few days."

Gavin asked the next question on everyone's mind. "So if Denton isn't on Dr. Kindred's device, then where is he?"

Isaac looked down at the second device in Charlotte's hand. "He is on the drive that I gave Charlotte at the lab."

Charlotte swallowed. "I don't think he is, Isaac. I tried to activate it earlier, but…"

"Ah, yes. I implemented a failsafe. Denton's sequence can only be accessed when connected locally to the device holding my sequence."

Amid her friends' incredulous stares, Charlotte connected the cable to each device, and everyone jumped as Denton's likeness appeared beside Isaac. "I am here," he said ambivalently.

"So we did it?" Grinning exuberantly, Gavin looked around the circle. "We should celebrate!"

"We did, and we should, but perhaps at another time," Isaac said with a smile before looking at Marissa. "I think you have some guidance for what needs to happen next?"

Marissa paused, choosing her words carefully. "My department has raised concerns about how the androids are being treated under Dr. Kindred's leadership. He seems to be making some decisions that are not aligned with the stated goals of the program. Once I started working more closely with Dr. Menta, I learned that she also shares these concerns. There's a secret group, outside of Cognation, who is working to protect the androids. Dr. Menta planned to transfer Denton to this group; now, getting Denton away from Cognation, away from Dr. Kindred, is the top priority."

"So do we give him back to Dr. Menta?" Chai asked quietly.

"No," Charlotte said. "I don't think we can trust her."

"I'm not sure that's true," Marissa said thoughtfully. "But it does seem like Dr. Kindred doesn't fully trust Dr. Menta, and that's a problem. It's probably safest if we keep Denton's sequence to ourselves, at least for now."

"Obviously," Denton said at the same time that Isaac said, "I agree."

Ignoring Denton, Isaac continued, "The next step is to get this device away from the campus."

"Luckily, we're all heading out tomorrow." Marissa checked her watch. "Charlotte and I board the hypertrain to Boston in about twelve hours. We'll just need to stay undetected until then."

Denton offered a final sarcastic thought before disappearing. "How wonderful. I have always wanted to go to Boston."

Throughout this exchange, Charlotte had remained quiet, bothered by something in the back of her mind. "Isaac, I was just with you. How could your sequence be on this device and in your body?"

"This version of me is a copy that I downloaded onto this device. If Dr. Kindred is successful in wiping my memory - something he has only a 2.76% chance of - then reuniting this copy with the sequence in my body will restore my records."

"Whoa," Jace marveled. "There's two of you? That's so cool!"

Cool is not how Charlotte would describe it, but before she could dwell on the duplicity of Isaac's sequence, Marissa brought the group back to the present.

"You should all probably return to your dorms. We don't want to raise any suspicion. Isaac, how certain are you that Dr. Kindred won't figure out the decoy before tomorrow morning?"

"I am 98.91% certain."

"Okay." Marissa thought for a second. "That's an acceptable risk. Charlotte, we'll meet at the aerotram at 9am tomorrow like we planned, all right?"

"We're leaving then, too, so we'll be on hand if you need any backup," Jace said, dramatically deepening his voice.

The boys fist bumped their agreement, and Chai nodded. Charlotte was grateful for Chai's small sign of solidarity, even if she still displayed some reluctance toward being involved.

Marissa chuckled in spite of herself. "I don't think we'll need that, but thanks."

As they stood, Charlotte realized this was goodbye again for Isaac, and she couldn't stop herself from saying, "I wish you had told me you were working with Dr. Menta."

Isaac nodded. "I am truly sorry that I omitted this information. As you are my best friend, I wanted to tell you, but the principles prohibited me from disobeying Dr. Menta's order."

Best friend? Flattered but embarrassed, Charlotte didn't know what to say. This would need to be a longer, and more private, conversation some other time. For now, though, she was relieved to know that Isaac wanted to be honest with her.

Avoiding eye contact with her other best friends, Charlotte smiled self-consciously. "I'll see you soon, Isaac."

As Marissa deactivated the vieweroom, Isaac vanished, leaving Charlotte with only the memory of his parting gaze. Turning away from the sudden emptiness, Charlotte slipped her hand into her pocket and wrapped her fingers tightly around the most precious possessions she'd ever held.

CHAPTER 54

THOUGH THE CONSTANT ebb and flow of adrenaline had left Charlotte's body exhausted, she doubted that she would be able to sleep tonight. A soft, rippling snore always accompanied Chai's first moments of slumber; judging by the silence from Chai's side of the room, she wasn't sleeping either.

After their late-night meeting concluded, Jace and Gavin had insisted on accompanying the girls to Lyra. Conscious that the woods might have ears, they spoke only about trivial things - plans for the break, whose pitch they liked the best - but Charlotte could barely follow the conversation. Every snap of a twig, every rustle of leaves, made her clutch the devices, and she only realized how jumpy she was when Gavin lightly wrapped his arm around her shoulders.

Once in their room, Chai and Charlotte said little as they got ready for bed, but it was an easy silence, the type of companionable silence they hadn't shared in a while. Later, as they both lay wide awake, Chai's voice came softly from across the room. "I'm sorry, Charlotte. I'm...I'm trying."

Charlotte waited a moment to see if Chai would add anything else, but she didn't. Maybe she didn't need to. "I know,

Chai. I'm sorry, too," Charlotte said, and she could almost feel Chai's smile in the dark.

As her eyes began to droop, Charlotte held onto the devices that now hung from a chain around her neck. Perhaps she would be able to sleep after all.

In what seemed like the next instant, Charlotte felt Chai nudging her awake, and she jolted upright, surprised to see sunlight coming in through their window.

"This must be a first," Chai said, making them both laugh more freely than they had in months. Their relationship may have been strained this semester, but Charlotte was thankful that it had not been crushed.

Unfortunately, they had no time to dwell on the fragile restoration of their friendship. Given that they had to leave in less than an hour, the two girls rushed around, frantically getting ready and double checking their packed bags before the autocart came to collect them.

Leaving the dorm with just enough time to reach the aerotram on schedule, the girls ran into Jace and Gavin when they stepped outside. Jace greeted Chai with a brief kiss, a ritual that Charlotte was only starting to get used to.

"I thought we were meeting you at the tram," Charlotte said to Gavin.

"We got ready early and thought it'd be nice to walk together." He winked, which made Charlotte smile.

"Thanks, Gavin. For everything. You've really been the best through all of this."

He shrugged off her compliment. "Getting to hang out more with you is all the thanks I need."

Holding in a laugh, she shook her head and tried to ignore the fact that a single butterfly in her stomach fluttered to hear him say that.

They quickly reached the entrance to the Academy, where Marissa and their aerotram waited. With the precision of a mother hen, she herded them toward the spiral path to the tram. The rational side of Charlotte knew they probably had nothing to worry about, but that didn't ease her tension, which grew with each ascending revolution; the closer they got to freedom, the more she couldn't shake the feeling that they would be stopped.

They filed into seats along the back, and Charlotte suppressed a groan as two additional passengers hopped on before the doors closed. Settling across the aisle, Beckett and Athena continued their conversation without acknowledging anyone else.

"Really, when you compare the pitches last night to previous years, it's not like the androids added much. So if they're not worth all the trouble they cause, then why should we have to deal with them?" Beckett's supremely self-confident air, as usual, grated on Charlotte's nerves.

"You're so right. Hopefully they won't be a problem after next semester." Athena looked knowingly at Beckett.

You're the problem, rose to Charlotte's lips, but from the corner of her eye, she saw Marissa shake her head. They weren't worth making a scene. Charlotte instead pressed her fingers against the chain hanging under her shirt. Athena and Beckett might think they had insider knowledge, but they really had no idea what they were talking about.

Less than two minutes later, the tram slowed to a halt, and Charlotte followed her sister and friends onto the platform. She crossed off another item on her mental checklist, leaving *board the hypertrain to Boston* as the final step.

The Ternion station buzzed with students, faculty, and staff about to leave for the holidays, and for a moment, Charlotte let herself think back to last year's winter break, when everything was blissfully uncomplicated. She wondered if her world would ever be like that again.

Too soon, Chai glanced down the platform at the arriving hypertrain. "I think that's us." She, Jace, and Gavin were heading on the same line for the first leg of their trips. "Is your train here yet?"

Charlotte shook her head. "It'll be here in a few minutes. You all should go. I don't want you to lose your seats."

Chai and Jace folded into a big group hug around Charlotte; after a moment's hesitation, Gavin joined.

"I'll miss you," Chai said when they all let go.

Charlotte nodded and smiled. "I'll miss you too, but we'll be back here before we know it."

"We'll be expecting updates about, you know, your holiday plans." Gavin's expressive eyebrows made Charlotte laugh despite her nerves.

"Don't worry. I'll keep you in the loop." It seemed silly to get sentimental about saying goodbye before a three-week break, but a strange heaviness settled over Charlotte as she watched her friends walk away. They turned to offer one more wave before disappearing into the crowd, and Charlotte held in a sigh as she and Marissa moved toward their own platform.

"It shouldn't be long now," Marissa said, her eyes pointed vigilantly forward. As if on cue, their train slid smoothly up to the station. Marissa guided Charlotte toward the seventh car and through the narrow hallway to their reserved two-person cabin. Expecting Marissa to move into the room once the door opened, Charlotte instead smacked into her sister, who froze unexpectedly.

"Ow!" Charlotte rubbed her nose where it had connected with Marissa's skull. Just as suddenly as she had stopped,

Marissa pulled Charlotte into their room and locked the door behind them. Once Charlotte saw what was on the table by the window, she froze as well.

Charlotte recognized the object right away, but it took her brain a moment to reconcile the impossibility of it.

"That's one of Dr. Coggins' journals," Charlotte said, her voice barely above a whisper.

"I know," Marissa whispered back. "What I don't know is what it's doing here."

They both moved forward cautiously, as if the journal might bite them. When she got closer, Charlotte noticed the number etched onto the book's spine, and her hand flew to her mouth. "Marissa! This isn't just any journal."

"What do you mean?"

"When Isaac first read through the journals, he mentioned that the forty-second volume was missing. This is it!"

Giving in to the irresistible pull of curiosity, Charlotte reached forward to open the cover. As she flipped the first page open, a message simultaneously appeared in both sisters' viewers.

Though only for some eyes to see, this holds the hidden gems you'll need. Keep it with your treasures dear; with elders' wisdom, all is clear.

"Wait, what?" Through her confusion, Charlotte saw that Marissa looked thoughtful. "You know what this means?"

"No...but I have a hunch." Marissa's eyes brightened. "It has to be from Dr. Menta."

"Dr. Menta?"

"I think so. When we first started working together, she talked about looking for clues to explain the anomalies in Denton's sequence, and she used the term 'hidden gems.' Plus, besides you, she's the only one I spoke to about the journals."

"But why would she give the journal to us?" Charlotte asked slowly.

Equally bewildered on that point, Marissa shrugged. "I have no idea."

"And what other treasures does she mean?" Charlotte clutched her chain. "Do you think she knows what we took?"

"It's possible. If that's true, then maybe she wanted us to have the sequences." Marissa pointed to the part about elders' wisdom. "Our elders could be Mom and Dad, right?"

"Could be," Charlotte agreed reluctantly. That thought reminded her that in less than six hours, she would have to explain to her parents that she willingly stole two android sequences from Cognation. Though comforted by the fact that Isaac and Denton would remain safe in her possession, she knew that her parents might not support her actions, whether or not Dr. Menta approved. She could only hope that they would understand.

In the meantime, though, Charlotte needed to clarify her own understanding. Removing the chain from around her neck, she set her illicit devices next to the journal. "Marissa, I think we have a lot to talk about before we get to Boston."

Marissa nodded with a wry smile. "I think you're right, Char."

As the hypertrain pulled away from Ternion, away from the Academy, away from Cognation, Charlotte took a deep breath. No matter what happened next, she still believed that she had done the right thing, for better or for worse.

Or, more likely, for better *and* for worse.

Acknowledgments

A year and a half ago, I decided to write a novel, for better or for worse. Or, more precisely, for better *and* for worse. On the days when putting a single sentence on the page seemed like an impossible battle, I didn't know if I would make it to the final chapter. Luckily, I didn't have to go through this process alone, and I am deeply grateful for everyone who helped this dream become a reality.

To Dylan – Thank you for being my partner in life, love, and all of our creative pursuits. You believed in this story long before I did, and my favorite part of the writing process was hiking through the woods with you while dreaming up Cognation's campus. You are also the best editor and science advisor any sci-fi writer could ask for; thank you for saving me from violating too many laws of physics. This book simply would not have been written without you, and I can't wait to start working on the next one together.

To Mum and Dad – Thank you for showing me the world throughout my childhood and for indulging my voracious love of reading. You have always supported me in everything I set out to do, and I love that I can always count on you to be my biggest fans. Dad, thank you for the rigorous notes on your read-throughs, and Mum, thank you for marketing this book to everyone you know even before it was published.

To Millie and Ron – Not everyone is fortunate enough to have wonderful in-laws they enjoy spending time with, and I know that I am one of the lucky ones. Thank you for your excitement for this story and your typo-finding skills. And of course, thank you for raising such an amazing son.

To my family and friends – I am incredibly fortunate to have so many caring friends and family members who have supported me in this work. Writing a novel requires a daunting leap of faith, but your encouragement made me feel like this wasn't such a crazy endeavor after all. Thank you especially to everyone who read early drafts; your thoughtful feedback was immensely valuable for my final revisions.

To my teachers – I would not be the writer I am today without the many exceptional teachers who helped me grasp the power of language. You not only inspired me to become an educator but also gave me the skills and confidence to write stories of my own. To you and to all teachers who are empowering students to find their voices, thank you.

To my readers – A book is nothing at all without a reader. Thank you for taking a chance on a first-time author and spending some time at Cognation Academy with me. I hope you will join Charlotte and Isaac as their story continues.

Last but not least, to Asimov – Thank you for keeping me company during computer time and for purring away my moments of writer's block. As you like to say, a cat is a writer's best friend.

–

ABOUT THE AUTHOR

Though it's impossible to know for sure, Nicole Marie is fairly certain that she is not in fact an android. She is, however, a former English teacher who loves literature and believes that stories have the power to change the world. When she's not reading or writing, she enjoys exploring new places, and she comes up with her best ideas while taking long hikes with her husband. *After Intelligence: The Hidden Sequence* is her first (and hopefully not her last) novel.

ABOUT THE PUBLISHER

Tandemental
sharing stories to shape the future

Charlotte and Isaac's adventures continue in the
next book of the *After Intelligence* series!

Visit <u>www.tandemental.com</u> to learn more
and stay up to date on all future releases.

CPSIA information can be obtained
at www.ICGtesting.com
Printed in the USA
LVHW110039140121
676399LV00004BA/114

9 781952 862021